Byte Marks

She's his match—but he's not in her business plan.

Hereditary witch Dominique LaPierre has always refused to use her powers, especially when it comes to business. Until now. Her new company, a computer dating service that hooks up the San Francisco human and para communities, thrives on crossing that boundary. Business is great despite opposition from the arrogant and conceited Antoine Thierry, a leader in the vampire community. And, to her irritation, she finds she's got the hots for him.

Antoine doesn't like or trust witches. Nor does he like the growing power of technology; real vampires, in his view, don't need it to have a social life. Besides, if he can't control the game, he doesn't want to play—except with Dominique. The heat between them could melt down any hard drive. She pushes his buttons on every level, from the board room to the bedroom. But he's holding out, especially when she looks to him to support her new business.

Antoine wants it all. His way—and his woman.

Warning: This title contains hot sex and lots of it!

What's a Ghoul to Do?

She's the only mate he wants. But love isn't on the menu.

Lilith P. Graves needs to get a life. A social life. This shouldn't be a problem, since she's partnered with her best friend in the "Fangly, My Dear" dating service. Problem is, she keeps falling for the wrong guys, and they don't get more wrong than the super-hot alpha Rafe Graywolf.

With the history of bad blood between her kind and his, the message is clear: Vegetarian demi-ghouls need not apply.

Obeying the call of duty, Rafe took the role of alpha at a rough time for the pack. For the sake of stability, the elders insist he find a mate. Now. A dating service isn't normally his cut of steak, but he has little time—or choice.

But Lilith...now there's a choice morsel he could sink his teeth into. Too bad they're on opposite ends of the ghoul-werewolf social spectrum. Not to mention the food chain...

Warning: This title contains several heaping helpings of hot, sizzling sex!

Playing with Matches

In a battle of wills, only one can be on top. Right?

After an investigation goes horribly wrong, former journalist and brand-new vampire Gabe Morrow wants to get a life. A social life, that is.

Fresh from the vampire halfway house, he's ecstatic—and a little wary—when Fangly, My Dear fixes him up with San Francisco cop Tanith Kalinski. Although his last investigation had him tracking corrupt cops, one night with this detective blows him away.

Vampires have always both repelled and fascinated Tanith. She figures one date—one long, passionate night of hot sex—will finally get the creatures out of her system. Then she meets Gabe. Their instantaneous attraction is so intense that instead of curing her of her obsession, their one night together makes it stronger than ever.

What's worse, Gabe wants more than she's willing to offer. With his murderer still on the loose, keeping Gabe at arm's length risks more than her heart—it could mean her life.

Warning: This title contains plenty of hot vampire loving.

Look for these titles by
Mardi Ballou

Now Available:

Possession

Fangly, My Dear

Mardi Ballou

A SAMHAIN PUBLISHING, LTD. publication.

Samhain Publishing, Ltd.
577 Mulberry Street, Suite 1520
Macon, GA 31201
www.samhainpublishing.com

Editing by Heidi Moore
Cover by Scott Carpenter

Byte Marks, ISBN 1-59998-939-5
First Samhain Publishing, Ltd. electronic publication: May 2008
What's a Ghoul to Do?, ISBN 1-60504-142-4
First Samhain Publishing, Ltd. electronic publication: August 2008
Playing with Matches, ISBN 978-1-60504-234-3
First Samhain Publishing, Ltd. electronic publication: November 2008
First Samhain Publishing, Ltd. print publication: October 2009

Contents

Byte Marks

Dedication

To Lee, in appreciation always for all the lovely bytes

Chapter One

Vacation? Dominique wanted to excise that word from her personal vocabulary. She hated taking time off from her businesses, but she'd forced herself to because her best friend needed her. On the plane from Boston to San Francisco, she'd obsessed over why Lilith sounded so depressed but had come up empty. The moment the plane landed, she took off like a shot.

"Over here!" Standing just behind the barrier, Lilith shouted and waved.

"It's great to see you!" Dominique hugged her friend hard.

"Welcome to San Francisco. I'm glad you could tear yourself away. I was afraid you'd never be willing to leave work." Lilith's grin didn't quite reach her eyes.

"You're impossible to resist."

"Every eligible bachelor in the Greater Bay Area seems to have no trouble doing exactly that." Lilith's laugh sounded dry and decidedly unfunny.

"And here I thought the expression on your face meant you were having second thoughts about my coming out." Her friend's evident pain rocked Dominique. She'd made the right decision to come now.

Lilith shook her head. "Are you kidding? This is the best thing in months, maybe years. Ignore my whining. I'm just letting an unrealistic expectation of a social life get to me. Come on, let's get down to the luggage carousel so we can blow this joint."

"Great idea. You know, when it comes to having a social life, I'm rowing the same leaky boat as you," Dominique admitted as they walked. But evidently not having a man in her life impacted her much less than Lilith.

"Wait a minute. Weren't you going out with Mark? I thought things were hot and heavy between you two." Lilith led Dominique to the escalator down.

"*Were*. Emphasis on the past tense. That's been over since before I started negotiations with Zigmont, Ltd. to buy Lady Tech. By the way, that deal went better than expected. That's why I can come out and play for a few days. I hope you have lots of good stuff planned."

"Lots," Lilith echoed with a discouraging lack of enthusiasm as they neared the carousel. People milled around waiting for their suitcases.

"I hate having to waste my time waiting." Dominique frowned at the carousel that bore only one cardboard box and a guitar case. "The only time I'm tempted to resort to witchcraft is when my luggage is held up."

"If I had the gift, I'd be using it all the time."

Dominique rolled her eyes. "Trust me, you wouldn't. I can see the price the women in my family pay for plying the craft. It's not worth it."

"As family backgrounds go, I'd trade with you in a minute. Guys might find witches sexy."

"More like scary."

"Maybe. But no one finds ghouls sexy. Not even other ghouls." Lilith's mouth formed a grim line.

"You're only a half-ghoul on your father's side. And you sure as heck don't look anything like him."

"Thank the gods."

After only a few minutes with her friend, Dominique understood the causes of her depression. A stalled social life could mess with anyone's mood. What bothered her even more was Lilith being so down on her family. Now that Dominique understood what was going on, she'd be able to come up with a plan to pull her friend out of the doldrums.

Once they retrieved her solitary suitcase, the friends took the elevator to the garage.

With the suitcase loaded into the trunk of Lilith's late-model BMW, the two women got on their way. In several minutes, Lilith had them out on the freeway. "We'll be at my place soon. Once you get settled, we can figure out what to do tonight. I know you must be jet-lagged."

For Dominique, who traveled all the time, the three hours' difference between the coasts seemed trivial. Her friend's depression, on the other hand, didn't.

"How long since you've been in San Francisco?" Lilith asked as she drove through the late June evening traffic. Rush hour was past, but the sun hadn't set yet.

Dominique couldn't remember. "It's been years. Not since Harvard. I only saw you when you came out to Boston."

"Right. You were never willing to make the trip out here."

"Hey, I'm here now."

"Sorry. I guess I'm feeling rejected and unwanted." Lilith bit her lip.

"I want to know what's going on with you. The good, the bad and the ugly. Weren't you seeing some guy you liked a lot from Stanford?"

"Dylan. A surprise visit from Dad sent him running for the hills—permanently."

"I'm sorry." Lilith's father was lovely, as ghouls went. Of course Dominique had been prepared before she first met him. But she could see how his thick blue skin, red eyes, claws and growl might put off any but the most committed of his daughter's boyfriends.

"Yeah, I should've warned him. But damn, I want a boyfriend who can deal, even without preparation." She pounded the steering wheel to emphasize her point.

"I can see that, but I'm not a disinterested observer. I mean I've had lots of time to get to know and love your family. All things considered, somewhere down the pike you might decide you need to compromise on that point, maybe not use it as a litmus test for men."

Lilith sniffed. "Since Dylan took off, I haven't had a single date. I don't even have to question how much to tell potential boyfriends about my family because there aren't any. Boyfriends, that is. I've got tons of family here."

Dominique stole a look at her friend. Even from the most objective of standards, at age twenty-nine, Lilith Graves should have been fighting off hordes of guys lining up to take her out. A blue-eyed blonde who favored her mother, Lilith was blessed with long legs, generous curves and height, creamy skin. Even better, she had a great personality, and was a hundred percent loyal and generous to the people she cared about. And then there was her Harvard degree and tons of old money. "That's hard to believe."

"Thanks, Dominique. You're good for my ego."

"Here in San Francisco, the world capital of diversity, I'd expect a beautiful demi-ghoul to be Ms. Popularity."

"Actually, I thought by distancing myself from the parts of my heritage that put guys off, I'd get past negative stereotypes. But that hasn't happened."

"Cripes, Lilith, you may be the only vegetarian demi-ghoul most people will ever meet. Even if you weren't gorgeous and fantastic, I'd expect the curiosity factor alone would get you some dates."

"Well, you'd be wrong. Do you find your being a witch puts guys off?" Lilith turned and glanced at Dominique.

She shook her head. "It doesn't come up because it's not part of who I am. The craft has no significance in any part of my life except for occasional interactions with my mother, grandmother and aunts."

"So you really don't tell guys about your family background?"

Dominique shrugged. "It just doesn't come up. Maybe if I ever got serious with anyone to the point where we talked about meeting the families, I would. I'd have to. But having a mostly absentee witch mother and totally absentee father is not the same as living in the same city as a father who's a ghoul and a mother who's human—and having both meddle in your life constantly."

Lilith sighed. "Oh, look. I shouldn't be bringing all this up now, anyway. You're on *vacation*, and here I am yammering about my petty stuff. It's not like we're going to solve anything today. Dominique, do me a favor and forget my bellyaching. I don't want anything to interfere with your having a good time. Heck, I figure if you do, you might come out more than once every five years."

They both laughed and turned to gossip about friends they had in common. Despite her stated intentions, Lilith seemed to sadden when they spoke about people getting engaged or married. She even sniffled over a friend getting a divorce.

Turning off what she saw and heard was not easy for Dominique. After she'd freshened up and put away her stuff, she joined Lilith in the gorgeous living room of her friend's Nob Hill house for some wine.

"To a great visit and lots of fun!" They toasted each other with a Pinot Noir from Lilith's family's Napa winery. Delicious.

"If you're up for Italian food tonight, we can go to this place I love in North Beach," Lilith said. "After, if you haven't crashed, we can check out some clubs."

"Italian sounds perfect. And trust me, Lilith, I'm up for whatever. I won't be crashing any time soon. Bring on the clubs." The way Dominique felt, she could go all night.

"Okay. If you're not trying to hook up with a guy for anything more than some laughs or a one-night stand, the social life here in San Francisco is world-class."

As this trip was a chance to cheer up her friend, Dominique hadn't given any thought to meeting guys. Still, she wouldn't say no to some flirting—as long as it didn't hurt Lilith. "Let the good times roll."

Talk about rolling. By the time she finished gorging at Cassio's North Beach, Dominique thought Lilith would have to roll her home.

"What are you in the mood for?" Lilith seemed happier after they'd eaten.

Dominique shrugged. "Whatever. It's all new to me."

"Being you just got here, I'll spare you Ghouls' Night Out. There are clubs that cater to just one group population, others that attract a cross-section."

"If they cater to just one group, does that mean we wouldn't be welcome?"

"There's always wiggle room for tourists." Lilith paused. "Any group that's going to be hard-nosed and strict about access would go private. In the public ones, even when there's a predominant group, anyone can drop in to have a drink or a bite to eat." She giggled. "In some places, an unsuspecting tourist might *be* someone's bite to eat."

"I'm sure there must be some controls." Dominique shivered with delicious curiosity at the prospect of a walk on the wild side.

Lilith nodded. "All our creatures of the night are supposed to be on their best behavior in public, especially around the tourists."

"Sounds intriguing and loads different from Boston."

"Do you want to try a witch club first? There's a small one here in the city."

Dominique shook her head. "Anything but. You did mention a ghoul club? I wouldn't mind."

Lilith rolled her eyes. "I just put in my obligatory monthly afternoon with Dad's family. I love them, but when they get a bug up their collective asses, they can be hard to take. My being a vegetarian has never gone over big, and these days I'm everyone's number one matchmaking challenge. I'd just as soon skip the family haunts tonight."

"It's all new to me. Introduce me to San Francisco nightlife. I hope I'm not underdressed."

Lilith, in black leather, fishnets and stilettos, shook her head. "You look amazing as always."

Dressed in a red cami and black silk pants, Dominique figured she looked like a grown-up, practically Lilith's chaperone. Maybe she'd treat herself to a more interesting wardrobe while she was here.

"Let's check out Club Red," Lilith said at last. "That's a vampire club. Antoine Thierry, the owner, has a reputation for the best of the best. Of course I'd understand why you might not want to hang around with vampires, given the bad blood, so to speak, between vamps and witches."

Dominique groaned. "There you go again, putting too much importance on my family background. I don't know what you're talking about with that 'bad blood' stuff. Back home, some of my best friends are vampires, not to mention how much I love doing business with them. San Francisco vampires. How can we go wrong?"

The night-darkened streets resonated with the energy of beings in search of diversion. Dominique, feeling as close to mellow as she could remember, drank it all in. Everyone moved, talked and laughed. Clothes ranged from elegant to bizarre with many gradations between. She saw hair every color of the rainbow, some all the colors of the rainbow. Creativity and energy flowed, inviting her to become part of the fascinating scene. Caught up, Dominique felt her mood lighten—and, as she'd hoped, the same seemed true for Lilith. Her friend's smile looked wide and genuine.

Revelers crowded the entrance to Club Red and spilled onto

the sidewalk in front. Dominique couldn't be completely sure who was a vampire and who wasn't. Though the other women in her family had a highly honed instinct to identify para beings, she'd suppressed that ability. Unless someone flashed some fang, she couldn't be sure.

Lilith knew one of the bouncers well enough to get them preferential entry. Once inside, Dominique's business brain kicked in. Was this a successful operation? If yes, what made it so? If not, what could be changed? Judging by the crowded dance floor and busy bar, Club Red looked profitable.

"Want a drink?" Lilith asked.

That would be the perfect prop for a tour of the club.

"I'll buy. What are you drinking?" Remembering where she was, Dominique added, "Is this a full-service bar?"

Lilith laughed. "No one's going to expect you to drink the stuff from the blood bank."

Though they had to wait to order, Dominique noted that the staff handled the crowd with brisk efficiency.

"What'll it be, ladies?" Their bartender looked like a run-of-the-mill frat guy with a crew-cut until Dominique caught a wink of fang. Fascinated, she forgot to order.

"I'll have a virgin Bloody Mary," Lilith said. *Sotto voce*, she added to Dominique, "Here virgin means without the blood."

"A virgin margarita," Dominique said.

The bartender nodded. In moments he'd placed gorgeous drinks before them. Dominique whipped out her credit card.

"It's on the house." The deep masculine voice came from behind them.

"Right, Mr. Thierry." The bartender snapped to attention.

Dominique turned to see who was treating. Tall, dark, dressed in Armani, longish black hair and dark gray eyes. He struck her as a cross between Frank Langella's Dracula and Johnny Depp's Captain Jack Sparrow. He had the slightest accent—it should be French according to his name, but she wasn't quite sure. He looked and sounded exotic—and hot. Though her body had been in shut down mode since her break-up with Mark, dormant nerve endings sprang to alert. Amazing that she would cream with desire over a man—a vampire—she'd just met.

The frenetic beat of the music was just enough to encourage dancing and drinking without making conversation impossible. Antoine Thierry surveyed this part of his domain and judged what he saw to be acceptable. Never one to be complacent, his mind jumped to what he could do to make Club Red better, hotter and more attractive to San Francisco's sophisticated nightlife population—most of all to his fellow vampires.

As he made his way through the crowd, he listened to snippets of conversation, greeted friends old and new and kept an eye out for anything that fell below his high standards. He also kept an eye out for attractive females, for he hadn't yet decided who he'd share after hours with.

Lola Vasquez, a companion of many congenial nights, flirted with him from a corner table. It was too early for him to commit, but he'd consider Lola.

Approaching the bar to buy a drink for an old friend, Antoine spotted Lilith Graves, a sweet demi-ghoul—he'd have thought that description an oxymoron before he met her. Though Antoine tried to be reasonably tolerant, he preferred to socialize with other vampires and structured his life along those lines. Lilith was one of the few non-vampires he'd welcomed to his inner circle. His interest rose when he saw her striking companion. A stranger in town or someone who'd evaded his personal radar? As Keith, his bartender, started to ring up the women's tab, he stepped in.

Both Lilith and Ms. Breathtaking raised glasses to thank him. When Lilith's friend smiled, she nearly broke Antoine's heart. She also revealed she wasn't a vampire. Regular human? Antoine didn't sense any shifter vibes from her. He also didn't see her as a ghoul, not even a rare demi like Lilith. But there was something about her—and he intended to find out what.

"Thanks so much, Antoine," Lilith said when he'd gotten close enough for conversation.

"The pleasure is mine, Lilith—and I don't believe I've met your friend."

Lilith clucked. "That's 'cause she just got to town. This is my dearest friend in the world. Dominique LaPierre meet Club Red's owner, Antoine Thierry. Don't call him Tony."

He inclined his head, took Dominique's outstretched hand and savored the warmth of her smile. Dominique was tall, coming to right below his chin, and willowy. Two skillfully placed combs swept long raven tresses back from her finely chiseled face. Her eyes, of an icy blue rare for a brunette with olive skin, shone with intelligence and good humor. The moment he saw her, he hungered to taste her full, sensuous lips. His body began to thrum with his desire to gain intimate acquaintance with her luscious body and the strong pulse beating at the base of her long neck. "Enchanted, Ms. LaPierre." He kissed her hand, startling at the buzz that sparked between them.

"Please call me Dominique." Though her words were cool, a delicious blush colored her cheeks.

"Dominique," he repeated, his voice a shade above a whisper. "Do you live here or are you visiting?"

"I'm visiting."

"Tell me more. Where are you from?"

As Dominique had just taken a sip from her drink, Lilith answered. "Dominique and I went to Harvard together, undergrad. Roommates from freshman year on. I was content with a BA. Dominique went on for an MBA."

"Really."

Dominique rolled her eyes and started to speak, but Lilith cut her off. "She's a rising star in the business world, a major entrepreneur. I'm lucky she's decided to take a rare vacation from starting, running and selling multi-million dollar businesses."

"Very impressive." Despite the praise in the words, Antoine took care to keep his voice neutral. "And where are you based now?"

"Boston. As you might be able to tell, Lilith, in addition to being my dearest friend, is also a one-woman cheerleading squad."

Antoine noted her voice was low pitched, polished, sexy and very much in harmony with her looks. Anything less would have been a deal breaker. "From my experience, Lilith gets things right."

When Dominique smiled at him, for a moment he could believe he would do anything to please this woman—a thought he classified as "scary" and unacceptable. Though he'd grown jaded and immune to the charms of beautiful women, Dominique affected him like a breath of fresh air, which also put him on guard. Most frightening of all, in addition to his sexual excitement, an indefinable frisson of some other emotion flashed through him. Not being a man to back down from a challenge, he would spend private time with her—his first step would be taking her home with him tonight. Once he'd made her his, he'd face the unfamiliar sensations she evoked in him— and master them.

Just a few moments in Antoine Thierry's company helped Dominique understand the phrase *hypnotic vampiric gazes*. It took an effort to tear her eyes away, especially since she *wanted* to keep looking at him, no matter what games he was playing to rivet her attention.

"How long will you be in San Francisco?" His words flowed into her and took up residence in her most intimate core. This was nuts. All he'd asked was a simple social question.

"My original plan was to stay a week, but I'm flexible."

His eyes glittered, and she winced at the possible erotic images *flexible* could evoke. Great. Why did she tell him that? It was as if she were saying, "Hey, guy, I'm available." She wasn't. After her break-up with Mark, she'd decided it would be a long, long time until she put her heart on the line again for any man. If ever. Logic told her Antoine Thierry was a heartbreaker. She sensed he could damage her in ways that would make Mark's abandonment look like a romp at the beach.

"I'm glad to hear that. A week isn't nearly long enough to sample all we have to offer." He looked toward Lilith, who nodded in confirmation.

Time to nip this in the bud. "Though I'm between businesses right now, I still have obligations that might require me to cut short my vacation."

He had the most amazing, expressive eyes. "San Francisco is known to charm visitors into changing all sorts of plans."

He took her hand and rubbed one finger along the lines and flesh of her palm. The simple motion, perfectly acceptable in and invisible to mixed company, felt downright erotic.

Dominique figured she should pull away, but she didn't know how to do that without looking ungracious, so she let him continue and struggled to hold on to her senses. She swallowed hard. "I'm sure Lilith has made lots of plans for us."

"I would consider it a great privilege if you would allow me to give you a special tour of the city tonight. I guarantee I will show you a San Francisco few tourists ever get to visit." He continued stroking her palm and part of Dominique wanted to agree to anything he was offering.

But then reason returned. She was Lilith's guest, for crying out loud. Antoine's invitation had not included her best friend— the same best friend who'd just been crying on her shoulder about her lack of a social life. How crummy would Dominique have to be to abandon Lilith on her first night in the city?

She managed to extricate her hand. He seemed to sense the instant she started to withdraw. "That's very kind and generous, Mr. Thierry."

"Antoine," he murmured again.

"But you see, I've just arrived. In my part of the world, it's late. I'm sure jet lag is going to strike with a vengeance any minute." There. She'd managed to come up with a polite and plausible excuse without using Lilith as a shield.

"Of course the invitation includes Lilith," he said smoothly.

Now he mentioned that. It was okay. She could still claim jet lag. For the rest, Dominique sensed something dangerous about Antoine Thierry. She wasn't scared of him as a vampire. But as a man, he threatened her hard-won equilibrium. After the recent disaster with Mark, she valued staying well-balanced. "If Lilith wants to go with you, that's fine. I expect after this drink, I'll be ready to call it a night."

Lilith laughed and shook her head. "No offense, Antoine, but I can see you any time. Dominique and I have a lot to catch up on. But I will take a rain check on that tour. I bet you could show me things most natives haven't seen either."

"Any time." Antoine, looking the height of elegant nonchalance, nodded. "I look forward to spending more time with both of you. Welcome to my club. I hope you will be my guests here often. And now if you'll excuse me—" In moments he'd vanished into the dense crowd.

"Are you really tired?" Lilith had drunk about half her virgin Bloody Mary.

Dominique had to stifle a yawn. "Yeah, much more than I thought I'd be. I'm ready to call it a night."

They finished their drinks and made their way through the room, now much more crowded than earlier. They returned to Lilith's car, which she'd managed to park a mere three blocks away.

Enroute back to Lilith's, her friend said, "Antoine seems quite taken with you."

"He struck me as a major player. I imagine he pulls that same Don Juan act with lots of women." Dominique squirmed.

"He hasn't pulled it with me, but I agree. He likes the ladies, and it's usually reciprocal. That said, I think he appeared genuinely taken with you. So what did you think? Would you go out with him?" Lilith chuckled.

Dominique knew her friend would not let her change the subject without getting an answer. In fact, if she tried to put Lilith off, the stubborn Taurus would dig in and insist on a response. "Please. Like I don't have enough complications in my life. The last thing I need is to get involved with another player."

"Oh. You never told me that about Mark."

"I wanted to spare you. Anyway, as I'm not into bicoastal relationships, it's a moot point. I live in Boston, Antoine's in San Francisco."

"I'm not asking if you're interested in a lifetime commitment. Just about going out with him while you're here. Heck, you could have a fling. He strikes me as the perfect guy to have an intense but meaningless affair with."

Dominique shook her head. "I meant what I said. I'm on an extended hiatus from any kind of social life. I'm not about to change my mind for Antoine Thierry."

"I think my lady protesteth too much."

Dominique was about to protest some more when Lilith pointed out there was no need. "I won't bug you any more about him. But have you ever been out with a vampire?"

"No," Dominique admitted. "You haven't either, have you?"

"Oh, yes," Lilith said.

"How come I didn't know about that? Since when do you hold out?"

"It must have been while you were tied up in one of your business deals. Unfortunately, the whole thing didn't last long—

just like all my relationships. But you know what? It's true what they say. They are the most amazing lovers."

Of everything Dominique didn't need to hear tonight, Lilith's comment topped the charts. "You've been with lovers from enough groups to make a judgment like that?"

"Almost," Lilith said. "Pretty much everyone I want to date except shifters."

"It doesn't sound like your social life is as sorry a mess as you were saying earlier."

Lilith snorted. "Any statements I make are based on my excellent memory, not recent experience."

They'd arrived back at Lilith's place. Dominique found her friend's situation intriguing enough to stir thought processes. Besides, concentrating on problem solving would occupy her mind. She needed to keep from focusing too much attention on Antoine Thierry and imagining herself between the sheets with that sexy vampire.

Chapter Two

"So, Antoine," Lola Vasquez purred at him over a drink. "My plans for the rest of the night fell through. That means I'm footloose and fancy free." She stared at him, her brown cat's eyes brimming with a promise he knew she could amply fill. She licked full red lips and smiled. In her skin-tight gold *lamé*, Lola looked like a Christmas gift just waiting to be unwrapped—again.

Antoine never went home alone after making the rounds of his clubs. The night had flown by before he'd chosen a companion. Lola would be superb company. But tonight, something weird was going on with him. He felt preoccupied and restless—way different than before he met Dominique LaPierre. Since that electrifying moment, something fundamental inside him had shifted. His lack of interest in the beautiful women around him was just a symptom. Contrary to his typical superb self-control, he couldn't stop thinking about her. All the other women now seemed insipid.

He took Lola's hand and kissed the elegantly jeweled and manicured fingers. "I wish I were also free."

She raised a perfect arched brow. "I thought you were."

"The grapevine has it wrong tonight." He conjured up his most mysterious, guarded look.

She pouted, displaying her ruby lips to full advantage. Before she could press for further details, he excused himself and made his escape.

Dominique LaPierre. The merest memory of their brief encounter aroused him. His cock, semi-erect from the first moment, throbbed with insistence at every thought of her. In addition to her physical beauty and her impressive intelligence, some other quality he couldn't identify drew him. He shook his head to clear the image away, but it persisted. Deciding to call it a night far earlier than usual, he drove home alone.

What made her stand out? Antoine wasn't in the habit of kidding himself, especially about women. Bloody hell, he felt like some horny adolescent, turned on by the images in his head. Unlike the horny adolescent he'd been too long ago to think about, he typically satisfied his sexual hungers and moved on. Frustration was no longer part of his personal experience.

Or it hadn't been until tonight. But he wanted Dominique with a stark desire strong as a physical ache. Dominique, who'd turned down his invitation with claims of jet leg. Plausible, of course. For most men. Except that women didn't turn him down. This one, however, didn't appear to experience a moment's hesitation before she'd refused. He was not one to take "No" as an answer. In the privacy of his Mercedes, he growled his rage.

If she were as exhausted as she claimed, she must have gone to sleep hours ago. He, on the other hand, would not go easily to his rest. Once home, he paced like a madman. He'd have to seek release.

Fortunately, her waking or sleeping was no obstacle. Since he'd long ago perfected the art of dream visits, he could be with Dominique tonight. As this mode required a great deal of psychic energy, he indulged on the rarest of occasions. But possessing Dominique would be worth whatever he must expend.

He would never force himself on any woman, whether in a dream or waking state. He never had to. But his instincts told him Dominique wanted him. A dream visit would remove all obstacles and allow them both to act on their attraction. As he geared himself to go to her, excitement spiraled outward from deep inside him. By spending this night with her, he would achieve exquisite satisfaction and get her out of his system.

At an early age, Dominique decided to suppress her witch's heritage and identity. Her maternal grandmother, Maeve, warned that no matter how much Dominique tried, she would never be able to distance herself completely from who she was. But the women in her family were strong-willed. Dominique put as much energy into rejecting her heritage as the women before her invested in guarding it.

Maeve and Siobhan, Dominique's mother, did not take her decision lightly. When they challenged her motivation, Dominique raised the banner of rationality. If she couldn't analyze witch magick and understand its components, she didn't want it in her life. As she saw it, taking part in the family tradition would force her to invoke elements beyond her control—a practice she refused.

Instead, Dominique insisted on creating her own identity and resolved to make business her life's work and mission. Maeve pointed out that she could shape her own practice of witch magick to be a component of success in business. But Dominique made a solemn vow never to resort to magick in any of her business dealings.

The only family tradition she kept up was a night-time ritual that soothed her like a fuzzy, cuddly teddy bear and affected only her. Before she went to sleep, Dominique would visualize what she wanted to dream of. Often her dreams inspired some aspect of her work and provided a touch of free-spirited originality she found acceptable.

But tonight, her usual routines seemed to elude her and her mind refused to behave. No matter how she tried to steer her thoughts, one image claimed control—Antoine Thierry. Her fixation on him ran counter to everything she believed in and felt committed to. She concentrated her energy on evicting him from her mind's eye. For the first time ever, she failed to meet a self-chosen challenge.

Exasperated and trying to blame her lack of success on jet lag, Dominique forcibly focused her consciousness on the image and sounds of ocean tides. The sun burned bright on the horizon before ceding to a silvery moon. Rays of moonlight flowed down to a white-sanded beach where a tall figure strode, arms out, coming ever closer to claim her. Antoine. Gritting her teeth, she shook her head. No matter what she tried, she couldn't banish Antoine from her thoughts for more than a fleeting moment.

Exhausted, but still focused on him, she decided to give up on her ritual and let her mind drift. She would see him again tomorrow, armed with the intentional goal to cure herself of her ridiculous, obsessive attraction.

She'd succeed—tomorrow. But right now she thrashed in a strange bed. What was wrong with her? She never had trouble sleeping. Knowing how late her internal clock thought it was, she couldn't begin to understand why sleep wouldn't come. The night felt like a vast, unfriendly desert she was stranded in.

She visualized them back in his bar. Gazing at her, lips parted, Antoine held out a drink. Dominique looked around for Lilith who, she saw, was talking and laughing with other friends and didn't seem to miss her. Determined to break away from him after one drink, Dominique accepted. Forewarned was forearmed. Prepared to deal with the sexual excitement his presence aroused, she steeled herself to use the full force of her will to resist his attraction.

But when she got close to Antoine, the power of his piercing gaze didn't diminish. The exact opposite. His eyes seemed to penetrate all her facades and secrets. Though he didn't say a word, she understood she could hide nothing from him. Far from being revolted, she welcomed his intimate scrutiny and opened herself to him in complete surrender.

Her hand trembled so that she nearly spilled her drink, bringing her back to her senses for a moment. What was she doing? What was happening to her? She had to find a way to distance herself from him. With great effort she managed to raise her drink to her lips and take a sip of the excellent virgin mojito. Wishing she'd worn shades, Dominique brazened out meeting Antoine's gaze.

"Tell me about your business."

That was not what she'd expected him to say, but she felt almost grateful to him for attempting to diffuse the sexual tension—at least for the moment. But each mundane word went straight to her core. He may as well have asked, "Want to fuck?"

She braced herself to resist the erotic thrum of her traitorous thoughts. "Yes. I just sold a business I started right out of graduate school, and I've decided to take some time off before I decide what's next." Nothing like babbling.

Then his unbusinesslike fingers traced a path down the side of her face, and thoughts of business flew from her head. His touch awoke and aroused her. Her clit throbbed for him when all he did was stroke her burning cheek. She pressed her legs tight.

His smile got her even hotter—if she could call the spare movement of his sensuous lips leading to the slight upward quirk at the corners a smile. More than his glittering eyes, that movement of his mouth told her he'd read to the bottom of her soul and he wanted her. Despite Antoine's sophisticated veneer, Dominique intuited the pulse of his primitive hunger for her, and she responded with a subliminal rhythm in exact harmony.

"Is there any possibility we can *tempt* you to start a business out here?"

The question left her breathless. At the moment, he could probably tempt her to try to fly to Mars. His power over her took root and grew despite her vows to resist. She made a noncommittal reply, just enough to move their conversation along.

"I find you very intriguing and want to get to know you better. Let's go somewhere to be alone." Antoine's soft utterance melted what remained of her resistance.

She could think of nothing she desired more. Without uttering a sound, she agreed.

He scooped her up, lunged to the club's exit and, in moments was soaring high above San Francisco with her cradled in his arms. "This is one of the most romantic cities in the world, but we natives never take the time to enjoy it until a visitor arrives." His words caressed her as they flew high above the urban landscape. Despite the night's mildness, Dominique burrowed into Antoine's warmth.

"That argues for remaining a visitor instead of taking up residence," she whispered.

He kissed her then, his lips first brushing hers with the lightness of a sigh. She'd never kissed a vampire before and had always wondered if the fangs might intrude. They didn't, at least not in this gentle meeting of lips.

Curious to touch his fangs, Dominique deepened the kiss, pressing her mouth against Antoine's and forcing his lips open. He moved his head away for a moment and regarded her with obvious amusement in his eyes.

"Your fangs," she whispered.

"Yes, what about them? Did I bite you?"

"Not yet." She blushed, a reaction she despised but couldn't seem to break herself of.

"Would you like me to?"

She couldn't believe she'd all but *asked* a vampire to bite her. "I expected your bite to be unavoidable during the course of a kiss."

"So you've been thinking about kissing me. All you needed to do was ask."

Embarrassment heated her. "Curiosity," she rasped.

He laughed. "Believe it or not, I don't know the answer. In the interest of advancing knowledge, in addition to your being so beautiful you take my breath away, I'd say a deeper, longer kiss is called for."

Her heartbeat accelerated as he closed his mouth over hers. He opened her lips with his questing tongue and teeth. Resolved to remain alert even as her body claimed precedence over thought processes, she focused on the sensations of their contact. Antoine smelled and tasted sexy. She couldn't analyze the exact components of his physical presence. She could only identify how the combination made her feel.

His teeth—whether his fangs or his other teeth, she couldn't tell—grazed over her lips and tongue, stimulating and arousing her, feeling nothing at all like a bite. More like a sexy nibble.

As she continued to research her question, she followed him into a deeper, more intimate kiss that left her gasping and hungry.

When he moved back from her, she longed to lunge after him. "What's the verdict?" His eyes glittered.

"May I touch you there?" Her voice quivered and her hand shook.

"You want to touch my fangs?"

Fingers outstretched, she nodded.

"This is indeed an intimate gesture. I would have to feel very close to anyone I allowed to perform such an action."

Was he mocking her or was everything she'd ever learned about vampires rubbish? Before she could ask, he continued, "Lucky for us, I feel very close with you." His deep voice grew even lower as he said the last words, which resonated through her like a lover's breath. Her heart expanded at the notion of sharing such closeness with him, but a sudden attack of shyness kept her from admitting so.

"Please, go ahead and touch me." He grasped her fingers with his hand, and the warmth of his touch surged through her. Then he opened his mouth, and Dominique saw the two pointed fangs gleam in the late-night darkness.

With extreme caution, she placed a finger on the tip of one fang and tested its sharpness. When Antoine ran his fangs and teeth over first her finger, then her lips, the contact felt soft and sensuous. Yet she knew these same fangs could pierce her. Though vampires didn't have a reputation for being gentle, he treated her with great tenderness. So many misconceptions. How lucky she was to be in his arms to learn the truth.

Once he'd entered Dominique's dream, Antoine congratulated himself for following his instincts. The arousal he'd experienced when they met turned out to be no fluke. In her presence, he discovered she was even more unique and intriguing than he'd first realized. Her true nature remained a mystery, which fascinated and intrigued him. What caused the vibes he got from her? She fit into no category he could yet identify. Always eager to master a challenge, he knew he would figure her out before long.

Meanwhile, their kiss turned him on with far more power than anticipated. He wanted to know this woman on every possible level of intimacy, up to and including the vampiric embrace that would uncover the most intimate secrets of her heart and soul.

He brought her to her room in Lilith's house, though he wanted to bring her to the innermost chamber of his personal quarters. This desire rattled him, for he wasn't a man to bestow such tokens of affection lightly.

Accustomed to holding back in every intimate encounter, Antoine found himself tempted to lower his usual barriers. Of course, this meant he would have to erect them even higher. He drew her to him. "I open my life to you and invite you in."

She laughed. "Antoine Thierry, you are the most closed-off man I've ever met."

"Open me," he commanded. He would allow himself this new experience this one night. Tomorrow, when he'd had his fill of Dominique, he'd return to normal—stronger than ever.

She melted into his arms with a sigh and a whimper, allowing him to enjoy the life force of her body, her strength and vitality.

His acute senses drank in the regular drumbeat of her heart, the warmth of her breath, the sensuous pressure of her high, firm breasts molded against his chest. He needed to see those breasts and stroke the nipples into excitement. He took off her white lace nightshirt and watched with pleasure as she shivered with delight in a slight draft.

His cock had gone from half-arousal to the full deal as soon as they were alone together. Antoine Thierry was not one for delayed gratification, and he'd never been hard for so long without satisfying his lust.

But with Dominique he savored the lust and even the tension that pushed him to satisfy his sexual hunger. Much as he wanted to make love with her—it wouldn't be a simple fuck tonight—every step of their being together had to be memorable. After all, he had no guarantee she would decide to stay in San Francisco for any length of time, and Boston wasn't for him. This night—this dream—might be their only time together. So, despite the urge to gorge himself in a marathon fuck fest, his wiser self squelched that impulse. Even if it killed him, he'd proceed at a slow pace. Whatever was about to happen between them would be extraordinary.

When he touched her breast for the first time, Dominique sucked in her breath so hard, he at first feared he'd hurt her, maybe pressed too hard. Other lovers had told him he didn't know his own strength. But the feel of her skin, the exquisite responsiveness of her pink nipples and the areolas made his intention to move with infinite slowness a challenge of vampiric proportions.

"I want to touch your nipples too," Dominique announced.

Just the prospect set his blood to coursing. Even before she touched him, his nipples pebbled into hardness.

She followed his every move as he tossed off his black silk shirt and stood bare-chested. She drank him in with her eyes before she touched him. When his nipples dug into her palms, she raised an eyebrow and smiled. She ran her hands over his chest and Antoine realized he would not, after all, be able to continue his delaying tactics.

Dominique had never before *ached* to have a man between her legs as she now ached for the feel of Antoine's hard cock deep within her. Goddess knew he'd been hard since their first moments together—she'd snuck glances at his crotch, and then she'd felt his tempting bulge pressed against her in each embrace. He seemed huge, restrained within his still-fastened pants so that she feared he might explode before she ever got him inside her. But, judging from his movements and his sounds, her wait was about to end. If not, she'd have to take matters into her own hands.

His eyes wide with invitation, Antoine pressed her hand exactly where she wanted it—over his bulge. To show her acceptance, she squeezed him there and then unzipped his pants. When Antoine's erection sprang free, they both sighed. His cock rose thick and long, so appealing she wanted to get on her knees and take him into her mouth. When he realized what she planned, Antoine shook his head. "Tempting as the prospect is, I want this first time to last. If you take me into your mouth, it won't."

She loved knowing how much she turned him on, what power she had over Antoine. What clothes they still had on interfered with this power. She needed to be naked with him now. Eyes fixed on his, she stripped and threw her clothes aside. He growled as he swallowed her up with his eyes. Lips locked with hers, he backed her to the king-size bed covered with black silk and laid her down.

Her heartbeat careened out of control as desire swept through her. Antoine groaned, rubbing his erection along her belly, down to the warm wetness of her pussy. With her body on fire, she met his longing with her own, relying on instinct to lead her. Antoine pulled away from her for a moment, and Dominique thrust her hands out to draw him back.

"I want you," he whispered.

"I'm yours," she whispered back.

He started to say something else, then appeared to change his mind. Instead, he laid his head on her breasts. She burned for him to possess her. He traced a line down her belly to her sensuous core, and Dominique sucked in her breath hard.

Already wet and hot for him, she'd die if he didn't possess her completely.

But now Antoine began to act as if he had all the time in the world. Maybe he did—but she didn't.

"Touch me." Though she despised her neediness, Dominique whimpered the words of desire.

"With delight, my lady. I am yours to direct."

Right. The last thing this man would ever do was obey. But he flashed a smile. She'd never understand this man who seemed to know all her secret desires. With his mouth and hands, he dared her to dance to his erotic beat.

She squirmed with intense need, which seemed to feed his huge ego. But she could worry about that later, much later, when she'd achieved the satisfaction only he could bring her. Quivering, she placed his questing hand where she most needed it. "Here," she ordered, except her request came out as a gasp. If he refused her, she'd wither into a little pile of ash.

"As you wish, my beauty," he crooned before he expertly flicked her clit with his large thumb. Still trying to hold on to a shred of dignity and control, Dominique bit her lip. She wanted to cloak herself with an icy mantle. Like an empress entwined with a commoner, she'd command him to fill her wishes. But at this point she couldn't even dredge up the right words. Though she longed to come in his arms, she didn't want this man to realize the extent of his power over her—a losing battle, she suspected.

The sensuous pressure of his fingers tracing the contours of her pussy, playing with her folds and her clit, distracted her from further thoughts. The sharp, thrilling sensation of his touch, the overwhelming promise of his presence filled her. At this moment, she would give herself totally to the physical wonder of being with him. Later, she'd have too much time—the rest of her life—to analyze what had happened. She would be with him only once.

Antoine slipped a finger into her, teasing her with a foretaste of the satisfaction she craved. She moved her hips to maximize the sweet pressure of his touch inside her.

"The things you do to me, Dominique." He took her hand and splayed her fingers around his aroused length.

The feel of his erection, rock hard and throbbing against her hand, tantalized her beyond endurance. Why was he making her wait? She wanted to take him completely inside her, needed him so much. Her pussy clenched and tightened, holding his finger hostage.

Now that she'd felt the dimensions of his erection, his finger could never be enough, no matter how great his skill as he played with her. Dominique had to have his cock in her right then. "Come into me."

He rose and for a moment stared at her with such intensity, she swore he'd swallowed up her soul. Then with a growl, he lowered himself to her again.

She wanted to seize every moment so she would always remember the sensation of his skin heating her, his hard muscles pressed against her own firmness and softness, his mysterious scent, the pungency of being with him like this. Just the two of them alone together in their own world.

Her hand trembling, she squeezed his aroused length, making him even harder. The veins and cords of his cock stood out along the marble of his shaft, and all she could think was how she wanted to take him into her in every possible way. She longed to taste, smell, lick and nibble this beautiful man's body. Much as she yearned to tongue him and cover his cock with love bites, her pussy would not be denied. Still lying on their sides and facing each other, Antoine opened Dominique's legs and positioned his sex at the apex of her need.

One hand on his cock and the other on her ass, Antoine filled her feminine opening with the thick head of his engorged penis and gently probed. Dominique gasped as the movement unleashed sensations she'd gone too long—maybe forever— without. In reaction to her shudder and her soft growl, he clasped her to him and thrust his huge, hard dick deep inside her.

Dominique came close to weeping at the wonder of how she felt with him inside her. Though she'd anticipated the pleasure of his intimate touch, nothing came close to the wonder of the reality. She closed her legs around him as if to hold him forever, though she'd never before imagined forever.

In a moment, he'd intensified their contact and slid even deeper inside her. With both hands clamped on her ass, he held her tight, as if he also had no intention of ever letting go. Little movements she allowed herself set off sparks of pleasure that radiated outward from her core. But she couldn't pace herself.

Her breathing went ragged with her effort. She needed more from him, harder and faster, though giving herself such freedom might force them far too quickly to their peak.

In this erotic interlude with this man, she escaped beyond all her usual limits and inhibitions. Being with Antoine was the ultimate one-night stand.

With a slight nudge, she got him to turn over. Driven by a pulsing desire, she mounted him. A surge of sensation gripped her as she slid down him. Growling with joy, she went for the ride of her life. Antoine clutched her ass, holding her so tight there couldn't be a single iota of space between them. Closer, closer, closer. His cock was buried so deep inside her they truly were one. Everywhere he touched raised such arcs of pleasure that she couldn't pause, couldn't stop to savor the wonder. More, more, more.

Nearly drunk with pleasure and with greed to fully experience all he had to offer, she lay down flat on top of him so they were skin to skin. She had to kiss him, to rub her lips over his, to feel his heart beat against hers. He adjusted to her shift by tightening his hold. All the time, he stroked her ass as he pumped himself ever so slowly into her, thrusting his cock in, pulling back, outlining subtle movements with his hips that left her gasping.

Her kiss began tenderly as she tasted his lips with the tip of her tongue. Despite her desire to linger as she would over a rare, fine wine, her need to drink more deeply impelled her to raise the heat. And so she rushed from licking his lips to a tangling of tongues. Though Antoine appeared to exercise almost maddening control, his breathing accelerated as his cock grew harder and more insistent. He pressed his own demands for complete intimacy as his fingers teased the crease and hole between her cheeks. Even the slightest touch heightened her arousal. Soon she'd blasted into orbit, floating among the stars and planets of darkest outer space.

When she could no longer hold back, a soul-shattering climax engulfed her, shaking her from the tips of her toes to the top of her head. "I'm coming," she sang out to Antoine and the rest of the universe. He smiled and stroked her, smug in his knowledge of exactly what he was doing, of what she felt. Through her paroxysms of pleasure, he remained rock-hard, urging her on to this ultimate orgasm.

Shuddering in his arms, all that remained for perfection was to feel him explode in her, come deep inside her. First, he'd come the way other men did. And then, from what she knew of vampires, there'd be the final act, the unique vampiric bonding that would seal their union and leave her forever in his thrall.

Curious but just a little afraid, she overcame her slight hesitation to open to the total experience of being with him. She rode him and rode him, but still he remained rock-hard. Like some super man, he held firm and didn't come. Damn it, he had to come, or she wouldn't be complete. She gritted her teeth and dedicated her entire being to making him come. She rode and rode and rode...

For the first time ever, Antoine took in far more energy than he expended—psychic and sexual. She turned him on so, making the pleasure of their lovemaking last instead of surrendering to a hasty come required great focus. Fortunately, he was the perfect man to meet this sublime challenge. By dint of his superb control, he'd transcended ordinary limits and transported them both into a new realm. With this beautiful woman in his arms, he could soar beyond even the boundaries of his imagination. With little effort, he could have lasted until dawn, except...

Except that, even though Dominique vibrated with pleasure at each caress, he sensed her need for what only he could offer. She needed to feel him climax, to know him in the throes of his orgasm. Attuned to her with every fiber of his being, he intuited her craving for the vampiric kiss. When his thoughts went there, his arousal thrust him beyond the limits of control.

But there was an indefinable something that shielded her from his full vampiric power. The mystery he'd sensed earlier intensified. Soon, he would know all about her—including the name of the hidden power that hindered her complete surrender. She craved what her nature wouldn't let her have. Locked in their embrace, he shifted them so she lay under him. Her beautiful long legs joined around his waist, and he felt her muscles tense as she tightened her hold.

Lying with her beneath him, Antoine penetrated even deeper into her welcoming embrace. To his amazement, she opened herself yet more, responding to his movements with renewed energy and drawing him to unexplored layers. Warm and dewy from her exertions, she thrashed and writhed in acceptance of his total embrace and their profound erotic intimacy.

Overwhelmed, Antoine at last relinquished control. Unleashing himself with a howl, he let her know he was coming. With an explosion of passion that started deep inside him and gathered force, he drove himself into her, again and again and again—until there was nothing left. The universe around him shattered.

Dominique held him through the storm of his orgasm, clinging to him as his movements became wilder and more frenetic. Spent, he clasped her without words as the tide of sensation began to recede.

"Are you all right?" he murmured when his brain resumed functioning. He kissed her hair, the sweet smooth skin of her forehead.

"Funny question. Why shouldn't I be?" She studied him quizzically with her beautiful blue eyes, no longer icy.

"That was kind of intense." The word sounded lame as he pronounced it.

"I thought *intense* went with the turf when one hangs out with vampires."

"I suppose. Sometimes, when it's the first time, non-vamps feel overwhelmed."

"The first time? That has implications..."

Usually his partner would be the one speaking about "the first time" and trying to ascertain if there would be more. The desire to be with Dominique beyond tonight both excited and disturbed him. Needing her, wanting her would threaten his habitual control, make him vulnerable—a unique situation that should make him run like hell in the other direction. But the only running he wanted to do was to her.

Time to change the subject. Now came complete revelation time. "What are you, Dominique LaPierre? I sense you have special powers, but not what they are. I've never before encountered anyone like you. I hadn't expected ever to be surprised anymore."

From the way her facial expression altered, his question did not please her, which, of course, amped up his curiosity.

"I don't understand what you're asking." Her voice sounded falsely neutral.

The room had just grown ten degrees colder. He admired that kind of ability. He stroked her face, letting his fingers slip down to the tender spot where her jugular pulsed, and he hungered. Much as he burned to drink of her, her powers would complicate the final embrace. "I think you do. There's very little that gets past you. Tell me, what are you? Surely not a demi-ghoul like your friend, Lilith? No. I don't get a sense of your sharing her nature."

She pushed away from him, sat up and drew the sheet around herself. "I don't know what else your radar is telling you, but I'd advise you to get it adjusted."

He shook his head at that. "The signals are getting stronger. I'm totally intrigued, even more than before. There's nothing you could say that would diminish my regard for you."

She shrugged. "Think what you will. I suspect that once you form an opinion, you're not one to be swayed by information that doesn't support it."

"You haven't answered my question."

"Your being here in Lilith's house with me was a big mistake. Leave now." Her eyes were an even icier blue now than when they'd met.

"You choose to push me away rather than tell me the truth."

"There's no truth to tell you, except that I want you to leave." Despite the confidence of her words, her face reflected conflicting emotions. "I don't want to be with you any more. Leave me." Her vehemence and agitation grew with each word.

Dominique evidently had a lot invested in not revealing herself. That she could keep this secret from him, despite the searing intimacy between them, aroused his curiosity the way her beauty aroused his lust. Intrigued before, Antoine viewed her secrecy as a personal challenge. He would find out what she was guarding with such ferocity. Then he would know how to proceed.

But nothing more would happen tonight. Fangs throbbing, he exited from her dream and hovered near her just long enough to see her fall into a deep sleep. Then with a strange sense of bereftness, he wrenched himself away and made his solitary way home.

Chapter Three

Dominique woke the next morning feeling weird, hung-over, well-loved—as if she'd had the best sex of her life—and inspired to start a new business. Considering she'd just arrived in San Francisco, she'd already gotten a lot of mileage out of her trip.

As she brushed her teeth, her face grew hot with a bright red blush. Startling, detailed memories of a particularly vivid dream rocked her. She put down her toothbrush and gripped the edge of the sink. In her remembered dream—nightmare—Antoine Thierry had insinuated himself into her bed. He'd made passionate love with her, taking her to new levels of sensuality and satisfying her on every level except... Waves of heat coursed through her as the memory unspooled like the film reel from hell.

Then a pang of regret chilled her. He'd stopped short of the vampiric kiss, leaving her frustrated. She clutched her throat, unable to believe she'd ever want such a kiss. Maybe she couldn't dream a vampire's feeding because she'd never experienced one. On the other hand, she'd never before had such over-the-moon sex, but she'd been able to dream it. What could this mean? Slivers of the dream kept springing to mind, disturbing her. Remembering the intensity of her climaxes—definitely multiple, also a first—she blushed harder.

Despite the emotion in her dream, she shivered with distaste at the prospect of the averted kiss. Vampires, even sexy ones, weren't her type—and Antoine was Exhibit A to justify her opinion. She valued her independence too much to get entangled with a macho control freak like him. A mere dream about him shook up her world. All her instincts screamed that the reality would be much worse.

Even in the dream, he'd become a serious threat to all she cherished. When she'd abandoned her deepest principles and surrendered to him, he'd pressed her to reveal her identity. His untimely insistence broke the mood and freed her from his enchantment. He'd wanted total consummation as much— maybe more than she had. She'd kicked him out rather than tell him who she was. End of dream.

Why had this question come up in her fantasy? Her lineage was not relevant to her life. When she should have gone through her coven's coming-of-age ritual, she'd refused. To her family's regret, Dominique renounced her heritage. She didn't follow any practices, didn't hook up with other witches and didn't let her past influence the present.

Though she'd inherited her identity, Dominique viewed being a witch as different from being a vampire, a shifter, or even a demi-ghoul like Lilith. Dominique's body didn't change with the moon's phases, her teeth didn't grow, dawn or dusk made no difference to her... To control her ghoul nature, Lilith had to be a strict vegetarian. All Dominique had to do was say "No"—never a challenge.

So why had her true identity come up in her dream about Antoine? Totally weird.

Bemused, she showered, dressed and prepared for the day. She didn't like the implications of her dream. In fact, the seed of danger she'd sensed around Antoine had blossomed into a woman-eating weed she'd better avoid. She knew she shouldn't underestimate the strength of his appeal. Antoine Thierry avoidance was a powerful motivator for keeping her vacation in San Francisco short. Knowing Lilith would be upset if she left too soon, Dominique's guard went up—she hoped not too late. After all, her primary reason for coming was to cheer up Lilith.

Her dream and Lilith's laments percolated in her mind like morning coffee. An idea tugged at her entrepreneurial heart. She sensed she could start a successful new business and help her friend. The chance to do both would be hard to walk away from.

By the time Dominique got to the kitchen, Lilith was already dressed and eating breakfast—a lot of fruit, a small amount of cereal, yogurt to hold the combination together and a heavenly caffeine-rich brew. Huge red strawberries, plump blueberries and raspberries, orange and green wedges of melon.

Dominique's stomach rumbled. New business ideas always made her hungry.

After she had helped herself, she sat down across the country French table from Lilith.

"How'd you sleep?" her friend asked.

Dominique choked on the coffee she'd just sipped. She considered lying to her close friend a slippery slope she didn't want to set foot on. Rather than decide whether to tell her about the dream—and if she did, how much detail to go into—she redirected the conversation.

"I have an idea for a new business."

Lilith rolled her eyes. "I can't believe it. I thought you were going to take some time off for bad behavior. You haven't even been here two days. Now I feel like I've messed up in my mission to help you unwind and have a good time."

"Don't be silly. Actually, Lilith, you're the inspiration for my new business idea."

"Even worse. Not only have I not encouraged you to take a break, talking to me has made you run, not walk, to another work opportunity." She groaned.

"We'll have to work on banishing that guilt, girlfriend. So, you want to hear about my idea?"

"I know I shouldn't encourage you in this, but, yeah. How can I resist? You amaze me with how you can come up with million-dollar business ideas at the drop of a hat." Lilith refilled her coffee cup and offered to top up Dominique's. "So tell me."

"I've been thinking about what you said—about the shortage of great dates in the San Francisco area. If a woman like you can't get a decent date, something is out of whack."

"You don't think it's just me that's out of whack?" Lilith's voice had a pleading note in it.

They'd also have to do something to lift her low self-esteem. If Dominique's business could accomplish that, she'd consider it a success—which didn't preclude making a profit. "Of course not. Lilith Graves, guys should be lining up around the block to get you to even consider going out with them. Objective opinion. You're intelligent, beautiful, smart, have a great sense of humor. All that plus a fabulous trust fund. I mean, come on. What's the problem?"

Lilith shrugged. "So, what exactly does my lack of a social life have to do with starting a business?"

"After you described your situation, at first I thought there must be a shortage of eligible men. After last night, I don't think that's it. But for some reason, the terrific guys and the terrific women aren't meeting."

Lilith looked less than impressed. She shook her head. "You know I'm your biggest fan, but I think you're off here."

Dominique frowned. "What do you mean?"

"There are already lots of dating services here in San Francisco and the whole Bay Area."

"Yeah, so why doesn't a fantastic woman like you have the dates you want? There are available guys out there..."

To Dominique's dismay, Lilith's eyes filled with tears. *Rats.*

"Sorry for the water works. Look, the short answer is no service I know of will find dates for ghouls—even vegetarian demi-ghouls." She blew her nose.

"What?" Dominique couldn't believe her ears. "You mean they refuse to allow you to register?"

Her friend wiped away tears as she nodded.

"How can they do that?"

She shrugged. "The official word is that the ghoul population is too small to be profitable for them. If we want a dating service, we should start our own."

"Are they saying ghouls should date only other ghouls?"

"Not in so many words. But they claim other groups show little interest in dates with ghouls, so it's not cost effective to keep us in their databases."

Dominique slammed her mug down so hard coffee sloshed onto the table. "Not cost effective? What did you say when some creep told you that?"

"What could I say? I thought about organizing a multi-ghoul protest march, but I haven't gotten past planning." She sniffled.

"Well, you should do it. Heck, I'll march with you. You know what? You're my first client."

"Your first client? Won't that set you up for your first ever business failure?"

"Failure? I never heard of that word." And she didn't intend to start now.

"Well, stick with me, and you'll soon learn the meaning."

"*Au contraire*, my friend. Stick with me and you'll forget

that nasty word exists. I've got my first client. Now all I have to do is set up the business."

Lilith almost smiled. "Heck, I don't want to be just your client. I want to be your partner and first employee. I've been looking for interesting work." She paused. "Does this mean you're moving out here to San Francisco?" Her eyes danced.

Move to the West Coast? "Hmm. I hadn't thought out that part of it. These days it's easy to conduct business long distance. But for the time being, yeah. I'll be out here until we're up and operational. After that, who knows?"

Lilith whooped. "Hell, even if you don't get me any dates, which is a distinct possibility, I'm in. It'll be great having you here for as long as you stay. But, aside from having me as a client and you as the business brains, what will set our service apart from all the others?"

"We'll have the most up-to-date computer matches, cutting-edge tech."

"I repeat my question. Don't forget, Silicon Valley is here. The latest high tech is everywhere."

Dominique's ideas were at a very preliminary stage. This was how she always started off, taking the germ of a concept and brainstorming like crazy until she had a firm plan to work from, so Lilith's objections didn't faze her. "For one thing, the service will be open to every kind of being—including ghouls. And beings can be matched with other beings of their choice. As long as our programs find them compatible, we'll match them."

"Even witches?" Lilith gazed hard at her.

Dominique winced. Lilith was one of the few people outside her family who knew the details of Dominique's true identity. On several occasions, her friend had expressed concern about her rejection of her family traditions.

"If I can accept my father's family, surely you can accept your mother's."

Lips pursed, Dominique nodded. "Even witches." Hopefully, none would actually sign up—but she'd deal with that possibility when she came to it. The two women ate the rest of their breakfast in companionable silence. Lilith's mention of witches reminded Dominique of Antoine's probing.

Since the probing had occurred in a dream, she shrugged off the uncomfortable memory and forced herself to think of other matters. "I'd like to get started scoping out how to do this.

What do you think? How should we begin?" She finished her coffee.

Her new business partner thought for a few moments. "Let's meet with leaders of the different communities to get precise information about how many beings from their groups would be interested. Also, we can get an up-to-date census of single men and women. I'm assuming we'll also make gay matches."

"Of course. That's a great idea about meeting with the community leaders for an initial survey. So, what are the groups and who are their leaders?"

Lilith grabbed a pad and listed them all, after which she read out what she'd written. "Of course, you've already met the most influential vampire leader—Antoine Thierry. We can catch up with him again tonight."

"Isn't there anyone else we can talk to in the vampire community? I got the impression it's pretty large." Dominique's heart sank when she thought of seeing him again. She'd be so focused on not blushing, she'd fumble in her efforts to be professional. Vampires were reputed to be great mind readers... Her face grew hot at the prospect.

Lilith's brows drew together. "Hey, I thought you two hit it off."

"It's just that I've already met him. I figured it would be good to diversify my contacts." *That sounded convincing, right?* She squirmed under the other woman's scrutiny.

"Yeah, that would be good. But Antoine's the top go-to man for the vampire community. Anyone else would be a distant second. If you have a problem with him, you really need to work it out."

All right. When it came to business, she was a pro. If she wanted to pursue this idea, it looked like she couldn't avoid Antoine Thierry. She'd deal.

And, after all, last night had really just been a dream, right? All in her head. Why was she letting the memory get to her?

"Not that way," Antoine growled when he saw how his host

had arranged the tables for a large party at Club Red. "Fix it the way we agreed."

"Right, boss." His employee looked at him as if he'd sprouted a third fang. The table arrangement wasn't that far off. Usually Antoine kept his temper in check and picked his battles, but he wasn't in the habit of waking up with a raging hard-on for the wrong woman. After his dream encounter with Dominique LaPierre, he was supposed to be over her. But his obsession had grown stronger after the first contact, after she'd booted him out. She was getting on his nerves.

"I'll be in my office," he muttered.

He sat down at his desk and tried to figure out what he was doing wrong. He should have fed off her when he'd had the chance, despite discovering her natural resistance. A little hypnotic suggestion, a few piercing gazes and she'd have forgotten she'd ordered him to leave and begged for his embrace. Together, they'd have gotten past her defenses. But he'd gone along with her protest and left. Only that failure could explain why he couldn't evict her from his thoughts.

What was her identity? Who was she? He'd never before taken this long to figure out what a being was. From the way she'd turned frosty when he probed, she had some major hang-ups. Usually that turned him off, but he was more turned on than ever.

This had to end pronto or it would drive him crazy. Once he knew who Dominique LaPierre was, he would move on. He was sure of it. He was about to dial Lilith Graves's number when his personal line rang. "Thierry."

"Antoine, it's Lilith Graves."

He smiled. Fortuitous timing. "Ah, I was just thinking of you."

"You were?"

No need for further explanation. "What can I do for you?"

"You remember my friend Dominique, the gorgeous brunette I introduced you to last night?"

Better than he remembered his own name. "I never forget a beautiful face."

Lilith laughed. "I've heard that about you."

"My fame precedes me."

"Well, I have some fabulous news. Dominique has a

business idea she'd like to develop here in San Francisco. As is her usual style, she wants to get started quickly. Did I tell you she made a thirty-million dollar profit when she sold her last business?"

"Interesting. Are you calling because you want me to help with this idea?"

"Yes. We'd like to talk to you about it tonight, if we can steal a few minutes of your time."

Surely the gods were smiling. But it never paid to be too available. "I have a very full schedule, so I'm not sure I can squeeze you in."

"Please try. I know you'd have a lot to contribute."

Flattery never hurt. "Hmmm, I'll see what I can shuffle. A business idea? Can you be more specific?"

"She'd be a lot better at giving you information, so it would be best all around if we can meet."

It would suit him to play hard to get. "You know, I'm fully committed to my current businesses. Much as I'd like to help the two of you, I'm really not in the market to invest in any new opportunities right now."

"Antoine, I'm putting this badly. She's not looking for investors. Dominique wants to talk to you about her idea, especially how it relates to the vampire community. I told her you're the go-to guy. All we need right now is a quick appointment."

Could he make room in his schedule for Dominique? Did the sun set in the West? "For you, Lilith, I'll see what I can do."

"You won't regret it."

"Club Red at midnight?"

"See you then."

So Dominique was going to stay in San Francisco. He glanced at the clock. It was already 10:30. He had to get moving so he could clear his schedule to fit her in. The prospect of seeing her got his cock hard and his fangs throbbing. Tonight he wouldn't need to resort to a dream visit. They'd be together in every way—he took a solemn oath. And then he'd be free to move on.

Antoine swore with frustration at the problems he

encountered at each of his clubs. Usually he breezed through the early check-ins, but tonight nothing went right. So, despite his firm intention to be on time, he didn't get back to Club Red until 12:30. He'd phoned his bartender with instructions to take care of the two women and put their drinks on his tab.

Dominique wasn't smiling when their eyes met. She stood ramrod stiff, fists clenched, eyes shooting sparks. He'd use her obvious agitation to his advantage.

"I hope I didn't get the time wrong." Lilith looked apologetic.

"I was held up at my other clubs. Ladies, let's go to my office." He gestured to the back.

The two women moved through the crowd with Antoine close behind. He admired how Dominique's ass contracted when she walked. Once inside his office, he invited them to be seated. Aware of his erection, he sat behind his desk and composed his features into an authoritative mask.

"Tell me about your business proposition." He sat back to listen.

Dominique winced at the word "proposition". He could sense her struggle not to think about her dream, to focus instead on the business that brought them together. Maybe some day he'd tell her the truth about the night before. That would be after she revealed her identity. Then he'd explain about the dream visit as they lay intimately entwined after hot sexy... His cock twitched, and he wrenched his thought processes back to the discussion at hand.

Dominique began with a quick outline of her plan for an inter-group dating service. Lilith listed all the San Francisco community leaders they'd already contacted and those they'd lined appointments up with.

"Thank you for including me. As I mentioned to Lilith earlier, though I wish you both luck, I'm not looking to invest in any new businesses at this time." He leaned back in his chair.

"As I believe Lilith already told you, we're not looking for financial investors." Dominique's voice dripped with irritation.

"What we want is your cooperation as a community leader," Lilith added.

"What exactly do you mean?"

Dominique started to explain when Lilith's pager went off. She excused herself. While she was out of the room, Dominique and Antoine sat in a silence he figured he enjoyed more than she did. Bloody hell, she was spectacular. Though he didn't think much of the business the two women wanted to launch, he might just allow himself to enjoy her extended time in San Francisco—despite his abhorrence of anything that smacked of relationships or entanglements. Damn how she messed with his head.

Looking sheepish, Lilith popped back in. "I am so sorry. Family crisis. Dad and my two uncles have been arrested. I need to go bail them out."

Ghouls. Antoine shook his head. Hard to believe Lilith sprang from that sorry lot.

Dominique rose. "I'll go with you."

Lilith shook her head. "Thanks, but there's no need. I've done this before, and I'm sure I'll do it again. I know exactly where to go and what to do. It won't be fast or pretty, but I'll get the guys out. Though I'm tempted to leave them in. Aargh. Stay here and finish explaining everything. And then, Antoine, can you get Dominique back to my place? This will probably take hours."

"Of course." He bit back a very large smile. His dick twitched in happy anticipation.

From the look on her face, one would think Dominique wasn't at all thrilled, but he could read her better than that. When Lilith had left, she picked up the thread of the conversation. "We were talking about what we'd like from you, Antoine, as a vampire community leader." She ran her tongue over her beautiful full lips, and he had to grip his chair to keep from leaping across his desk to ravish her.

"Yes. You have the most amazing eyes."

"We need to keep this conversation professional or I'll leave."

"But I promised Lilith I'd escort you home, so you can't."

"I'm sure I can get a cab. As I was saying, you're a vampire community leader..." She appeared to lose the thread. *Must be his hypnotic gaze not to mention his animal magnetism.*

"I'd love to help you, but I don't see how. You see, vampires don't need dating services. Not to brag, but we have no problems getting dates. Quite the opposite."

Her aura bristled with bright crimson anger. Lovely. "But there must be some vampires whose social lives are less than satisfactory all the time."

"I doubt it. I don't know of any losers like that." He came out from behind the desk and took her hands in his. "But I want to hear more. Let's go somewhere more comfortable to continue our talk."

Her brows furrowed and she pulled back, putting up surprising resistance considering how much he'd turned up the charm. It had never failed him before except—

Suddenly the pieces of the puzzle came together. "You're a witch."

He'd been with another witch years earlier, before he knew better. While not quite as low in his personal estimation as ghouls, witches were on his To Avoid list. Their particular talents for magick made them unpredictable. If he couldn't predict a pattern of behavior, he couldn't exert effective control. While in most other beings he'd find this a challenge, in witches it morphed into a source of frustration. Getting past their psychic shields could tie a man up in knots. Once he knew who she was, his erection should have gone south. Perversely, she fascinated him even more.

She flinched back as if he'd splashed her with scalding water. "My personal data is none of your business."

"Look again, witch. With powers like yours, I'll bet you're in a top spot in the hierarchy. Witch royalty? Your identity is my business because you asked for my help as a community leader. Not to mention..." He cleared his throat, forcing himself to stay focused. "You need to answer my questions before we go any further."

"They sound more like accusations." With an almost violent jerk, she broke eye contact. "I am not a practicing witch. That is my irrevocable choice. So though you've somehow picked up traces of this hereditary identity, for all practical purposes your perceptions are off."

"No, they're not. I'm right on the money. No matter how much you protest, you've got witch branded on you from the inside out. Why deny it? Explain."

She glared bombs at him. "I came from a line of witches and chose to opt out. That's all you need to know. It's more than you have the right to know. And that's all I'll ever say on the topic. End of conversation."

Her words might have been more credible if she made a move to leave, but she seemed frozen to the spot.

"You can take the witch out of the tradition, but you can't take the tradition out of the witch."

"What?"

He shook his head and laughed. "I can't believe I didn't see it the moment we met. I must be slipping. My darling Dominique, you vibrate your identity, whether you want that to be true or not. And I made a solemn vow after my previous encounter with one of your kind that it would be the last. So despite your appeal, I will now take you back to Lilith's and say good-bye." He had every intention of doing as he said. He led her out to his Mercedes and helped her in.

When he'd started the engine, she broke the silence. "How did you know?"

"The more relevant question to ask is why it took me so long to get it. You, Dominique LaPierre, are a total witch. Your identity is not something you can put on and take off like a hat. "

She squirmed. "What do you mean it took you so long? We haven't spend much time together."

He nearly told her then about the dream visit. Since she was struggling to deal with being unmasked, he figured he should forego shaking her up any further. "If you're serious about opening your dating service, you need to sharpen your own identification skills. Some clients from the lower status groups might try to disguise their true natures. You need to know whom and what you're dealing with."

"My service will be based on respect and acceptance for all. I will not tolerate intolerance."

"What do you mean by that? Are you going to dictate which groups clients will be allowed to choose dates from?"

"No, never. My clients will be free to specify whom they want to date."

"And which groups they don't want dates from?"

She nodded vigorously. "Of course."

"Then I don't understand what you mean about the tolerance thing."

She shifted in her seat. "Letting people choose whether or not they want to date people from specific groups does not imply disrespect or intolerance or any kind of ranking. It's personal taste. But my stated policy is that beings from all groups will be welcome to participate and can feel confident they will be accepted."

"Even witches?"

Dominique did not respond with words, but her blush confirmed what he suspected, that she was very conflicted. *A case of "Do as I say and not as I do," eh*?

When they got to Lilith's, Antoine told himself he should see Dominique to the door and get the hell out of Dodge. But it was clear that their conversation disturbed her. In addition to her being desirable, he now saw a vulnerable side that intrigued him even more than her beauty.

He parked his car and walked her to Lilith's door. She unlocked the door and turned to say good night. He started to respond the same. Without conscious thought, he found himself joined to her in a liplock that unleashed the full force of his lust.

Chapter Four

How long could Dominique blame jet lag for her weird state of mind? Was it jet lag that made her invite Antoine into Lilith's house after he drove her home? How could she account for her confusion when he fired difficult questions at her—and, even worse, for how incredibly attractive she found him despite his despicable behavior? Though she knew letting him come in had to be one of the worst ideas ever, an invitation came out of her mouth in her voice. If this was jet lag, she had the worst case in recorded history.

Once inside the condo, she caught the look in his eyes, a mix of desire and lust that filled her with a bizarre sense of *déjà vu*. He kissed her again, then moved his head back and raised his hand to trace the outline of her lips. His erection, which threatened to burst through his elegant slacks, felt huge pressed against her. Enormous and so tempting she could scarcely breathe. She swallowed hard and willed herself to get her act together. The weirdest thing was that nothing about their being together seemed strange, but it should have because she'd never been alone like this with him except... Her weird illusion found words. "Something about you seems so familiar, as if we'd been like this before." No sense being coy or pretending what was going to happen wasn't.

His grin looked wolfish. "Maybe in your dreams..."

Her face burned with another disgusting blush. How could he know what she'd dreamed the night before? Was this a flagrant example of his ability to mind read? Vampires had to be the most amazing lovers if they could key in so accurately on what a person was thinking. Hell, he'd been a fantastic lover in her dream, though she kept reminding herself that wasn't him—that he'd been a figment of her overheated imagination and libido—right?

To avoid having to answer her own questions, she kissed him. Fortunately, he was very distractible this way.

"I want you, my witch, even though I know I should run. In every way a man can want a woman, I want to make love with you."

She quivered at the sound and meaning of his words. If she hadn't snagged on his use of the word "witch," she'd have melted into a puddle of sticky goo. His insistence on stressing her identity stiffened her will, at least for the moment. "Don't call me *witch*. I've renounced that label. It's not who I am."

He wound her hair around his hand and drew her closer. They were skin to skin. "I accept you, my pet, even your witch nature. As to the details, I'm more than willing to postpone that discussion. I'm not willing to postpone this." He thrust his penis harder into her softness and she creamed her panties. Trembling with the force of her desire, she whimpered. She wanted him in her, and she wanted herself around him with a fierceness that coursed through her like a rampaging river.

"You desire me too, don't you, my lovely one?" His words bit into her and she savored their tang.

"Yes, oh yes." Her answer came out on a sigh, barely audible.

With a grunt, he lifted her and held her to him as he raced to the guest room. He knew which door was hers. If she wasn't careful, she would get too used to having her mind read like this. On the other hand, she had to watch her wanton thoughts when she was so exposed to him.

The feel of his arms around her, his lips on her, his cock throbbing with desire—it all continued to seem familiar, yet so exciting, arousing her to new hungers.

"Dominique, you are so beautiful. I couldn't wait any longer. Thank you for your invitation."

Though his words sent a shiver of fear sparking through her, her yearning for him proved stronger. Giving a vampire an invitation meant what? Voice as steady as she could make it, she asked.

He laughed, a sensuous sound she wanted to catch between her lips and drink into her.

He traced the contours of her face with his long,

aristocratic fingers. "This invitation is your way of saying you're open to the many experiences I can show you." His fangs gleamed in punctuation, and she felt a corresponding pulse of surrender race through her. She wanted him to taste her, to put his lips and teeth on her and to take her life force into himself.

When he set her down on her feet, they both realized she was too wobbly to stand. She hooked an arm behind his neck and held on until her legs could support her.

"Will you allow me the pleasure?" His fingers brushed the neckline of her suit jacket.

"Yes." She wanted his hands on her, taking off her clothes with meticulous care and focus. His touch surprised her with its gentleness as he removed her jacket and laid it neatly on the small desk in the corner. He kissed her then, and a locked place in Dominique's heart opened, as if she were coming home after a long, lonely journey. Everything about his touch resonated in her. His mouth fit perfectly with hers, and she wished the kiss could last forever. His hands on her breasts stimulated her through the raw silk of her shirt and bra and made her yearn for him to undress her with no further delay. Even hidden under cloth, her nipples beaded at his slightest touch, and she wanted him with a ferocity that took her breath away.

With a gasp she pulled back, arose and under his watchful, smiling gaze, drew off her shirt and bra.

"You stun me with your beauty," he whispered, as if he were present at the unveiling of an art masterpiece. "And you're so impatient. I like that in a woman. But I wanted to be the one to take your clothes off."

"Your turn." She held her hand out. "You can undress yourself."

"Only if you will allow me to remove the rest of your garments afterward."

"You drive a hard bargain."

"That's far from all that's hard." His grin left nothing to the imagination. Dominique eyed his burgeoning erection and licked her lips.

"Agreed."

He threw off his clothes—and she experienced a wave of *déjà vu*. How could this be? She'd seen him like this before in her dream, and somehow she'd gotten every detail right, managed to imagine his magnificence even though he was more gorgeous than any other man she'd ever seen. His body, buff and muscled, left her panting and weak with passion. And his penis, as promised by his bulge, jutted out big and hard from his dark mass of hair, inviting her to touch and taste and feel.

She didn't refuse, couldn't refuse. Throwing aside her strange sense of the uncanny, she knelt before him, held his cock in her fingers and examined him as if to commit every furrow and ridge to memory. When he twitched in her hand, revealing an excitement stronger than his air of *savoir faire*, she couldn't hold back. She began to tongue and lick the rigid shaft. He put his hands on her head, running his fingers through her flowing hair.

Antoine, wound tight as a coil about to spring, moaned his approval, and his cock grew in her mouth. While she licked his erection, Dominique put one hand on his high, tight balls and squeezed. Her other hand began to explore the crease between his cheeks. Antoine arched his hips, moving deeper and harder in her mouth as he wriggled to allow her fingers to play.

Dominique was getting into it when Antoine abruptly withdrew. "I don't want to come yet," he whispered, "as the night is still young and there's much for us to enjoy. But my lady, you're something else."

Antoine stretched out and pulled her down on top of him. But she wanted to feel his weight solid on her, grounding so she could believe what was happening was real—in contrast to her previous fantasy. The more they kissed and caressed, the more she experienced his body with hers, the harder it was for her to let go of the surreal feeling that she was again in a dream. But he was so solid to her questing fingers and lips. His scent, the special musk of his arousal, had her head spinning more than champagne. She had no doubt his lovemaking would propel her into a new world of being. For now, she maneuvered to pull him on top so she could stay rooted to the earth.

With skilled, sensitive fingers he skimmed over her pussy, and Dominique sucked her breath in hard. Her clit ached for his attention, which he teasingly provided. She squirmed and had no shame as she maneuvered to experience him in all the ways she burned to. He played her, bringing her to the edge of madness. "I want you inside me now." She clamped her hands on his ass to underscore her words. He got it.

"Your wish, my delightful lady, is my command."

She doubted that, but she appreciated Antoine saying so. She imagined herself on the verge of some dramatic flight, a step off a cliff, an experience beyond any she'd known before. This coupled with the ongoing sense of *déjà vu* kept her head in a whirl. Thank goodness, in moments he'd slid his enormous dick into her hot, wet sheath.

"Dominique," he whispered, her name sounding like the secret code for all that was precious and rare in the universe. Her chattering brain at long last switched off.

With him, she'd returned to some primitive state of being and become attuned to the sensations thrilling her. She had to remind herself to breathe, to remember her body consisted of more than her pulsing, ravenous cunt. His touch had woken her there as if she'd been a sleeping beauty, and he inflamed her so that she had to move in response. She had to find a way to quench her all-encompassing hunger and thirst for this man. Her sensitized clit vibrated at the merest suggestion of his touch. She could have sworn he was coming at her from many different angles, now harder, now softer, as the pleasure whirled out from her center in erotic shock waves. How could she have dreamt this?

Wanting to please him too, she resumed her finger play in the crease of his delicious butt, touching the opening between his cheeks, pressing harder when he wiggled his ass in response. "Antoine," she moaned. When her lips formed his name, she imbued it with all her conflicted emotions. How could mere words begin to express her desire, the erotic pleasure of their being together and all the confusion of her emotions?

Her intimate muscles began to contract, the first sign she'd soon rocket to the stars in a breath-taking climax. She didn't want to come yet because that would signal the end of their being together like this. They might be together other times, in other ways, but never again would she experience the special magic of this moment. If only she could make their intimate joining last.

As he'd been reading her all night, he must also have sensed her hesitation. "Don't hold back," he exhorted her, his voice harsh and rasping. "There will be more, I promise. Give it up, Dominique, let it flow."

She required little encouragement to do what her body

cried out for. His words provided the nudge that pushed her over the line. With a gasp, she did just as he said, crying out the release that had been building in her since his first intimate touch.

"Yes, my precious," he purred, urging her to ride out her come. Every word and move enthralled her, and yet that sense of having been here with him like this before lingered.

By now he filled her, rock-hard and immense deep in her, surely on the brink of coming himself. But when she slowed her own movements and then subsided, he lay still with her.

She started to move harder so she could bring him to his climax and share that peak experience with him, but he had other ideas. He planted his hands on her hips and held her in place, throwing her into profound confusion. Could this be another way vampires differed from other men? "But don't you want to come?" She'd never met a man who didn't.

His eyes smoldered. "Words can't express how much I do. And I will. That's inevitable. In the meantime, I want us to stay as we are and savor the pleasure in the moment."

How could she not melt at these words? With a pang, she realized that she and Antoine would never again be together like this—except, maybe in her dreams, which he couldn't know about. She shivered at that thought, a reminder of how dreamlike everything tonight had felt since his first touch.

Right now, she didn't want to think of a time after the interval they would spend in this bed together, cocooned in their own little world. But she was a realist and couldn't keep reality at bay forever. She sensed he was the same. An affair between them wouldn't fit into either of their lives. For one thing, Antoine Thierry was a player and she'd be a fool to think he'd change. He had a lifestyle he'd gone to great effort to build, and he appeared to have a lot invested in keeping the status quo.

As for her, she found relationships completely consuming and, ultimately, draining. After the destructive effects of the last one, she'd taken a solemn vow to keep her life simple and solo. She liked herself much better when she wasn't devoting time and energy to trying to figure out how to deal with the man in her life—and keeping entanglement-free made her more productive at work. So tonight's pleasure would be ephemeral.

She also realized how fleeting this special time would be. So now they would squeeze all they could from every moment. "I'm ready to be with you in this way," she whispered back.

With a moan, he held her and lay still, hugging her. She became familiar with the rhythm of his heartbeat and his breath. Maybe they could stay together like this all night, intimately joined but lying with exquisite stillness. Dominique fantasized about them staying in bed like this forever. Lilith, such a good friend, would organize necessary services. They'd have meals brought in—the usual take-out for her and the stuff Antoine required. But didn't vampires also have a strict dawn curfew? Antoine didn't seem to have any such concerns now.

He began to move in a slow but exquisite back and forth dance with his hard dick in her hot wet softness. She shuddered with renewed pleasure. After she'd come earlier, she figured she'd just go along for his ride, but Dominique soon realized they'd be sharing this one. With his magic touch, the rhythm of his shaft moving in her intimate core, there was no way he'd come alone.

"I can't resist you," he murmured. "Dominique, my lady, all for you." He howled his release as he pumped his essence into her.

Dominique followed his lead again a moment later, grasping at his cock as her muscles contracted with her own release—to her astonishment, more intense than the first time, which had nearly knocked her head off. The sense of *déjà vu* almost overwhelmed her along with a frisson of disappointment that she couldn't understand.

And then a deep sense memory came over her. Vampire intimacy went beyond conventional orgasms. For their lovemaking to be complete, Antoine would also have to feed from her. But her dream hadn't included this consummation.

Trembling for this completion, Dominique surrendered to Antoine. Eyes glazed with lust and fangs gleaming, he lowered his lips to the pulsing base of her neck. She tightened in anticipation of a sharp bite. Would there be much pain? Her muscles contracted and she had to remind herself to relax. Though she couldn't have said why, she trusted Antoine not to hurt her.

He didn't. After the abrupt sting of the initial contact between fangs and skin, a strange and delicious warmth and lassitude began to flow within her. Aware of his lips clamped to her, of the way he sucked at the wound he'd produced, Dominique had never been more conscious of her entire body. In addition to the sexual glow enveloping her, she experienced a sense of well-being and an acute appreciation of who she was. For just this moment, she accepted herself as a witch, as a total being. Only she in the whole universe could give Antoine this special gift right now. Close as they'd felt while they made love, at this moment the intimacy between them grew more intense. They were together in every possible way, and her soul vibrated with heightened perceptions of him, of her, of them.

She was drifting down a river of life and light, color and sound, and she'd have been content to linger in its rare waters forever.

Far sooner than he wanted to, Antoine licked Dominique's wound and healed her. Now that he'd taken her well beyond the boundaries of their mutual dream, he felt closer and more enthralled with Dominique than the reverse. Though she denied her identity, her magick enveloped and surrounded him. Such power could only be the work of a witch immured in her tradition. He'd gotten beyond her witch barrier to a place of beguiling charm.

Not what he'd intended. With every other woman he'd known, feeding had been a definite last step that bolstered his resolve to move on. With Dominique, however, the more he tasted, the greater his hunger grew. If he'd realized how dangerous this beautiful witch would be to his equilibrium, he'd never have crossed her threshold. He couldn't remember the last time he'd been such a fool.

Unable to tear himself away, he gazed down to where she lay beneath him, her eyes closed and her breath gradually returning to normal. He'd never known anywhere close to the same level of completeness. Antoine took great care as he rolled off to lie next to her. When he moved away, she whimpered softly in her dozing state and reached for him, and he allowed himself to snuggle with her. *Allowed* himself. The truth was, he couldn't hold back from extending their contact. She turned to him. He stroked her beautiful face and wished things between them could be simple. But he knew better.

Somehow, he'd have to shift them back from this unique intimacy to the professional distance they both claimed to want.

When she woke from her post-coital doze and began to

speak, he cupped her chin and raised her face so they could gaze into each other's eyes.

"Antoine, I have to ask you something."

"What is it, Dominique?"

She pursed her beautiful lips. "I've had the weirdest feeling all night, as if I'd dreamed everything that was going to happen tonight—well, not the way we lay together after... after I *came*, and not the feeding. But all the rest. It's the strangest sense I've ever had, not at all usual for me."

He loved the way she blushed. All that delicious blood flowing...

"A dream?" He ran his fingers down her cheek, delighting in the warmth of that blush.

"Yes. I've told you I'm not familiar with vampiric ways. Is this something you've ever experienced before, this kind of pre-dreaming?"

Timing being everything, he didn't feel this was the optimal moment to tell her the truth. Despite their intimacy, he didn't know her well enough to predict how she'd take what he had to say, but he suspected her reaction might ruin an otherwise beautiful evening. Though he hated lying, even by omission, he wasn't prepared to sacrifice their joy. Besides, he fully intended to tell her the truth sooner rather than later. Just not yet. "I'm not sure I understand exactly what you mean. Unfortunately, while I would like to explore the question, I won't be able to stay too much longer."

"Ah, yes, your curfew."

"I prefer to think of it as the parameters of my schedule. But before I go, I want you to think about what I asked earlier. About the proposed tolerance for all groups in your forthcoming business. Does that extend to your own identity?"

"I'll take a leaf from your book and table that discussion. Antoine, I feel too muzzy right now to answer sensibly."

"Fair enough. Muzzy it is. On that note, I'll leave you for now."

She sat up in bed and watched him dress. When she made a move to go with him to the door, he signaled her to stay where she was. She didn't look displeased.

He dropped a kiss on her cheek. It would have been very easy to go for more, but he had to leave.

"You never did tell me how you'll be able to help me with my business," she said as he was leaving.

No, he hadn't. That omission had not been unintentional.

Dominique lingered in a state between sleep and wakefulness after Antoine left. Her bed, so warm with both of them in it, now grew cold. She hugged herself and remembered how he'd felt in her arms.

She couldn't believe the emotional turmoil she'd been through since they'd met. She didn't relish being on the roller coaster of sentiment he'd awakened in her. The only way she could figure out to get off that roller coaster was to make sure she kept her life relationship-free. The irony of her attitude in light of her new business wasn't lost on her. Actually, she saw no inherent contradiction. After all, the world was full of successful businesses whose owners didn't use their products—book publishers who didn't read, rock promoters who listened to Beethoven, physicians who abused alcohol and drugs—wasn't it?

A man like Antoine could wreck her plans. She could easily envision a trail of broken hearts fluttering behind him. Plump hearts red with the blood that colored his most intimate moments. Well, hers wouldn't join that trail. All she had to do was strengthen her resolve. A little selective amnesia wouldn't hurt either.

She tossed and turned for another few minutes before surrendering to the night's inevitable insomnia. If she wasn't going to sleep, she might as well get up and work until she got sleepy enough to crawl back into bed and shut her eyes.

She woke her computer and opened the promo file for her new business. Hmm. "New business" would not do as the name for the dating service. What were the salient points to include in the name? "Tech", of course. "Dating", "matches", "guarantees". What name would reflect the uniqueness of her business? "Magick"?

Maybe it was the lateness of the hour or her being in a weird state of post-orgasmic vulnerability, but thoughts of her grandmother Maeve's legendary matchmaking prowess took residence in her head and wouldn't leave. Maeve certainly hadn't relied on tech to make matches, but she'd been known to find mates in cases considered hopeless. How had she done it? Dominique discounted witch magick and figured Maeve had some natural ability to sense the connections that would translate into reliable matches. Certainly Maeve's instinct for keying into people, her deep caring and her romantic nature— she probably combined all those elements in just the right proportion when she came up with her matches.

For a moment, she considered conferring with her grandmother. But once unleashed, Maeve would probably want to play an active role in the new business, which might not be a bad thing. Maeve's talents would give the business an edge over competitors. Unfortunately, though, she'd also attempt to find a match for Dominique and bring her back to the fold.

She had to be more tired than she'd realized—how else to account for even *thinking* about Maeve? What was it Antoine had said about self-acceptance? Damn, she needed to shake that thought too. She could turn her back on her witch self— her choice—same as she could choose where to live and make all the other decisions that shaped her life.

Despite the slight headache forming behind her left eyebrow, inspiration struck. *Two-by-Tech.* Catchy, short and a name that said it all—or said enough. *Two-by-Tech.* Clean, cutting edge. She liked it. She yawned. Later in the morning she'd run the name past Lilith.

Good. With a name for their business, they could move forward. She yawned again and her eyelids fluttered closed. Maybe she'd get a few hours' sleep after all.

From the moment he woke up the next night, a lingering sense of unease dogged Antoine, his cock hard for Dominique LaPierre. While a wake-up erection was business as usual, his ongoing fascination and obsession with her wasn't. Delightful as he'd found being with her, he was not about to repeat an experience so threatening to his self-control. If Dominique stayed in the area for any amount of time, maybe he could be with her again sometime in the far distant future. But he wouldn't let that happen until he was over his current weirdness and could put being with her in perspective.

He made short work of the erection, trying not to think about her as he stroked himself to a quick come. Then he raced through his shower, dressed and fed before he headed to Club Red. First order of business would be to reroute his lust to a more amenable target for after hours.

He drove to the club and parked. Almost on automatic pilot, he took a rapid visual survey of the public area on his way to his office. Though it was still early, his eye snagged on several beauties—some he'd spent time with in the past, some new to him. Good. He shouldn't have any difficulty finding a suitable playmate.

After a quick review of phone messages—none from her, he was glad to see—he returned a few calls and checked email. Quickly discarding whatever SPAM his filters had let through, he read the real messages. Despite his best intentions, his heart skipped a beat when he saw one from her. He read:

Dear Community Leader—obviously not a personal note—good.

I would like to take this opportunity to inform you about Two-by-Tech, a dating service for all members of the larger San Francisco community, which will be open for business soon. As the name indicates, this will be a tech-based dating service. What makes Two-by-Tech special is that it is open to clients from every group and that matches come with a money-back guarantee. His eyebrows shot up. She expected to make a profit?

Since you are a valued community leader, I'm seeking to enlist your aid and support in promoting Two-by-Tech to your group. I'm sure you'll agree we can provide services to enhance the quality of life for members of your community. I'd like to meet with you as soon as possible to further discuss the best way to meet your group's needs. Thank you in advance for your support.

In the meantime, please contact me with any concerns, insights or thoughts.

Dominique signed her name after a closing salutation that promised her words were sent "*sincerely*".

No, no, no. Everything about Dominique's business idea offended him. Despite modern society's growing reliance on tech, he did not believe it belonged in every aspect of life. Though he had difficulty believing any beings couldn't find their own dates, the existence of services meant some poor slobs might require help. As far as he knew, no vampires fell into that category. But if help was needed, sentient beings—not machines—had performed matchmaking services for centuries and should continue to do so. Bloody hell, he himself had matched up several couples.

Therefore he would not encourage any vampires to sign up for this service. Though vampires did date beings from other groups, that shouldn't relegate them to a database of the lovesick. Participation in this dubious enterprise would sully the vampire image and give the public a distorted image of the community. A vampire who needed this kind of assistance was a substandard anomaly, almost a disgrace to them all—a loser.

There was no way he'd agree to help Dominique. When he met with her, he'd tell her exactly that. With any luck, his refusal would make her angry. They'd fight and break off any future contact—which would simplify his life.

Too bad his dick and his head were in complete disagreement. Determined to find a much less challenging companion, he shut down his computer and headed out to his club.

Both Lilith and Dominique worked past the dinner hour. Lilith looked up from her computer screen when Dominique came into her office and dropped down in a chair. "I can't believe how much progress you've already made on Two-by-Tech."

Dominique smiled tiredly. "*We.* All the progress *we've* made. I really couldn't have done any of it without you—heck, you provided the initial inspiration."

Lilith's face lit up. "Thanks for the kind words. It's funny, people can never know what they might say that will inspire you to start a new business."

"Not everyone inspires me as much as you. By the way, what happened last night when you went down to the jail?"

She rolled her eyes. "All things considered, it wasn't horrible. At this point, I have to bail someone out so often, I'm the leading authority on getting ghouls sprung. Heck, I've memorized the steps for all the necessary procedures and who to call for what. This time, I've gotten Dad to promise he and his gang will show up for court and behave between now and then."

"I hope they appreciate you."

"Fat chance of that. But speaking of appreciation, we've heard from all the community leaders except Antoine. Everyone else is interested in learning more and willing to meet with us." She rubbed the back of her neck. "It's bizarre that Antoine didn't respond. Usually he's pretty good. Should I contact him again, or do you want me to look for another leader of the vampire community?"

Dominique's heart skittered at the mention of his name. Seeing him was definitely not part of her game plan for the night. "I don't know, Lilith. You understand the dynamics of the communities out here so much better than I. What would be the most strategically correct thing to do?"

"A dangerous question." She laughed. "Actually, I'm surprised Antoine hasn't answered you because I sensed some definite currents between the two of you."

Currents? That was one way to put it. Dominique mentally squirmed. She hadn't yet decided how much to tell her friend— none of the alternatives appealed to her. "I don't know. You said he is the recognized leader of that community. Wouldn't it hurt us to try to bypass him?"

Lilith appeared to consider that. "Excellent point. Do you think it's possible he just hasn't checked his email yet? It isn't very late yet in the vampire day."

Though Dominique would like to dismiss his non-response so simply, she couldn't. "I imagine he starts his night with a message check like everyone else."

"Hmm. Uh, did something you haven't told me happen between the two of you? It was so late when I got home, I didn't want to disturb you."

There it was, a direct question. She figured she'd best give Lilith some information while she tried to sort out what to do. "I had an interesting discussion with him about the business plan. He seemed to get stuck on our principle of welcoming every group as clients."

"That sounds about right. He tends to be a bit ethnocentric about vampires. So what was your discussion like?"

She snorted. "Ethnocentric? Oh yeah. Somehow he realized

that I'm a witch. And he asked if the tolerance I propose extends to my group."

Her friend's eyes widened with surprise. "He figured all that out about you already? Wow. I always thought he was a little scary—now I'll change that to very scary."

Dominique fought back the impulse to fully explain matters. "Some people just have well-developed instincts. I wouldn't let him impress me—or scare me."

"He does have a point about your rejection of your identity. For those of us who don't have that luxury, it seems kind of weird that you can."

"I don't want to discuss this now."

"Or ever," Lilith finished for her.

"We've gotten sidetracked. What are we going to do about getting a vampire community leader to work with us?"

Lilith shook her head. "There's no way anyone would cross Antoine. If we don't get his support, we might as well write off the vampires."

"I'm not about to do that. If he's going to ignore my email message, there's only one thing to do. Let's confront him in person. We'll be much harder to turn down that way." *Actually impossible.* She was not about to admit defeat.

"I'd love to go with you, but I'm busy tonight."

"A date?"

Lilith spluttered. "Only if you'd consider a revolting dinner with G. Nash Grubb a date—may I never be that desperate."

"G. Nash Grubb?"

Lilith shook her head. "The leader of the ghouls in the local community. The only way he'd agree to support us is if I said yes to dinner. Oh well, given the über-carnivore restaurant he'll take me to, at least it'll be easy on my diet."

"I owe you one."

"I'll collect." They hugged before Lilith headed off.

Though it was the last thing she wanted to do that night, head high and business instincts primed, Dominique headed off to Club Red for a face-to-face with Antoine.

Chapter Five

Antoine was still debating with himself as to which of two women would be the night's date when Dominique entered Club Red—and all bets were off.

After taking a moment to orient herself in the room, her eyes locked with his and she headed straight for him.

"A pleasure to see you again, Ms. LaPierre." The perfect host, he took her arm and led her to the bar. "What can we offer you tonight?"

She shrugged off his arm. "Nothing to drink, thank you. If I can have a word with you in private."

He glanced at his watch. "I was just leaving for Scarlet, one of my other clubs. If you'd like to ride with me, we can talk in the car."

She nodded.

In true gentleman mode, he helped her into his car. The brush of her hand on his, the brief contact of skin to skin, jolted him like an unwelcome electric shock. Okay, so he knew she was incredibly attractive. He could deal. "What do you want to talk about?"

"Why didn't you answer my email?"

"Your email?"

Her brow furrowed. "I'm sure you must have received it. I contacted all the community leaders to ask for their help and support to get my business started."

"Even the leader of the witch's community?"

"Witches don't operate that way, as I'm sure you must be aware. There's no real witch community here in San Francisco, just some stray individuals."

"Like yourself?"

"We're getting off topic here. My question was, why didn't you respond?"

He could continue playing this game, but he needed to be clear about his own goals—such as cutting short interactions with her so he could return to his usual life. "I bundle non-pressing emails and respond once a week, twice if my schedule's light."

She frowned. "Non-pressing? Antoine, I want your support. Given the large number of vampires in San Francisco and their popularity as potential dates, I want to count on them using my service. We now have a name—Two-by-Tech."

"Two-by-Tech?" He managed to sneer the name.

"Yes. I want our clients to realize the centrality of tech in our procedures."

"That centrality doesn't impress me."

"What?"

"When it comes to matching people for romance, I prefer more traditional approaches. If you were using intuitive methods, I'd be more inclined to support your business."

"I see," she said frostily. "The Troglodyte objection."

That got both eyebrows up. "Troglodyte?" No one had ever called him that before, and he didn't like it.

"I didn't expect that sort of objection here in Silicon Valley, but I can see location is no predictor of attitude. Once we have our programs set to go, would you be open to seeing what we do—with the possibility of changing your mind?"

"I'm always open-minded." To a degree. Didn't she know the full definition of being open-minded was having a hole in your head?

She made a small snorting noise. "Debatable. Do you have other concerns?"

"Actually, yes. You see, even though vampires socialize with other groups, we're really not open to the kind of interaction you envision for Two-by-Tech."

"What do you mean? Vampires participate in social life with beings from every group."

"Yes, we do. But in the grand scheme of our society, that's the exception rather than the rule. Vampires prefer to be with other vampires. There's so much about our world that's unique.

Trying to acclimate outsiders to our realities can be complicated, and the payoff is often not worth the effort."

"You speak for all vampires?" Her eyes were wide with surprise.

He shrugged. "No one can speak for *all* vampires. We are individuals."

"Right. And recognizing that different individuals have different needs, can't you see Two-by-Tech becoming an important resource to the community?"

She sounded so earnest, he was tempted to agree just to see her eyes light up with triumph. But therein would lie disaster. He needed to distance himself from her. "No. The rare vampire who can't manage to put together a satisfactory social life on his own is far too pathetic for a simple dating service to help."

"Spoken with the smugness that comes from an inflated sense of superiority." She scowled in apparent disgust, which struck him as even more delicious than her previous good humor. "Pull over and let me out now."

"Pull over? Here? That would not be a good idea. We're close to my club. Let me drive you there. Then, if you want, we can call a cab."

"I've got a cell phone. I can call a cab here."

He drove faster. "This is not an area where a beautiful young woman should wait for a cab alone."

She looked out the window. "It doesn't look that bad. I can take care of myself."

"I know you can, but indulge me in this. We're three minutes from the club."

Lips pursed, she pushed against the back of her seat.

As soon as he parked, she raised the door handle which he controlled the locks for.

"Just a minute."

"What? We're here. I'll call a cab." She slid toward the door, though in the confined interior of the car her move accomplished little to increase the space between them. Her warmth tantalized him.

"That's it? Are you giving up so easily? I'd have thought with your track record you'd be a more determined sales person."

She snorted. "When you start describing vampires who might sign up for my service in terms like 'pathetic', I figure there's no room for discussion."

"What can you do to convince me I'm wrong?"

She looked at him for a long moment, too long—as if she were taking his measure and he came up short. He'd resisted her valiantly, but every man had his limits. Cursing the dimensions of his car's seats, he reached for her and drew her into his arms.

Antoine Thierry had to be the most crazy-making individual she'd ever encountered. Sexy as hell, powerful, smart—he had everything going for him, and the chemistry between them sizzled. But his Neanderthal attitudes trumped all. And then he kissed her, and all that chemistry sparked to explode her indignation.

His lips on hers were soft, warm, hard, cold—expressing promises and demands she couldn't ignore. With one hand poised on the back of her neck and the other at the top of her thigh, his powerful fingers felt like they would burn through her wool suit skirt and singe her tender skin.

Dear goddess, he distracted her. How could she be clearheaded? In his embrace, her awareness of the erotic flame between them flared and spiked. Quite simply, she wanted this man. She reveled in his wanting her, no matter how much it complicated her life. He deepened his kiss, thrusting his tongue into her mouth to take full possession. He swept his tongue with slow deliberateness across her teeth, her tongue and the soft inner surfaces of her mouth. His teeth and lips were like finely tuned communicators, relaying messages that aroused her beyond bearing. How could she find herself so completely in sync with Antoine on the sensual level when his attitude drove her bonkers?

Amazing as his kiss was, Dominique wanted much more, even though her rational inner voice was begging her to cut and run. But she broke away from his lips only when she had to take a breath. Judging from the erection tenting the fly of his pants, he also wanted more. Her pussy grew moist and creamy with desire, and the prospect of having him touch her there with his bulge had her pulsing with anticipation.

"Oh, lady, you are beyond desirable," he whispered. As his lips brushed hers again, his fingers walked up her leg, moving ever closer to the place she wanted him. She arched her hips forward to meet his hand, and her legs splayed open, testing the limits of her pencil skirt.

When his fingers brushed the sensitive skin between her upper thigh and her pussy, Dominique nearly wept. She wanted him to touch all her sensitive spots with his magic fingers. At first he stroked her hot, moist slit through the thin silk of her panties. When she felt his fingers there, she'd have gasped if she could make a sound. Even through the barrier of silk, his fingers seared her with pleasure as he stroked her intimate folds.

From the pressure of his touch, the panties molded to the sleek contours of her cunt. Focused on satisfying her hunger, Dominique aggressively pressed her mound to his fingers and moved so he could stroke all the places she desired. Her clit throbbed from the arousal and when he massaged her there, the sensations almost pushed her over the top.

Never breaking the seal of their kiss, Antoine insinuated his fingers inside her panties and stroked her. Goddess, she was so wet. Dominique knew she must be saturating his fingers with her intimate juices. Her whole body now pulsing at a high level of arousal, she grew taut as a guitar string. Her nipples pebbled hard against her silk shirt, and just when she bit her lip not to moan with her need for his touch there, she felt his caress.

She wanted to get her hands on him too. When she reached for his cock, he shifted out of range. He moved his face back from hers a bit. "Much as I want your touch, this time's for you," he whispered. "Just pay attention to everything you need and want for your ultimate pleasure."

She started to protest that her pleasure included having the chance to touch him, but he nibbled on her lips before resuming the kiss, and she was lost.

Though she'd have been more than happy to let him stroke and pet her far into the night, she began to shudder with the upheaval of a toe-curling climax. He was so attuned to her, she'd have sworn he knew the moment she began to come. With his fingers, his tongue, his breath and the rasp of his teeth, he urged her to go deeper, higher, farther into a release that felt like it would explode out the doors and windows of the car. At the pinnacle of her orgasm, she threw her head back and just about howled. He murmured, telling her how beautiful she was, how it pleased him to have her come like this for him.

When the pleasure receded, the questions began. And the confusion returned with a vengeance. She was never one to take without giving, but that was what had just happened. Though the fly of Antoine's pants still bulged and his fangs gleamed, he held back from letting her satisfy him. Even after the way she'd just shattered in his embrace, Dominique felt strangely shy. None of this was like her.

"What can I do for you?" she asked, her voice sounding strange to her. Realizing her skirt was still hiked up around her hips, she wriggled to lower it to a more respectable level. Right. Who did she think she was fooling?

"You've done it already."

She turned and saw the big satisfied smile on his face. She nodded toward his cock. He shrugged. "What goes up must come down. I need to go check things in my club. Duty before pleasure."

She made a noise expressing skepticism as to how seriously Antoine followed this dictum.

"Would you like to come in with me?"

Realizing what a mess she must look like after their car sex, Dominique declined. "Unless we can talk about your participation in my business plan in your office here." She should be able to make a run for his office without attracting too much attention.

"Have you come up with some more points for your argument?"

"I will by the time you come to your office."

He nodded before he opened his door and went around to get hers.

His dick still ached for her, which was fine. Though Antoine had become accustomed to instant gratification, sometimes it felt interesting to defer his satisfaction. With its charm of rarity, he almost enjoyed remembering what it was like to have to work for culmination. Heck, he got a kick out of making Dominique work for what she wanted from him. Walking around with a hard-on reminded him what frustration felt like. Though he didn't appreciate experiencing that emotion, it did keep him sharp and on edge for his dealings with Dominique.

Business looked good tonight. The way business had been growing at all his clubs, he might soon consider opening a fourth. He greeted the night's customers, had a drink with a group passionately discussing a recent scandal and worked the room. He'd made it a point to hire the cream of the crop to staff his clubs and he paid top dollar. In view of how smoothly operations went ten out of ten times, he figured he'd hit on a winning combination.

Thinking about a new business led him right back to Dominique and her plans. Crazy as he was about her, he didn't like her business idea. For a moment, he wondered what difference it would make if he did find her idea appealing. Then he might be tempted to go into business with her, a far stickier proposition than a simple affair. He couldn't put off going back to his office and finishing their discussion. What he intended was to let her say her piece. He'd refute her points with his own brilliant arguments, then send her on her way. Maybe she'd even realize her idea was bound for failure and give it up. She might even go back to the East Coast. He swallowed back a pang of regret at the thought of her leaving.

Those were his intentions until he opened his door and saw her sitting on his desk completely nude with her legs crossed over her tempting core.

"I figured my clothes were too wrinkled." She uncrossed her legs, and he kissed his plans good-bye.

Dominique was determined to pleasure Antoine before she left him tonight. She'd taken great care to clear his desktop, which didn't require much effort, stepped out of her clothes, struck her confident pose and waited. Luck was with her as he arrived before she lost her nerve.

In a flash, he flew across the room and scooped her up. "You will have your way with me, won't you?"

From her sexy perch, she wound her arms around his neck and initiated a marathon kiss. When she broke away, she remarked, "One of us is dressed and one isn't. I consider that essential to fix, don't you?"

Chuckling, he deposited her back on his desk and shrugged off his clothes. He was a gorgeous man with a body that invited feasting—and not just with her eyes. She was gratified to see that his cock rode high and huge. Had he held on to his erection through the whole time in the club? She savored the small victory of knowing she aroused him to this level.

She hopped off the desk and stood before him, enjoying the feel of his cock on the sensitive skin near her navel. While she could get off by rubbing herself against his erection, she wanted to taste that delicious-looking dick. Reaching up to plant her hands on his shoulders, she walked him back to his ergonomically correct swivel chair and sat him down.

"I'm hungry." She licked her lips as she got down on her knees in front of him and opened his legs wide. Looking stunned, he raised an eyebrow and contemplated her as if in wonder.

She placed one hand on each of his knees and opened his legs wider. Then she winked before lowering her face to take his erection into her oh-so-eager mouth. If only she could watch his face as she went down on him but, alas, that was physically impossible.

Maybe she couldn't see him, but she could hear him and feel his response—and it was all good. As soon as she put her lips around him, he emitted a combination of gasps and moans that gave her goose bumps. Goddess, he was so big, she could scarcely get her lips around his engorged glans. No way his long, thick shaft would fit into her mouth unless she deep throated him in a way she'd never managed before.

He tasted and smelled wonderful, a combination of salt, musk, outdoors, leather and pure man. She loved the feel of his smooth skin over the steel of his erect cock and the ridges and veins that defined him. He pulsed with excitement. Her world narrowed to one goal—to pleasure him as much as he'd pleased her in his car. She wanted to lead the way, for him to experience that searing eroticism and the breathtaking climb to culmination.

Though she'd gone down on other men, she'd never before swallowed her lover's come, but she would tonight. She wanted to risk this intimacy with him, though she realized deepening their bond would lift their relationship to another level.

He kept his hands twined in her messy hair, but for once she didn't care how she looked. His grip tightened as he became more aroused and his breath hitched. She placed her hands on either side for a solid hold. Moving his hips back and forth, he thrust his dick ever deeper into her mouth then withdrew until he was almost out. Dominique ran her tongue around the engorged shaft and head, laving him everywhere. Conscious not to bite too hard, she nibbled on the plump underside, tracing the main vein with her tongue and teeth.

At one point, she desired to taste his balls also. Not wanting to leave his cock bereft, she slid her fingers along the slick surface. She licked his balls thoroughly before switching the positions of her mouth and her hand. Right before she took him back in her mouth, she saw a large drop of pre-come in the opening of his glans and tongued it off. Antoine moaned his appreciation.

"I'm going to come very, very soon," he whispered. He stroked her face before grasping the top of her head.

With her mouth now full again, she nodded.

"If you don't want me to come in your mouth, it's okay. But you have to let me know so I'll pull out in time."

She nodded again to indicate she wanted him to come in her mouth.

From the way Antoine accelerated his thrusts and his more frequent, louder grunts of appreciation, Dominique knew he was close to the edge. He also told her in words. She remained exactly where she was, sucking his cock with great deliberation.

"Now, my lady," he shouted. "I'm going to come now." He once more made as if to withdraw, but she held on for all she was worth. Just before he began to spurt his climax, he at last seemed to understand her intention. Releasing a long sigh of satisfaction, he spasmed in her.

At last satisfied, Dominique took everything he gave and encouraged him to come even more. When he subsided, he laid her head in his lap and caressed her face. But she didn't intend to stay there for long. She wanted the rest.

"I want you to feed off me now."

Antoine couldn't believe his ears. Though he'd had many other lovers who weren't vampires, Dominique was the first so exquisitely attuned to his needs. Satisfying as his climax had been, feeding off her now would put him over the top. His whole body geared up for the rush of sensation she offered.

"Are you sure?"

"Yes," she murmured, baring her lovely throat to him, "I want your pleasure to be complete."

His fangs thrummed with need. "It has been already." Despite his words, he ached to feel the orgasmic pleasure of her life force flowing into him. Straining not to hurt her by moving too quickly, he lowered his lips to her pulsing jugular and bit.

She flinched at the initial contact, and he winced. Her bright red blood oozed at the puncture site and he lost what remained of his self-restraint as the sensuous delights of her vibrancy enveloped him. Heady with the richness of her, he drank in her generous gift. So close to her, joined with her in an even greater intimacy than sex, he feasted.

But too soon, far too soon, he realized he must stop drinking and heal her wound or he would take too much. With an iron grip on his desires, Antoine drew back. After a flick of his tongue, her punctures disappeared and their bubble of intimacy evaporated.

Dominique looked stunned. As reality set in, he reluctantly admitted he needed to bring their wonderful closeness to an end. Though he'd have loved to play with her all night long and beyond, he remained painfully aware of their differences. More than anything, he didn't want her to feel used or betrayed when she realized he'd never change his opinion about the business that meant so much to her.

He handed her her clothes. "Beautiful as you look, you'd better put these on or I won't be able to do the rest of my work tonight."

She ran her hands through her still tousled hair. "Turn around," she ordered him.

He wanted to laugh. After the intimacy they'd just shared, he found it ludicrous that she'd develop a case of modesty.

"Why?"

"I've never dressed in front of a man, and I don't intend to start now." She draped her clothes before her.

Though he could have pointed out several hundred thousand holes in her logic, his gut told him not to. Considering they had no future together, he'd let her hold on to her self-imposed limits. He grabbed his own clothes and turned his back to her. "Do you mind if I dress while you do—or do you have some rules about simultaneous dressing?"

"You don't have to make me sound like some obsessive-compulsive just because I like to do things a certain way. Go ahead."

He did. When they both turned around fully clothed, it was as if all their earlier togetherness hadn't happened, and he regretted that loss. But he figured it would be simpler to bring a halt to whatever was developing between him before it grew much more. Otherwise, he suspected this woman would make mincemeat of the way he'd ordered his existence.

Chapter Six

Here came the tricky part—shifting to business talk after incredible sex. Maybe she'd be better off conducting all future business with him via email and telephone. Except, of course, he'd already demonstrated he could easily brush off both. Meanwhile, she'd have to ignore the musky scent of sex that filled the air to get her head straight. "I'd like to get closure with you about the vampire community and Two-by-Tech."

"I still have objections, which I don't believe you've addressed."

She gathered her scattered thoughts. "I don't know that I'm going to be able to change your opinions with words. Actions speak much louder, after all. So how about sending us a few clients—let's say three. To introduce the service, I'll waive the fee for the first three vampires you send. Then you can talk to them, see how they rate the experience. I'm convinced that, once you see us in action, you'll agree we're offering an important service."

"I need to give it more thought. But that's a generous offer. I'll be in touch, okay?"

She'd have preferred more of a commitment but didn't see any advantage to pushing harder. They spoke little when Antoine drove her back to Lilith's condo enroute to his third club.

The next month flew by in a flurry of activity. Dominique now really appreciated Lilith's joining her to get Two-by-Tech off the ground. Even with both of them working full-time, they put in long days and fell exhausted into bed each night. But when they opened for business in a converted Victorian a month after Dominique's arrival in San Francisco, they considered all their effort worthwhile. Between their generous intro offer and their solid public relations, they had a good base to work from. Regular people, shifters, ghouls, demons, witches, a small number of fairies—almost every segment of the population responded enthusiastically. They had clients from every group except one—vampires. The lack of vampires in their database was a giant gap that could undermine the business in the long run. Antoine had proven unmovable.

Once they'd fed all the new data into their computers, Dominique made a startling discovery. Her gut instincts led her to the perfect matches long before her computer program did. Sometimes, her gut overruled the computer matches and guided her to even better ones. With a sense of irony, she'd realized these instinctual matches might make the service more palatable to Antoine—if she ever got the chance to tell him. Reluctantly, she confessed her new-found skill to her friend.

"But this is great," Lilith bubbled.

"Great? Why would you say that? Doesn't it mean our computer program is off?"

Lilith shook her head. "I know you've got a lot invested in denying your witch powers, but this shows you can't. You know what I say? Why fight it? Your instincts are going to give our business an edge no computers could provide."

In her head, Dominique could hear her grandmother's voice confirming this gift. Tempted as she might be to try, she couldn't turn off her instincts. For now, she'd go with them. She'd deal with the bigger questions later.

But she couldn't avoid dealing with the vampire problem any longer. At first, whenever Lilith asked what was happening with the vampire segment, Dominique steeled herself not to get teary. Sensitive to her friend's moods, Lilith did not press the point.

Antoine had effectively dodged Dominique for the past month. Bewildered and frustrated, she'd forced herself to avoid going anywhere she might run into him. How could she deal with him—or forget what they had, so briefly, together?

Antoine planned to spend his time not thinking about

Dominique LaPierre and Two-by-Tech. Fortunately, between business commitments and his social life, he had more than enough going on to keep very busy. On the night of the Two-by-Tech opening, Fred Hopkins, the most bumbling vampire Antoine had encountered in more than a century, approached him at Club Red.

"What can I do for you, Fred?"

"There's talk about a new kind of dating service here in the city. I'm thinking about signing with them. Wanted to ask your opinion." He wiped his hand across his mouth.

That figured. "Why do you want my opinion? It sounds like you've made up your mind." Remembering Dominique's offer, Antoine realized Fred would be a perfect candidate to send her. If she could find a suitable match for a throwback like him, Antoine figured she was on to something. But he felt more vehemently than ever that vampires shouldn't rely on outsiders to provide matches. Using a service like hers was tantamount to admitting weakness and inadequacy—anathema to the vampire image.

"You think they could get me a date?"

Antoine shook his head. "Come on, man. You're a *vampire*, an immortal with the power to savor the world's greatest sensual pleasures. Women want to date us."

"They do?" Hopkins's beady little mud-colored eyes widened.

"Of course. Female vampires, women from other groups. Where have you been hiding? Books, movies, plays—vampires are romantic heroes women dream of."

Hopkins rubbed his hands together. "You mean all I have to do is ask and a gorgeous dame will say yes?"

Antoine supposed there'd be someone desperate enough to date him. "You just have to connect with the right one. But you know, it wouldn't hurt to update your wardrobe."

Fred looked down at his paisley polyester Nehru jacket and appeared to ponder Antoine's advice. "Maybe it is time to retire this."

"Treat yourself to some new clothes, get your hair styled. That kind of stuff impresses women. Once you get a new look, go for it. I'm sure you'll meet someone great without having to go through all the bother of signing up with a service and answering a slew of ridiculous questions."

Fred thanked him and went on his way.

Antoine watched him leave with a twinge of discomfort. The other man's mention of the dating service brought up unwelcome thoughts. Though Antoine went to great lengths not to admit it to himself, he missed Dominique. Sometimes he missed her so much, he found himself picking up the phone or preparing an email. But each time he stood at the dangerous edge, he pulled back. He preferred to keep his love life no-strings, which meant no-Dominique.

Maybe someday keeping her out of his life would become easy. Right now, Dominique-avoidance required every iota of his will.

Determined to continue holding out, he exited his office and went on his nightly prowl for a woman to distract him from the tug on his heart. In the weeks since he and Dominique last made love, he hadn't managed to connect with any of the women available to him. He kept comparing them to her and going home alone. But one of these nights, he'd break that particular curse and find a woman he could take home. Only then would he know he'd moved on.

As the business grew, Dominique realized she was letting her personal feelings impair her professional judgment when it came to solving the vampire problem. To her great relief, Lilith offered to deal with Antoine.

The night before her appointment with Antoine, a vampire who identified himself as Fred Hopkins contacted Two-by-Tech. When he begged for an after-hours intake appointment, they both agreed to stay in the office to meet him.

"Maybe Antoine's finally come through," Lilith said.

"About time. Better late than never."

However, Dominique felt less sanguine when she and Lilith met Fred. So much for her stereotype of handsome, elegant vampires. Still, Two-by-Tech billed itself as full-service. She and Lilith were committed to providing dates for all their clients, even challenges like Fred.

"How did you happen to choose Two-by-Tech, Fred?" she asked. "Did Antoine Thierry send you?"

He shook his head and made a face. "No. He told me no self-respecting vampire would use a service like yours for a date. So what'd I do? I listened to him. Got rid of my paisley Nehru jacket and bought this new suit." He pointed to an ill-fitting jacket and pants of a brown tweed that resembled industrial carpeting from the eighties.

The two friends looked at each other. Bad enough Antoine hadn't supported them, but now they learned he'd actually discouraged a vampire from using their service. Dominique willed herself not to react in front of the client. In fairness to Fred, she made him the offer Antoine should have told him about.

"You'll match me up for free?"

They both nodded. "Since you're the first, you qualify."

"You just made my day, uh, night."

Dominique vowed to find a perfect date for this lonely vampire.

By the time he left, she could no longer hold her temper. "That—that—I can't think of a name bad enough."

Lilith shook her head. "I'm really disappointed. Somehow, I thought he'd change his mind. I should have been on top of this. Well, there are other members of the vampire community who could help, though I'd have preferred not to go that route."

"Like whom?"

"Mirella Proctor. She's been in San Francisco forever, and she knows everyone and everything in the vampire community. If you want, I'll call her tonight, get things rolling. Unlike Antoine, she likes to reach out."

Dominique nodded. "Great idea. As for me, I'm going to give a certain club owner a piece of my mind."

He'd reached the end of his resistance. Antoine couldn't kid himself any longer. He needed to contact Dominique, tell her he missed her and find some way for them to be together. For about the hundredth time since their last night together, he had his finger poised to dial her number. Only this time, an incoming call came first.

"Antoine Thierry."

"Dominique LaPierre." From the sound of her voice, permafrost icicles should have formed along the phone wire.

"Dominique. To what do I owe the pleasure?" He swallowed hard.

"It's distinctly not a pleasure. A vampire came to Two-by-Tech this evening."

"Really. And how is your new business? According to the current buzz, you're doing very well."

"No thanks to you." Her voice grew quite loud, almost shrill, on the last word. "The vampire who came today? He's the first."

"We all have to start somewhere." He kept his voice low and even. "Congratulations."

"He told us you've been warning vampires off using our service."

Ah. The reason for the call. "Whatever. Obviously, this hasn't hurt you."

She made a very angry sound.

"I'm glad you called. Difficult as it might be for you to believe, I've wanted to call you many times and stopped myself. But I was going to go through with it tonight."

"Why? You like to torture people you're planning to betray?"

He deserved that. "No. I apologize for what I said to Fred. It was Fred Hopkins who came to you, right?"

"Information about specific clients is confidential," she snapped.

"Of course it is. Well, my apology holds. I'd like to see you so I can apologize in person. It would also give me a chance to say I have had a change of mind."

"Hah. The last thing I intend to do is see you again—ever. I just wanted you to know exactly what I think of what you did. And now I'm ending this conversation." She hung up with a sharper than necessary click.

Talk about timing. He'd meant what he said. All right, so he'd changed his mind because he missed Dominique and wanted to make things right with her. Judging from their conversation, that just might not happen. He'd really screwed up. But there had to be some way to fix what was broken.

And then it came to him. When all else failed, ask Mirella. If Mirella Proctor didn't know the answer to a question, it was really hopeless. Hat in hand, he dialed the number for the woman who was everyone's mentor.

Dominique fumed all night. Lilith tried to jolly her out of her bad mood with a wonderful dinner in North Beach. They even went down to City Lights and spent several hours browsing in the eclectic bookstore. Dominique was in such a rotten mood, she didn't buy a single book—unprecedented. Nothing lifted the dark cloud hovering over her. As the two of them indulged in bedtime ice cream sundaes, Lilith took her life in her hands and asked about Antoine. "He's really gotten to you, hasn't he?"

"What do you mean?" Dominique barked.

"You're taking what Antoine did very hard, aren't you?" She raised a spoonful of rocky road to her mouth.

"What do you mean?" Dominique glared at her friend. "What he did was horrible. He undermined us in the vampire community. I call that pretty major. We know what he said to Fred Hopkins because Fred told us. But how many vampires did Antoine Thierry poison against us?"

"We don't know for sure if there were any aside from Fred. Let's face it. A lot of what Antoine said is the truth. As a rule, vampires don't have trouble getting dates. Maybe it wasn't in the cards for us ever to have a large vampire clientele."

"Certainly not with his talking against us."

Lilith shrugged. "Again, we know he did it once. And, I have to admit, Fred Hopkins is not our most promising client." She held up her hands as if to ask Dominique to hear her out. "Look, you know I'm always honest with you. We're always honest with each other. That's what our friendship has been about since day one."

Dominique nodded.

"I think there's more going on here than meets the eye. As in, there's something between you and him. The chemistry was obvious whenever you were together. I figure something happened. Something I don't know about, and it involves a lot of strong feelings on his part and yours. Otherwise, you wouldn't be this hurt." She sighed.

Dominique bristled. "I don't want to talk about it."

"Whenever you do, I'm available."

Despite Lilith's sweetness, Dominique's nerve endings felt grated raw. "I'm sorry we wasted so much time waiting for Antoine to help us. I wish we'd gotten in contact with Mirella Proctor from the beginning. It would have saved a lot of wear and tear."

"We were better off waiting. We can tell Mirella everything, including what Antoine's done. She can handle him like no one else."

"Admirable woman." Though she hadn't finished more than a quarter of her sundae, Dominique looked at her watch and pushed the dessert away. "Let's call it a night. I have a feeling tomorrow's going to require lots of energy."

"That's why I'm finishing my sundae."

When Dominique got on-line the next morning, she saw she had an appointment with another vampire that night. Good. Antoine hadn't been able to sabotage them after all. She'd do the intake and Lilith would go to meet with Mirella.

After a quick dinner, Lilith left. Dominique checked on the progress reports of several matches and on the copy for upcoming ads. When she looked up from her work, Antoine was standing at her desk. Bloody hell. This was not what she needed right now. But goddess, he looked so amazing. Seeing him made her realize how much she'd missed him. Even now, angry as she was, she'd happily melt into his embrace.

"Why are you here?" Why did she ask him that? She needed to get him out before her potential client showed up. "Never mind. This is a bad time. I'm expecting someone else. Please leave."

"I'm your appointment." He eased himself into the visitor's chair and stretched out his long legs.

"What?"

"Male vampire wanting to sign up for your service. I made the appointment last night on your website." He grinned, showing a flash of fang. "I believe I'm one of the first three of my kind to apply. That makes me eligible for free service, right?"

Her mind was spinning in non-productive circles. Gripping the edge of her desk for strength, she shook her head. "Why are you *really* here, Antoine? In addition to being the least likely candidate ever for a dating service, you hate what we're doing." She narrowed her eyes. "Do you have some sort of plan to destroy my business from within?"

He shrugged. "I didn't like your ideas at first, but I've had a change of heart. It happens."

"Right." She rolled her eyes.

"But more than that, I've missed you. As in, nothing has had any flavor or spark since that night in my office."

She couldn't believe a word. He had that hypnotic gaze thing going. She had to tear herself away from his gaze and from the power he too easily exerted over her. But no matter how she tried to insulate herself, his words went straight to her heart and her sex. Frozen in place, she struggled to cross her legs hard and resist. "That's a pretty speech, but I don't believe you."

"Understandable." He reached across the desk and took her hands in his. "Now that I've had a taste of being with you, I want more. I can understand if you won't be with me anymore, but I figure if I'm lucky, you'll be able to match me with someone almost as wonderful as you."

"Really?"

"No. There's no one as wonderful as you. My favorite witch, you've cast a spell on me."

She growled. "I don't do spells."

"You do without even knowing it. Dominique, I've been such an idiot. You've opened my eyes in so many ways. Now that I've seen your light, I can't go back to the dark. Sign me up or, even better, let's make our own match—you and me."

That was it. She'd have to be made of lead-lined steel to resist him. She wasn't, and she didn't.

She met him halfway 'round the desk and made the match of her lifetime. They clung together in a kiss that sealed their pact.

"Contrary to what I said before, I want to be part of your business in any way I can. I'll throw the support of the vampire community behind you. You were right. Lots of people from the community could use your service, only most of them hesitate to. So, we owe you a huge thanks." He nuzzled her tender neck.

"I accept."

"Only one thing, my love," he murmured. She got all goose bumpy at his use of the word "love".

"What's that?"

"Two-by-Tech. That name sets my teeth on edge. I've got a better one."

"Which is?"

He grinned before he whispered the name to her.

Much later, after Lilith almost interrupted them in an intimate interval, the three toasted their new arrangement and their new name—Fangly, My Dear.

What's a Ghoul
to Do?

Dedication

This book is dedicated to all the wonderful readers out there—and to Lee, my first and always reader.

Chapter One

Rafe Graywolf scooped his gorgeous date up and kicked open his door. Her perfume fogged his brain as she nuzzled against him. Warm. Hot. His erection throbbed.

"I've been waiting all night to get you back here," he growled.

Lana licked his neck with her talented tongue and his balls contracted.

Then he made his first mistake. He turned on the light and saw them, waiting. August Graywolf and Benedict Volpe. Triple shit. How had the two elders, doddering and past their prime, managed to get into his cottage?

That was when he made his second mistake. He almost dropped Lana. Though he managed to hold onto her, her whimper came from frustration, not sexual desire. The mood was now broken, erection now history. He set her down and encircled her with a possessive arm.

August cleared his throat. "We didn't know you'd have company."

Right. Like he was supposed to check in with them about his social life. Rafe aimed his death glare at his uncle. "Unlike you, she's invited. As in, let me hold the door open for you. Tomorrow you can tell me why you busted in here while I was out."

"We apologize for intruding, but we didn't bust in." Benedict held up a key.

August cleared his throat. "I'm afraid we can't leave. A situation has arisen that needs—"

"You could have phoned." Rafe exercised excruciating effort to hold together the shards of his temper.

"We didn't want to leave a message on your machine. You didn't answer your phone or your page..." Benedict was looking at his feet.

Oh, yeah. The vibration. He'd figured that was part of Lana's charm. "Can't I ever take a single night off? I'm sure there must be someone else who can handle whatever's come up."

"No," August responded. "Maybe you should give the young lady cab fare home so we can tell you what's going on." August was Rafe's uncle. He and his fellow elders had convinced—more like coerced—Rafe to take up the position of pack alpha. After all their effort to get him to change his life plans and become alpha, Rafe expected the elders to be grateful. Yeah right. They messed up his dates, bugged him twenty-four seven and kept demanding more.

"Absolutely not," Rafe gritted out. He started to draw Lana closer, but she resisted.

"Maybe it's for the best that I go." Her husky voice gave him goosebumps.

Shit, shit, shit. This was the third date the two old men had messed up in the past two weeks. Rafe had told them, in short but expressive terms, that their interfering snouts were not welcome in his private life. As was all too clear, the message hadn't gotten through yet.

"She's staying and you're going. Unless it's life or death, whatever you want can wait until morning."

"It's life or death," August whined. "We wouldn't bother you for anything less."

Right. And they had some swamp land to sell him. He folded his arms in front of his chest and adjusted his face into his most menacing frown. "State the matter or leave. Better yet, do both. Now."

"We can't speak of this confidential matter in front of someone who's not a member of our pack," Benedict enunciated each syllable.

Rafe didn't believe a word either old coot muttered. On the other hand, could he take a chance? Maybe this time there was a modicum of truth in what they were saying.

"It's okay. I'll go," his date whispered.

No. His body screamed in protest. He didn't want to spend another night jawing with these two about pack politics and other crap that could wait for regular business hours. "I'll get rid of them. Lana, I don't want you to go."

She fluttered her lashes and licked her pouty lips, but the mood was gone. The two old men stood hovering like vultures.

He drew her away from their prying eyes and bent close to whisper, "I owe you, big time. Next time, let's go out of town so these two can't find us."

She kissed her fingertips, then pressed them to his lips. "I'll count on it."

"Want me to call you a cab?"

"Nah. I have a buddy who will pick me up." She went through the door, leaving behind a whiff of her scent to torment him the rest of the night.

Feeling murderous, he turned to the two old men. "Talk. This had better be very good."

"According to the latest intelligence reports, a pack down from Vancouver is planning to set up shop here," Benedict started.

Another pack was moving in. This was life or death news? "Calling them 'intelligence' reports is a gross misuse of the word. And I fail to see why this news provoked you to torpedo another of my nights off."

His uncle shook his head. "This is the same bunch that tried to home in on our turf twenty-five years ago. They're aggressive and ruthless. Last time, with your father leading us, we barely managed to repel them. All our sources say they're better prepared and more determined than ever before."

Despite himself, Rafe began to realize he should pay attention. He remembered when his father and the other males had to go on battle alert. The Vancouver pack, the Loups-Noirs, had come within a very short hair of defeating the Wentworths. Though the Wentworths won, males of his father's generation bore battle scars until the end of their days. His father, the pack alpha, had to struggle all his life to compensate for a painful limp.

Before Rafe assumed leadership, the elders had confided the shameful news that the other packs perceived the Wentworths as weak. They'd known he wouldn't be able to resist this challenge to the Wentworth honor. It fell to him to lead at this critical time when they'd have to rebuild their image and fight off the Loups-Noirs. Failure was never an option.

Having dedicated himself to right what had gone so wrong, Rafe lived and breathed pack business. The threats they faced were not so pressing and immediate as to justify the elders' intrusion. Still, since the night had been ruined, he might as well get to work.

"All right. Give me the reports." Neither of them moved.

"Come on. You got what you wanted. I'm now available to work on pack matters. So give me the reports and then you can go mess up someone else's date."

August looked at Benedict and nodded. Rafe's gut clenched. He braced himself.

"One more thing, Rafe. It's past time for you to choose your mate and get her established. Though most of the pack appreciates your taking on the mantle of leadership and approve of how you're handling things, there's always a group of malcontents. They've been talking, starting trouble."

Rafe winced. "I never promised to make everyone love me."

Benedict waved his hands in dismissal. "We're not saying you should. But, you see, they have a legitimate point, and thus they can complicate everything we're trying to do by directing everyone's focus the wrong way."

"Let's cut to the chase here."

August nodded. "The only way to silence the troublemakers is to take away their source of complaints. Namely, present your mate to the pack."

Damn. There it was, the real reason why they'd come. Well, he'd asked them to get to the point. "We've been over this before. I made it clear when I agreed to help out. I have no intention of hooking up with a mate now. Maybe in ten years, maybe never, but not now. You all agreed that would be okay because of the emergency."

"We've had to revise that stance. Your not having a mate is having a more harmful effect on the pack than we anticipated." August's lips trembled and his voice became quite weak.

Rafe bit back a harsh reply. Despite all his uncle's manipulative schemes and outright coercion, Rafe cared about the old man, about the pack. Still... "Judging from the way you reacted to her, I assume neither of you would consider Lana a suitable mate for the pack alpha."

Both men grew pale. "Are you planning to propose—" Benedict clamped his hand down over his heart as if to ward off cardiac arrest.

"I hadn't given it a thought. But, busy as I've been, I've hardly had time to look for dates, let alone potential mates." He furrowed his brow and then smiled, as if a great idea had just come to him. "It's time to think outside the box. I need to update the pack's ideas about the alpha taking a mate, starting now."

"No sense being hasty." August stroked his chin. "Let's talk. You see, Benedict and I have come up with some surefire ideas."

Determined not be railroaded again, Rafe sat down. He donned his psychological armor, folded his arms in front of him, and began to listen.

When she got to work, Lilith Graves checked for any news that had come in during the night. She sighed with a mix of contentment and a more complex emotion as she read the latest wedding announcement—yet another couple matched up by Fangly, My Dear. The agency her best friend in the world, Dominique LaPierre, had founded earlier that year was exceeding all their most optimistic projections. Dominique credited Lilith as the inspiration for the successful business, dedicated to helping beings from all the communities in the San Francisco Bay Area find their best possible matches. Though Lilith's generous trust funds meant she didn't need a job, she enjoyed her work at Fangly, My Dear and the office's upbeat atmosphere.

Since Fangly, My Dear had come on the scene, Lilith would swear the percentage of happy couples in San Francisco had risen. Even Dominique, who'd sworn off relationships after a string of disastrous breakups, had found her soul mate. The most hardened cases succumbed to Dominique's matchmaking formula—cutting edge high tech plus a good dose of old-fashioned white witch magick.

It seemed there was only one person in the San Francisco area they couldn't find a match for—Lilith P. Graves. She tried not to identify with the kid who had her nose pressed to the candy store window but never got any goodies. Still, despite Dominique's efforts to find her a match, Lilith often clunked out of the system like a fifth wheel. She dreaded that her name would never grace a wedding announcement. Wedding? Heck, at this point she was more likely to travel to Mars than ever be a bride.

She sighed. As a vegetarian demi-ghoul—her dad was a ghoul, her mom a human empath—Lilith realized she presented a matchmaking challenge of Olympic proportions. Her mom, with her exquisite sensitivity to everyone's emotions, was not the problem. People often wondered how she'd gotten together with Lilith's father—a real case of opposites attracting since his ancestors included creatures who hung out in cemeteries and ate the flesh of the dead. Then there was Great-uncle Henry who'd shapeshifted into hyena form to munch on the occasional lost traveler. Lilith recognized early that Dad's side of the family was different. They'd modified their diet to fit into modern society, but the old stigmas stayed with them. Though she loved her ghoul relatives as much as her human ones, Lilith realized society relegated her family to the lowest link of the status chain. Outside their own group, ghouls were not considered particularly desirable because of their dietary choices. Understatement. On the other hand, her fellow ghouls didn't look too fondly on Lilith's commitment to vegetarianism.

She might hold the world record for being a one-date wonder. No one in recent years had called back for a second date. When she'd seized the initiative and contacted guys she'd liked, their excuses for turning her down were legion. Heck, a girl could develop a complex. A solitary tear made its way down her cheek. *Oh great. Now I am going to mess up my mascara and have to redo my face.*

Dominique breezed into her office, looking like she'd just won the lottery. "You'll never guess who's coming to us for a match."

"Who?" Lilith turned her head to wipe her tear away.

"The Wentworth Werewolves." Dominique rolled her eyes. "I can't believe it. That group has been dragging their feet on getting with the program. Now that they've come around and gotten a whiff of what we can do for them, they want us. I'm psyched."

"The whole pack has signed up for matches?" That would be a coup.

Her friend waved a hand. "Not yet. But they will. They're

signing their alpha up. Imagine that, the alpha! Once we match him, it'll be a cinch to get the rest of the pack. Then our reputation will spread to other packs."

"What does that mean, 'they're signing their alpha up'? Isn't it his choice to come in? And isn't the alpha the big boss? How come he's letting someone else sign him up?"

Dominique shrugged. "I think you're looking at this the wrong way. You see, the alpha needs a mate. The Wentworths' alpha insists he can come up with his own mate, but he hasn't. He also says he doesn't want to follow the pack directives as to when he'll pick his mate. But according to pack rules, he needs to name his mate within a certain amount of time after he becomes alpha or he has to give up his office."

"Nothing like putting pressure on the guy."

Dominique eyed her. "That sounds like a very pessimistic interpretation of his situation."

"Well, I don't get the impression the alpha is up for a match. That might make our job tougher."

"But we thrive on tough. As to reluctant candidates, remember what a tough case Antoine was? But look at him now. Not only is he one of our biggest supporters, well, do I need to finish the rest?" Dominique blushed, which didn't happen often.

Lilith adored her friend and was thrilled that she'd settled in San Francisco and found Antoine, the love of her life. Still, sometimes all that positive energy could be grating, like when her own chin was dragging on the ground and there were no imminent signs of change.

"When's the alpha coming for his intake?" she asked. Lilith figured focusing on business would improve her mood.

"In about an hour."

"Do you want me to handle it?"

"Since this one's so important, I thought we should both be in on it."

"Okay. Do you have any background info you want me to read first?"

"Check out the pack online. Their website includes information about their traditions, including the requirements for the alpha and his mate."

"Gee, Dominique, it just hit me. This alpha's looking for his mate."

"His whole pack is behind him on this."

"That's a heck of a lot more serious than looking for a date for him." Even though many of their couples ended up in committed relationships, people usually started their search with regular dates—far less pressure.

Dominique nodded. "The alpha isn't looking for social connections. From what the pack's representative said, the alpha has no problem getting dates. But if a candidate isn't going to work as a mate, we'd be wasting everyone's time setting them up."

"What's his name?"

"Rafael Graywolf. Everybody calls him Rafe."

"Rafe. I like that. Rafe Graywolf. His name sounds sexy." Lilith went to her desk and got the website up. She didn't know any werewolves. Given her vegetarianism, she figured there'd be the same kind of obstacles to socializing with them as there were with the hugely carnivorous ghouls.

The Wentworth Werewolves were an old San Francisco pack with roots going back to before the 1849 Gold Rush. Just like many old San Francisco families, over the years they'd amassed great wealth and social standing.

The website featured photos of Rafe in both forms. He had the most amazing, piercing eyes, a gaze that compelled her even in a mere photo. As to his powerful body, as man and wolf, his sleekness and strength... It wasn't just his name she found sexy. She sighed and pushed that thought aside. Business is business, she reminded herself.

According to what she read, the requirements for the alpha's mate were quite rigid. Rafe had to look outside his pack for a bride. Being noble both by blood and by his position, Rafe had to choose a female of a rank equal to or higher than his own. As the agency designated to locate a mate, Fangly, My Dear would have to adhere to all the specifications. Much as both she and Dominique enjoyed challenges, setting up a search with so many stated parameters would be frustrating.

As she gazed at Rafe, Lilith sensed working with this man would be far more complex than she could imagine. She couldn't deny that he appealed to her in ways no one else had in a long time. With a pang she realized she wanted to be matched with him. Talk about a direct route to disaster. Almost all the other shifter groups viewed ghouls in a negative light. Many times in their long history, the other shifter groups—werewolves, all the were-cat groups, even were-snakes—had tried to overcome their own rivalries to unite and expel ghouls. In fact, werewolves had the reputation of being the ghouls' fiercest enemies—and had tried the hardest to remove them. The werewolves had never made peace with having ghouls in the shifter community. As an alpha, Rafe was an über werewolf. Even if she could somehow catch his interest, no way could he become involved with her—at this point, not even for one date.

Lilith tore herself away. Mooning over Mr. Inaccessible Alpha would be a sure path to depression. She needed to get to work and help Dominique find him a perfect match—and, no, it wasn't her. But her hormones raced and her heart yearned. She opened her arms wide to the universe and invited love to come her way.

Rafe Graywolf raced through the woods. The underbrush snapped and low branches tore at his face as he tried to outrun the frustrations of a long, sleepless night. If only he could stay in wolf form and turn his back on his complex responsibilities.

At age thirty-three in human reckoning, he was young to be an alpha, but he expected the pressures that went with the job would age him fast. Though his family had a long tradition of leadership, he'd assumed it would be years before he had to take his turn. The sudden, unexpected death of the previous alpha, his Uncle Jack, had started the pack's downward spiral. Then, under the acting alpha's regime, the pack had responded weakly to two bouts of aggression and lost a hefty percentage of their funds in bad investments.

With everything falling apart, there was no way Rafe could have turned down the elders when they'd tracked him to the East Coast and begged him to return home. The way they'd put it, only he could save the pack. The call of family and tradition had seduced him away from his very satisfactory life as visiting professor at a major university. As a guest of an old Massachusetts pack, he'd been able to limit participation in shifter politics to a level he found tolerable.

All that changed when the Wentworth delegation had

arrived and guilted him into becoming the pack alpha.

He'd returned home. In the two years he'd been away, the pack's situation had deteriorated almost beyond recognition. Teeth clenched, he'd set to work. In a short time, things began to improve. He even allowed himself to make tentative plans to return to the East Coast and resume his interrupted life there.

But Rafe hadn't paid enough attention to the details of his agreement with the pack. How had he overlooked the loophole naming him alpha for life? The real clincher for him was the thin veneer that separated success and disaster for his pack. After he learned of the horrors they would face if he didn't remain to follow through on the changes he'd made, he couldn't let them down.

Which led him to where he was today—signed up with a dating service to find a mate. Of all the ridiculous scenarios he'd ever imagined getting caught up in, none compared to a dating service. For a mate! According to the elders, he was supposed to settle down with this woman for life. It was the wolf way. *Grrrr.* He'd seen other good men laid low by the life mate thing and sworn it wouldn't happen to him—at least not until he was too old to care. But his uncle had started on him by invoking flattery and guilt. In Rafe's hands, his paws, whatever, lay the precarious future of the Wentworths. They needed to publicize that his appointment was alpha was for life—just like a prison sentence for a major crime—or their enemies would pounce.

To achieve maximum effectiveness, he needed to share his throne with *the* mate. The fate of his pack hung by this thread.

If he heard those words once more, he wouldn't be responsible for his actions. Just then a piercing whistle set his nerve endings on edge. The microchip implant he'd agreed to rendered him on call to his pack even when he'd taken his wolf form and was desperate for solitude. If they were once again summoning him to deal with a trivial matter, fur would fly. On the other hand, they all knew the story of the boy who cried wolf—

Swallowing a groan of frustration, Rafe returned to the designated meeting place, also the place where he'd stowed his gear, assumed an aggressive stance and glared. In moments, two messengers flanked him. They pawed the ground and emitted three short barks, signaling that they'd need to transform back to human form in order to convey their message. Crap. Rafe had been hoping they could simply communicate whatever the hell was going on in wolf form, after which he'd take off again. The need to revert to human form meant the message was complicated or that he'd need to handle the current crisis pronto. Maybe both.

Rafe completed his transformation first. He'd managed to pull on his jeans before the other two realized they didn't have clothes. Judging from the nervous expressions on both men's faces, neither had been too eager to come after him and he could see their nakedness added to their unease. He looked from one to the other. Two brothers, barely out of their teens, John and Keith Volpe. With a grunt, he tossed them extra clothes and shoes from his Jeep and waited till they'd dressed before speaking.

"What is it, guys?"

"You have an appointment," John mumbled.

"An appointment? With who? The governor of friggin' California?" It had better be at least that important.

The two brothers looked at each other. Evidently, Keith had drawn the short straw and had to talk next.

"Don't know. Your assistant told us to get you. She said you need to clean up. Something about Fangly..."

Fangly? *What the hell is Fangly—*

Then he remembered. That was part of the name of the matchmaking agency the elders had set him up with, like he was some weeping wallflower who needed a matchmaker to get him a date.

He started to growl his refusal to go back with them, but stopped when he saw John and Keith cringe. Rafe didn't consider terrifying the young part of the job description for alphas. Besides, his current mess wasn't the messengers' fault. Determined to assert his identity and have "no" mean "no" to his people, he'd make sure the right people got the message.

Rafe dismissed the young brothers, who looked relieved to go on their way alone. He envied them and their freedom.

Then, determined to reassert his own, Rafe got into the Jeep and drove back to his office.

When he arrived, the full band of elders awaited him.

August pounced first. "Where have you been? We had to twist arms to get you an intake appointment on such short notice." He looked Rafe up and down, seeming to take issue with his well-worn jeans and flannel shirt. "You can't go to Fangly, My Dear dressed like that. First impressions count."

Rafe folded his arms in front of him. "I don't recall agreeing to meet with Fangly, My Dear or anyone else tonight. And I'm going on the record now, when I'm out for a run, don't interrupt me for anything less than a major disaster—at least of six-point earthquake magnitude."

The four elders looked at each other as if acknowledging they were dealing with a dimwit. Benedict Volpe put a reassuring arm around August's shoulders. "We have discussed this. We realize that, as alpha, your plate is full and you haven't given top priority to the matter of a mate. But the time has come. If you don't choose a suitable mate, adversaries will have an opening to attack you."

Rafe could feel his mouth curl with contempt. "We've been through this, numerous times. We all agree that after everything I've accomplished in a short time to pull the Wentworths back from the brink of disaster, potential rivals have no strong platform."

All four elders shook their heads. "Rafe, you've accomplished wonders so far. But, as you young folks say, it's time for a reality check. There are packs just waiting to devour us and our resources. Granted, you put out the initial fires with your first round of action. You still have to realize, my boy, that there's no time to sit back and take stock. That was just a first round and our enemies are far from defeated. We're still vulnerable to hostile takeover, especially once the enemy gets to know you. Your not having a life mate is a major chink in our armor rival packs can exploit."

"I do not need to go to some dating service," he gritted out.

"We're not talking about you escorting some *girl* to a party," Benedict pointed out. "A life mate is serious. You haven't found her on your own and we're running out of time. This service, Fangly, My Dear, has an excellent reputation. Though they haven't been in business long, they've made several noteworthy matches."

"For losers," Rafe hissed. "Do you really want the Wentworths to get the reputation of needing some service to get us dates?"

August shook his head. "You've got it wrong, Rafe. Fangly,

My Dear is a high-class, cutting-edge operation. An expensive one. Our trusting them with the search for your life mate shows we're up to date with current trends and we're not afraid to invest in our future. It's more proof the Wentworths are top-notch all the way. Now, go change."

Rafe wondered what it would take to win any battle with August and the other elders. "My going to Fangly, My Dear would be one of the five most ridiculous ideas I've ever heard."

"It's a done deal," Benedict claimed.

"What does that mean?" Rafe asked.

"It means," August said, "we've already leaked the news of your going to the community."

Rafe felt a throb in his right temple. "On whose authority?"

August didn't waver. "Mine."

Marvelous. So much for any illusions as to who was in charge. "This wasn't your best idea," he muttered so just the two of them heard.

The older man shrugged. "Nothing else seemed to work. Go. Change into one of those elegant suits you brought back from the East Coast."

"I'm not changing."

At least August seemed to recognize when to fold so Rafe could hold on to a few delusions. Fifteen minutes later, August, Benedict and Rafe were on their way to Fangly, My Dear in August's Cadillac. Rafe thought with longing of the woods he'd been running through just a short time before.

In addition to reading up on the Wentworths online, Lilith and Dominique read up on shifters, especially the population in the Bay Area. "The more I read, the more fascinating Rafe sounds," Dominique said. "Though I still think this situation is too big for one person to handle, something's come up—and I need to leave you alone to handle Rafe. You're the only one I'd trust to take him on single-handedly."

"What's come up? Is it something serious with your family or Antoine?" Lilith knew Dominique didn't walk away from her commitments for anything less than life or death.

She shook her head. "Nothing like that. Antoine's running

into some snags with his half-way house for new vampires project. After one near disaster, he finds it's not as easy as he'd thought to get them started on a social life—and he's actually asked for help. This is one offer I can't refuse. I know I can count on you."

"Just another day at a big city dating service. Ho hum." Lilith tried to keep a straight face, but she knew her pretended casualness wouldn't fool Dominique. Lilith's sense of excitement at the prospect of meeting Rafe had her nearly bouncing off the walls. She had to keep reminding herself that this was *work*. Talking with him tonight was just part of her job. Right. On the other hand, she owed it to Dominique to remember she was a professional.

Determined to keep a wide emotional distance from Rafe, Lilith nonetheless wished she could have slipped back to her condo to change into clothes that would make her feel beautiful and desirable. Since she couldn't, she made do by snagging a few minutes to work on her hair and makeup. Next, she practiced asking the familiar intake questions, lowering her usual speaking voice to sound sexy. She also reminded herself that this was business and she was a professional.

Rafe was late. Watching the clock pass the appointment time, Lilith couldn't sit still. Her nerves were strung out, on the verge of snapping. When the phone rang, she jumped. Too agitated to answer—what if he was calling to cancel?—she let voice mail pick up. She held her breath until she'd listened to the message. August, Rafe Graywolf's uncle, said they'd been delayed but should be at the office in the next fifteen minutes.

Lilith listened to the message three times. Rafe wasn't coming alone. He'd have his uncle with him. Of course that fit with everything she'd read about family being the foundation of shifter society.

Lilith thought about her own family. Much as she loved them, she couldn't picture going for a dating service intake interview with any of her relatives—especially from her dad's side. The image of one of her cousins shifting into hyena form during the intake gave her a much needed laugh and helped her relax a bit—at the perfect time.

Just then, the shifter group arrived—two *mature* men and one total hottie—burst into the office suite. All her talk to herself about caution and the impracticality of becoming interested in Rafe except as a client evaporated as soon as she laid eyes on him. His physical beauty crashed over her like a tidal wave on an unprotected beach. Her knees buckled. She willed herself not to become tongue-tied and tried to tear her gaze from his.

Silence. Since this was her office and she was the professional in charge, it was her job to move things along. She just had to figure out how to pry her lips apart and act normal.

One of the older men cleared his throat. Lilith swallowed hard.

"Thank you all for coming here. My partner Dominique LaPierre, who couldn't be here tonight, and I are thrilled to take part in the search for Rafe's soul mate. Please don't hesitate to contact us with feedback, questions or whatever comes up. Now, before we start, does anyone have any questions?"

August spoke first. "We need to be very clear about the need to find a suitable life mate for Rafe. She must be able to take her place at his side as he leads the pack. Of course, with a blood line like his, Rafe must choose a worthy, suitable mate."

Lilith watched Rafe through this entire speech. Though his face remained neutral, her instincts said something far different was going on below the surface. Then Rafe turned and winked at her. For just a moment, it was like the two of them formed a unit, a couple. Her heartbeat sped up and her breathing got funny. How pathetic. A mere wink got her hot and bothered, fired her up her imagination and her senses, and almost had her panting. Talk about inappropriate. She really needed to get a life.

Thank the goddess she could busy her hands with her keyboard. No one could see how much she was trembling while she banged away at the keys and managed to pay full attention to whichever man was speaking. When the elders fell silent, she turned to Rafe.

"Now I'd like to hear from you. I need specifics. First, I'm going to ask some questions. These will enable us to create an accurate, thorough profile. Then we can talk about what you're looking for."

Rafe stretched his long legs out in front of him. His full, generous lips tightened into an almost grimace. Lilith, who had inherited empath genes from her mom, had grown quite adept at identifying who did or didn't want to be in their "hot" seat.

Like Dominique, she didn't relish working with a client who didn't want to be there. When a client seemed reluctant, for whatever reason, she or Dominique would have a good talk with him or her—and with whoever was applying pressure. But this situation was unique. The older men had warned the Fangly staff that Rafe would be a hard case—but much more than individual preference was at stake. The very fate of the pack demanded that all the players, especially Rafe, fulfill their designated roles.

Lilith remembered all the tales she'd loved while growing up. Princesses and princes in marriages arranged to ensure dynastic survival seemed romantic when they didn't involve real beings. The reality was grim, not glamorous.

"Anything you'd like to ask before we start?" Lilith focused on Rafe.

She loved how his facial muscles moved—also how they looked in repose.

"The elders are leaving first, right?"

The older men sprang to life and began to voice objections.

"This is Rafe's choice," Lilith told the hovering men. "If he'd feel more comfortable speaking only to me, I'm sure you'll understand and leave the room."

August pursed his lips. "If we're here, we can make sure Rafe's answers present an accurate portrait."

"Geez, Uncle August. You trust me to guide the pack but you think I can't answer a few questions about myself?"

Anger and frustration seemed to simmer right below the surface. Lilith wouldn't want to be the target of those feelings. Part of what she had to do was defuse his negativity about the whole process.

Benedict put a hand on his friend's shoulder to stop him from responding. "It's not that, Rafe. But the two of us know you and know enough about what's involved to provide the most accurate profile. Why don't you let us help you?"

Rafe rolled his eyes. "I think you two have helped me enough to last a lifetime. Now why don't you cool your heels in the outer office so we can get this over with? I do have other business to take care of and standing here arguing is just wasting my time."

The elders left the room.

Lilith asked, "Rafe, who is your personal hero?"

He shrugged. "In spite of what you've just witnessed, I'd say my heroes are the males of my pack. My ancestors, all the leaders and alphas who've brought us to where we are today."

Nothing unexpected in that answer.

"Who's your ideal woman?"

He winked at Lilith again. "When you can't be with the one you love, love the one you're with."

If only.

Chapter Two

This interview was not what Rafe expected when the elders set him up at Fangly, My Dear. Lilith P. Graves—her full name was spelled out in brass on the wooden plaque at the front of her desk—had caught his eye the moment he had stepped into her office. A blue-eyed blonde with sexy lips and a curvy body he wanted to get his arms around and his teeth into, Lilith appeared to have no idea of the monumental erection her scent aroused.

When he caught her eye, she blushed—making him even harder as he imagined all kinds of delicious ways to turn her even redder. He licked his lips.

"Why do I get the impression you're not taking any of this seriously?" she asked.

Serious? Poor Lilith. She seemed determined to come up with some result to make the elders happy. Fun as it was to give her a hard time—he'd love to give her the hard time of her life—Rafe didn't want to frustrate the poor woman any more than necessary. Too bad the two of them hadn't met somewhere—anywhere—else. Talk about the roles they were required to play... "Come on, Lilith. You're an intelligent woman. I don't believe you or anyone else can plug in a formula and make effective matches, plus there's the simple fact that *I don't want a mate*."

She frowned, bringing adorable furrows to her forehead. "I thought alphas are required to have mates in order to rule."

"True," he admitted. "I intend to have a mate. When I choose one, it will be for life. But as I've told my uncle and Benedict and the other elders, I'll choose my mate when I'm ready. You see, until recently I had no idea I'd be the alpha for my pack this soon. To deal with an emergency situation, we all have had to be flexible, bend some rules and traditions. I know the elders think it's crucial for me to have my mate now because that's what all the other alphas have done. I see this as one more example of our need to be flexible and find new ways."

"You're doing such a fabulous job for the Wentworths, they should be willing to accommodate you," Lilith murmured.

"Right. You'd think they'd appreciate what I've done and not try to coerce me into doing what I don't want to do yet."

"Okay," she said. "Rafe, your situation is unique. We're pledged to respecting our clients' rights, first and foremost. Since you're our actual client, your wishes take precedence over the elders'."

"Thanks for that. I appreciate your understanding. I know you have a business to run. There has to be a way for us to satisfy the elders and not waste my time."

"I hope so. They won't be happy if we don't find your ideal mate pronto."

"I'll deal with that. I'll make it clear that despite your brilliance and diligence, I'm the problem. No worries. I'll answer your intake questions. I'll even call the ladies you set me up with and go out with some of them. But, as far as lifetime soul mate choice goes, I'm in sole charge—on my own timetable."

"Fair enough. No one can guarantee they'll fall in love for life on command."

"Right. Speaking of orders, I'm starved. Right now, I want to order dinner. Come with me and we'll finish this intake over food." He grinned at her as she once again blushed.

Lilith couldn't believe her ears. Rafe had just asked her out, sort of. Not exactly as in a date, but beggars couldn't choosers. She hadn't seen that coming, but her usual empath senses seemed way off when it came to Rafe. This had never happened before and she had no idea what to expect. Later, when she had time to think, she'd have to figure out why her sense wasn't working. Later. Right now, he'd asked her out. She wanted to jump up and yell, "Yes!", but then she channeled Dominique and pulled herself together. "That's not our usual practice."

He shrugged. "I understand your business is new enough not to have a lot of established practices in place."

Good one. "I think that sounds like a great idea." Her voice sounded serene. She was going out with Rafe Graywolf. Even if it was only to conduct an intake interview, she could almost consider it a date.

His grin came slow and easy. "I take that as a 'yes'. Lilith, as you're doing me the favor here, where would you like to eat?"

Huh. She couldn't see Rafe going for Vinnie's Veggie Garden or any of her usual haunts. Weres went for red meat, cooked rare. Stifling her usual "ewww" at that prospect, Lilith reviewed a roster of possibilities. No way could she could endure a steakhouse. Then it struck her. She had to be upfront with him about not only what kind of food she ate, but who she was. "Before we go any further, I need to tell you some things about me."

A wicked grin lit up his face. "From the expression on your face, I'd expect you to confess to being a serial axe murderer or something along those lines."

At the moment, she'd prefer that identity to the one she was about to reveal. "I'm a vegetarian."

He cocked a brow. "So you won't ask to sample my barely singed filet. Can't say I understand why anyone would want to be a vegetarian, but I like a bit of mystery in women. Is that it? Are you ready to go?"

If only. "One more thing. The reason why I'm vegetarian. You see, I'm a demi-ghoul, on my dad's side. If I weren't a strict vegetarian—"

That rattled his cool. Lilith could see the precise moment when the truth of her identity registered—the moment he jolted back in his seat. What a moment for her empath skills to kick in. On the other hand, it wasn't like this had never happened before—or wouldn't happen again. Lilith held her head up and locked eyes with Rafe. She loved her family, both branches. Any guy who set a speed running record in his sprint away from her wasn't worth—

"That's a new one for me, Lilith. Anything else you want to mention?"

He wasn't running. She straightened her shoulders. "I'm also an empath from Mom's side of the family."

"Great. Then you realize I've got to eat pronto or I'll get crabby."

Her mind scrambled to come up with the perfect place to satisfy their needs. "Italian or Mex?"

"Italian," he snapped back.

"Cassio's?"

"In North Beach? Sounds great."

"But what about the elders waiting in the outer office?"

He looked at his watch and made a face. "They'll have to get their own dinner. I'll let them know. Ready to go?"

Rafe whipped out his cell, had a quick conversation with an elder and then phoned for a reservation. Before she could think of anything else to hold them up, they were out the door.

Seeing Lilith shuffle the lettuce, olives and cheese cubes of her vegetarian antipasto around her plate, Rafe figured she wasn't very hungry. At least she seemed to enjoy the excellent sourdough bread and Chianti. He, on the other hand, practically inhaled his steak and pasta.

He wondered what was bothering her. Lilith was an intriguing mixture of shy and sophisticated. Sophisticated wasn't hard to come by in San Francisco, but Rafe met very few people he'd consider shy. He liked that about her. He also liked the way he felt near her. Warm. Hot. She appeared to have no idea how damn sexy she was. He wanted to nuzzle the porcelain skin of her long, delicate neck. She brought out a mix of lust and protectiveness unlike any he'd ever felt. Pleasurable as these emotions could be, he also sensed he should be on his guard with her. Lilith P. Graves had him experiencing emotions very new to him. Most of all, though, she turned him on. He wanted to brush the blond curls back from her ivory cheeks and kiss the path they traced.

She'd cleared a spot on the crowded table for her papers and pen. "Before we have dessert, I thought we could get these questions out of the way."

He nodded to her still almost-full plate. "You didn't eat much. Didn't you like the antipasto? Do you want to order something else?"

"Busted. Now you know my guilty secret. I loaded up on the bread. It's my weakness and they just kept replenishing our basket. I couldn't resist." She smiled.

Talk about not being able to resist. The animal in him wanted to reach across the table and grab her, lay her down and ravish her. Of course, he had his inner animal well under control now. It wouldn't do to frighten her off, send her screaming into the night when she saw the power of his lust unleashed. His cock, fully erect for what felt like days, throbbed. He knew in very precise terms what he wanted for dessert.

Right now, though, he had to divert his blood supply from his erection back to the head on his shoulders.

"What is the physical description of your ideal woman?'"

"You," he whispered so softly, she almost didn't hear. "I like beautiful women." She shouldn't have needed the words to know what he felt, but her empath skills had deserted her just when she needed them most.

She rolled her eyes. "Can you be more specific. Eye color, hair color—that sort of thing?"

He grinned. "Let's see. Curly blond hair, down to about where you have it." He pointed to her. She gripped the pen with such focus, he wanted to slip it from between her fingers and suck on each one. "Big blue eyes that are true windows to the woman's soul. When I look in her eyes, I want to read her soul."

That netted him a look before she wrote.

"What about body type?"

"Female," he growled.

"Short, tall, willowy, more rounded—"

"Stand up so I can see."

Wonderful blush. She turned so red, he'd have sworn her blush must extend from the roots of her naturally blond hair clear down to her toenails.

"Rafe, get real. You have to stop kidding around, or we'll be here all night."

He lounged back in his seat. "You have other appointments?"

She turned away. "It's not that. I promised Dominique I'd get you to focus. The sooner we can get the forms done, the sooner we can input your responses and start finding matches for you."

"You're the exact image of my perfect woman. To answer your questions, just describe yourself. You're what I want, physically, socially and whatever other 'ly' you're looking for."

She pursed her gorgeous full lips. "Look, Rafe. It's not that

I'm not flattered. Heck, what woman wouldn't be? We can't forget, though, this isn't about us flirting and playing around. I understand where you're coming from about choosing a mate and I've agreed to help. Still, we at Fangly, My Dear have made a commitment to locate suitable candidates for you, even if you end up rejecting them all. We want the candidates to seem feasible. Please, cooperate."

"I am, Lilith. I want to go out with you. From where I'm sitting, you're the exact image of my perfect date, even if I didn't get your name from a dating service. Will you go out with me?" Though Rafe realized Lilith's family background made her unsuitable to be his life mate, and that his pack would never accept her in that role, he couldn't deny how attracted he was to her. He wanted her more each moment they spent together, even if she was a demi-ghoul. He had to be with her or he'd spend the rest of his life sure he'd missed out on something major.

She blushed even harder and batted her eyelashes. "This is so unprofessional. Not at all what I had in mind when I agreed to have dinner with you for your intake."

He waved away her objections. "Are you hiding behind your professional persona to say no?"

"God, no."

"Do you want to see me? Because Lilith, I want to be with you." He took her hands in his, dislodging the pen and crumpling several papers.

A series of emotions flitted across her face and he could smell the conflict brewing in her. All her pheromones told him she wanted him. She wanted him to fuck her and, though she was far more inhibited than he was, the notion of them taking each other amid the debris on the table turned her on. Her desire floated around her like an aura he could almost touch.

"Rafe, yes. I want to be with you. But I'm not a suitable candidate to be an alpha's mate and that's what I'm supposed to be helping you with." Her voice choked on the last words. Though he hated to cause her distress, he reveled in how much she wanted him too.

"Please. I must be able to input your answers in the morning. Please respond to my questions." Her eyes grew large.

"Come back to my place. We'll be much more comfortable there."

"Your place?"

"Yes. We can be alone, with no distractions. I'll answer all your questions and then you can stop worrying about those forms."

She thought for a moment. When she licked her lips with her little pink tongue, he knew she'd made her decision. "All right."

He paid the bill and got them out of Cassio's. Thank the gods, it was only a short drive to his place.

Everything was spiraling out of control. Dominique would never find herself in such an impossible situation. Even though Lilith's rational mind kept screaming that she should put a halt to what was happening right now, her heart and libido stomped all over the fading voice of reason. She wanted to be with Rafe Graywolf tonight. No way she could deny it, to herself or him.

He had to be the ultimate bad boy. Bad boy, bad wolf, bad client. He was trouble on two legs—sometimes four—and nothing good could ever come from letting herself be vulnerable to him. He could wreck her life, or at least seriously derail her for a long time. He could definitely make a hash of Fangly, My Dear and thus not only ruin the business, but destroy her friendship with Dominique. She could lose everything that was meaningful to her just to spend time with Rafe Graywolf. Lilith had to wonder if someone had been grinding up "stupid" pills and sneaking them into her food.

Still, she wanted to be with him. Though he went through women like other men went through newspapers, she could somehow believe that whatever happened between them would be unique. She could see herself playing Juliet to Rafe's Romeo—minus the nasty ending.

All he'd done was invite her to his place and she was rewriting Shakespeare to describe her emotions. She needed to get some perspective. He was flirting with her. He'd been coming on to her from the start, but he did that the way other men breathed. Of course, starved as she was for masculine attention, she ate up whatever he dished out. Rafe fed his huge ego off her obvious response.

Well, she needed to get them both back on track. She had a job to do and Rafe knew his limits. Flirting was fun, but she had to be sure neither of them took any of it too seriously. She had to be the grownup here, because he wasn't about to be.

First, she had to tamp down the ridiculous attraction she felt for him. Heck, a man this great looking and successful had women thronging to his side. No way could Lilith P. Graves compete—especially when the competition was beautiful, successful pack princesses, suitable candidates to become his mate for life.

"My humble abode." Humble? Not. Rafe's large cottage in the woods north of San Francisco surprised Lilith, mostly because she felt at home the moment she stepped across the threshold. Oversized, comfortable furniture filled but didn't crowd the living room. Judging by the artwork, Rafe had excellent, if eclectic, taste. Lilith wanted to linger over each piece, but time was fleeting.

How many other women had he brought back here with him? Whatever. At least she could be sure she was the only one who'd ever come with an intake questionnaire from a dating service. She always did want to be unique.

Rafe came up close behind her. She could feel his hot breath fan the nape of her neck before she turned to face him.

"*Mi casa es su casa.* Make yourself comfortable."

Yeah, right. As long as he stood that near her, *comfortable* wasn't an option.

"Can I get you a drink?"

A gallon of ice water might be a good start.

"We really need to finish the questionnaire," she murmured. "And it's getting late. I have to get home."

He got right in her face. "What's your first question?"

It's about the questionnaire. She swallowed hard. "What is your most important value?"

Instead of answering, he kissed her. His lips, full and well-formed, brushed across hers with unexpected tenderness. The element of surprise caught her off-guard and intrigued her. Though she should have known better, she pressed her lips back to his, which evidently was all the invitation he needed to begin a deep plunder of her mouth.

His powerful arms drew her to him as their mouths tangled. Was that his heartbeat or hers? In his embrace, she

117

lost track of boundaries. He felt so strong, so sheltering, as she burrowed in his arms. Her legs pressed against his, which he'd splayed in an effort to diminish the difference in their heights. She stood on her toes to reach up to him, but he still had to tilt his face down.

He ground his erection against the sensitive area of her lower belly and groin. She wanted to have him in her hot, wet pussy. She'd creamed so much already, the silk of her panties bunched up into her folds like a tease. She needed to feel him there, to wrap her legs around him and have him plunge his dick deep into her. Shivering with excitement and anticipation, she surrendered to the moment and the man.

Lips still latched to hers, he began to massage her back. The erotic friction of his hands on her, kneading her muscles and rubbing her, brought her to the edge of an orgasm. A hair trigger away from becoming a screaming meltdown, she imagined herself on a speeding train, out of control on lightning tracks.

"You're so beautiful," he whispered when they broke apart. Though her head told her he'd said the same words to many women and would say them to many more, they lodged in her heart and took root. He found *her* beautiful. He wanted *her*. Right now, it didn't matter what had come before or what would come afterward. For this moment, she was beautiful to him. She would cherish his words always.

For a moment, she tried to find a way to tell him to stop what was inevitable between them. Before she took him into herself, her rational voice chided, she still could hold something back. Once they became intimate, she would be lost.

She didn't care if she stayed lost forever. At this moment, she was ready to toss everything aside but the burning need for them to be together. He wanted her—completely, passionately, all the ways she'd always dreamed of being wanted. She could read his heart and soul with a startling clarity, each desire lit up with the light of absolute understanding. And she matched him in ardor. More than anything in the universe, she longed to expend her passion, her desire, on this man.

"I want to make love with you." His whispered words penetrated her soul.

"Yes."

Hand in hand, the two of them ran to his bedroom. His

king-size bed beckoned. In moments, he'd tossed back the blue and beige quilt to reveal pale blue cotton sheets. He tore off his clothes, then drank her in with his eyes as she gave up on a sexy strip and got naked.

Usually, she felt shy about being naked with anyone, but tonight was different. With Rafe she had the strangest desire to display herself with pride, to offer herself. The way he devoured her body with his gaze, Lilith could have sworn he was responding to her whacko emotions. Under Rafe's intense scrutiny, she unfurled herself, opening like a blossom at last encountering sunlight. His gaze warmed her. Though she didn't make it a practice to jump into strange beds, her leap into Rafe's bed felt exactly right. Kind of like Goldilocks. *Oof.* She wished her mind wouldn't play such weird tricks on her.

"I want to savor your beauty with all my senses." Rafe towered over her in his naked glory. Impossibly, the man appeared even more gorgeous in the actual flesh than she'd imagined. His body was the ideal. Not even Michelangelo could have sculpted such magnificence. Lilith couldn't decide what she wanted to do more—look or touch. Not to mention taste and smell. Like a starving woman invited to a rich one-time only banquet, she went into glutton mode and prepared to feast.

"I must touch you, now," he growled, climbing in alongside her.

Touching his skin set off electrical impulses within her. Before now, she'd never realized how much pleasure could come from simple skin-to-skin contact. Was it the wolf in Rafe that made him feel so different to her fingertips? Realizing this magnificent creature, this total man, contained within him a different nature took her breath away, exciting and terrifying her. She was completely out of her depth. But more than breath itself, she craved the erotic intimacy their being together promised.

"Lilith Graves, you are a very special, beautiful woman," he murmured, tracing the contours of her body with his fingertips.

She closed her eyes and focused her whole being on the moment. His masculine scent—pine and forest and something she couldn't name but found appealing—made her head spin. She wanted to remember that scent always, to imprint it within her so she could conjure it up, so she could summon up the sense memory of being with him every day for the rest of her life.

His breath seared her as he nuzzled the space between her breasts. She always felt self-conscious because she was bigger than most of the models in fashion magazines. Though people always said men liked big breasts, she hadn't found that to be true—until now. Rafe suckled one nipple with gusto while he fondled the other and appeared not only to accept but to appreciate her as she was. She moaned with pleasure in response to the way his hand and mouth moved, the things he did to her with each movement and breath. Most of all, she loved the way he savored her and awoke her to the wonders of her body. She'd never before realized how sensitive her breasts were, or how direct the connection was between her areolas and her clit.

"Mmm," she murmured. Her fingers wove into Rafe's thick black hair. With his ear near her heart, Rafe had to be able to hear what he was doing to her, how her heartbeat sped with arousal. His skin heated her everywhere they touched, as if he wanted to share his inner fire with her.

Never one to remain passive, Lilith reached for Rafe's flat, taut belly. Her hand immediately encountered his huge pulsing erection and they both moaned at the erotic contact. Rafe Graywolf was exceedingly well formed. His cock felt like velvet skin over a marble core. He responded to her slightest movement. With the thrusts of his hips and his deep growly moans, Rafe let her know how much she pleasured him.

"You are one delicious lady," he whispered. Using his talented tongue and teeth, he began to nibble the sensitive flesh of her breasts. She shivered. Moving with infinite slowness and deliberation, he began to work his way down her aroused body with his teeth and lips. At the same time, he caressed her vulva, his fingers darting to her clit, along the folds and on a foray deep inside her.

Goddess, she'd never before been so wet. She wanted him so much, he had to sense it in every fiber of his being. When his mouth touched her pussy, she had to hold tight to keep from flying off the bed. The pleasure of his tongue on her clit, his strong, sharp teeth nibbling at the soft, sensitive tissues and licking her wetness had her at the edge of a high precipice. Waves of pleasure radiated through her, from her feminine core outward, threatening to force her off that edge.

"I want you, Lilith. I want you to ride my cock until we both holler from the sheer pleasure of me being deep in you."

Hearing him put his desires into words almost brought her to tears. The fragility of the moment, of the bond between them, staggered her. This was the first time she'd ever experienced such perfect communication with any other being—as if their bodies were created for just this moment. She regarded her thought as silly, a mind blip caused by extreme arousal. There was no such thing as destiny, right? Yet her body thrummed with the wisdom that every moment in her life, all she'd ever been or done had led her to this exact time, this place, this man.

"I want you, too, Rafe." Her brain scrambled for something more memorable to say, but she came up empty. All she wanted now was to focus on him, on them, on what they could be together.

"I'm coming in," he groaned.

"Yes, oh yes," she breathed.

With a grunt he got to his knees and, in one smooth movement, wedged himself between her legs. He held his dick in his hand and Lilith nearly fainted from the pleasure of looking at him. Where was a camera when a girl needed one? Heck, she wished her eyes could become a camera to record the image of Rafe offering her his huge, hard penis. She'd have a special time each day for the rest of her life when she would dream over his picture and feast her senses on her memories.

With total focus, he positioned his glans between her folds and the contact set off sparks of pleasure that nudged her out of control. The pleasure of divine friction coupled with his scent shot through her. The way he sucked his breath in, with her empath senses going at full tilt, she could feel him experiencing the same level of sensation and delight.

"You feel so fantastic," he rasped. "So wet and warm, so welcoming."

"You're totally welcome to come into me." Her voice sounded surer and steadier than expected, considering how much she was quivering.

Now he braced himself with one hand on each of her hips and wedged the head of his cock the smallest bit into her. "Ohhh." This was the first time she'd ever had such a sense of intimate connection with a lover.

Too slowly, he worked his way into her. Every bit deeper opened her up to a whole new world of ecstasy. To her astonishment, the sense of intimate connection grew deeper as he claimed each inch of her.

"I feel like I've just found my missing half," he whispered.

Goose bumps sprang up on her arms and her back, despite the warmth the two of them generated. By sharing this profound intimacy with her, Rafe was inviting Lilith to a whole new dimension of being, one she'd never even imagined. He was showing her who he was and taking in the deepest knowledge of her. By participating with him in this almost mystical union, she welcomed him and agreed to their bond, the first time she'd ever felt this close to anyone—as if they'd become one. That realization scared and awed her.

When Rafe had penetrated to the deepest bit inside her, he lay perfectly still. Despite the impetus to move, to give themselves up to the full erotic pleasure of being together, she tried to follow his lead and remain still. If they stayed like this, they could prolong this magical joining. Could it ever be enough for her? Thinking that, she tilted her hip a fraction. He groaned and put his hand on her to still her.

If only she could turn off her mind and be in the moment. Despite the perfection of their being together, Lilith couldn't keep doubts at bay. After all, the ecstasy of their contact might blow her mind, but it might be just business as usual for Rafe. An unwelcome wave of jealousy surged through her, threatening this exquisite moment. It couldn't be this amazing for him with anyone else, could it? Lilith turned her head to clear away the disturbing thought. Just for now, she willed herself to turn off her mind and stop the questions that tormented her. No matter what, she would focus on being in the moment, allowing no thoughts of the past or the future or Rafe with another woman to intrude on the magic ride of the present.

Rafe grunted something and Lilith was afraid she'd messed everything up with her usual insecurities.

Then he said, "Much as I would love to remain like this forever, I've got to move. I've got to explore how it feels to plunge my cock in and out of you, to touch all the beautiful places inside you." He ran his strong fingers down her side, raising shivers wherever he touched.

"I want to feel the way you maneuver your cock in me," she

whispered back. She had her legs wound around him and he was so deep in her she imagined he could go no further. Nonetheless, she laid her hands on the firm cheeks of his ass and pressed him to her. To her wonder, this tightened their contact and sent new sparks of pleasure shooting through her.

In complete joy and togetherness, their rhythm perfectly in sync, they played out their intimate dance. They each touched more and more of the special places that rewarded their intimate exploration with ecstatic sensation. Lilith fell helplessly, ecstatically into the erotic mystery of being one with Rafe.

Chapter Three

Rafe had been attracted to Lilith from the moment they met, with an intensity that made previous attractions seem trivial. Though he'd made love with more women than he could remember, nothing about being with Lilith resembled any of his other experiences. The uniqueness couldn't be due to her being part ghoul, could it?

He was out of control, not at all a familiar experience. Holy shit. If he'd known making love with her would push his buttons to this extent, would he have given in to the erotic impulse—or run like hell? A woman like her, an interlude like this, could ruin him for being with other women. Talk about timing. Why had this woman come into his life just when he could no longer play around, when he had to search for his soul mate?

The way they moved together, the perfect rhythm and synchronicity between them, sparked a wild idea. All his instincts screamed that Lilith Graves was his mate. Except, how could that be? Lilith was possibly the most inappropriate woman in the universe to be a pack alpha's mate. For crying out loud, she was a *ghoul*, the absolute bottom of the evolutionary chain. To add insult to injury, she was a *vegetarian* ghoul. Not even the most flea-bitten, god-forsaken pack would lower themselves to accept her as their alpha's mate.

Though his rational inner voice kept arguing against the physical attraction that drew him to her, an overriding sense knew there was something more. Try as he might to be logical and listen to reason, he couldn't focus long on this glimmer of future trouble. He couldn't focus on anything that interfered with their being together. Right now, he'd be happy to stay forever in the pheromonic haze of their erotic coupling.

In addition to how he felt when he was with her—like he was bigger, stronger, handsomer and more fascinating than all the super heroes combined—he got off on the power of the chemistry between them. It was like they were the only two people in the world and they could happily recreate their own personal Eden.

Rafe took no small pride in pleasuring his sexual partners. That was one reason why they always wanted to come back for more. Besides, pleasure for pleasure fit with his notions of fair play. With Lilith, though, that impetus took on a whole new dimension. Pleasuring her became a mission he had to fulfill. Her reactions mattered because she did.

"Rafe," she whispered, stretching his name to several syllables as her body prepared to rise to her release.

The way she called his name, the way she clutched him, her graceful erotic dance—every nuance combined to sweep him up and carry him along in a flood of sensation. Now that he was sure she'd come first, he could let up on his iron self-control—he could unclench his teeth and begin to allow the gathering force of his own orgasm.

"Lilith," he murmured, stroking her hair. His thrusts and plunges into her became deeper, faster and ever more frenzied. The heat between them crackled and sparked, raising the stakes. Such intensity couldn't last, but before the flames subsided, he sensed they'd be forever singed in a mutual fire.

With Lilith now fully focused on the release she'd been building to, her face took on an especially sweet expression, almost peaceful. Rafe wanted to lick her rosy cheeks, her full, pouting lips, but he feared he'd burn her and scar her with the searing heat of his arousal. Later, he'd tongue her, taste her everywhere he longed to. For now, his own sexual wild ride threatened to engulf them. His cock had grown larger than ever before and, once he began to come, he'd explode into her, flooding her with the come she'd stimulated.

"Oh, oh, oooh." Lilith shuddered to a full-body climax that shook the earth and stars. He cherished each tremor and wanted to catch her moves and hold them to him. Breathless and stunned, he registered with shock what this woman did to his breathing and his heartbeat.

Right before he came, Rafe always had a moment when his inner wolf surfaced, fueling his orgasm with the powerful force of his dual nature. Though he didn't take on the physical aspect of his wolf self, for a time his heart beat doubled and his full soul soared. Then, after he gave himself up to his climax, as he lay in the glow of erotic satisfaction, his selves completed the journey to unity.

With Lilith, his wolf self lingered far longer than ever before. Reeling from all the shocks of their lovemaking, Rafe had no idea what to make of yet another first he was experiencing with her.

"How are you?" he crooned softly in her ear.

Rafe's breath tickled her ear. Lilith couldn't believe she had any nerve endings left to register sensations, but his warm breath proved she did. "Yum," she whispered back in brilliant response. Judging by his smile, he wasn't looking for brilliance just then, which was good.

Lost in a tide of pleasure with the merest touch of confusion, she fell back against the pillow. Her usual experience in the past was to find the after-loving moments to be a letdown, probably because she usually felt that she'd once more been with the wrong man. But with Rafe, who'd been the wrong man from the very first, Lilith couldn't bring herself to regard anything about him as less than right.

She had seriously underestimated how being with him would impact her. All she'd wanted, she told herself, was to break her long sexual dry spell. Rafe, who was totally out of her league for several million reasons, had seemed like her dream candidate for a quick but meaningless fuck—assuming they ever got that far, which had been a bit of a fantasy for her. But, goddess, she'd gotten far more than anticipated. Would the most amazing orgasm in her life turn out to be her biggest mistake ever?

As they clung to each other, limbs entangled, cocooned in the mutual musk of incredible sex, Lilith wished she could turn her mind off. Most of all, she wished she could make what they'd just experienced last. She'd never before made love with a shifter. Although she'd heard the same wild stories as everyone else, she hadn't believed them. When she and Rafe had come—their orgasms so close they'd been virtually simultaneous—Lilith could have sworn she'd sensed the life force of a big, powerful wolf hovering around her. She should have been scared, but instead, its presence seemed the most natural thing in the world. Heck, she'd shivered with disappointment when the sensation dissipated before she could examine it.

"I sensed the wolf," she whispered to Rafe. "Your wolf...you."

He brush kissed her lips. "He wanted to get to know you," he confessed. "And he will, but that wasn't the right moment. He likes you, a lot."

"Really? Is that usual?" She blushed, which was stupid considering how intimate they'd just been—still were. In some ways, lying with him like this felt even more intimate, considering that she had his leg between hers, wedged against her pussy, still creamy and sticky with his come. Yet asking the question made her blush.

He traced her areola, coaxing the nipple to bud into delicious hardness. Her lower belly clenched in renewed arousal. Lilith had always considered her ghoul self practically a nympho, which her human self made behave. Now, in contrast, she suspected Rafe was arousing both her inner girl and her ghoul. And considering that she'd just come, she'd have expected to need some recovery time. She felt good to go again and that just had to be completely wanton.

"No, it's not. Lilith, nothing about my being with you is usual. To be honest, I don't know exactly what to make of what's happened between us. My gut tells me that nothing you and I do together is wrong. You've hit me like a meteor from outer space, lady, and I can't ignore that."

He'd had that effect on her too.

And then she remembered. The questionnaire, the friggin' questionnaire. She was with Rafe to help him fill out the intake interview questions so she could help locate his perfect mate. Not her. Everything she was doing tonight threatened her agency, her job there and maybe most importantly, her friendship.

Still, what was happening between her and Rafe seemed even more important than her forever friendship with Dominique—which stunned her. Until now, she'd never have believed that anything could be more important to her than that friendship. Of all the inappropriate, unprofessional and disloyal behaviors. How could she have let this happen? How could she have fallen into bed with the most unavailable client in the universe?

The return of her thought processes sent Lilith's spirit plummeting back to Earth like a rogue elevator, down from the fuzzy, dreamy height of her fantasies.

Conflicting voices raged in Rafe's head—a variation on the usual "angel" and "devil", because this time, it wasn't at all clear which was the devil's voice. Was it the one behind the loud chorus urging him to extend his intimate interlude with Lilith? He loved everything about being with her like this, the two of them floating in their own unique world, buoyed by the incredible affinity that had sprung up between them. Being with her felt anything but wrong. On the other hand, the voice of reason, the one programmed by the elders, provided a much different message—"Run!"

So why wasn't he moving?

Rafe ran his eyes over Lilith's luscious body. Her clothes camouflaged her lovely body—sinfully hiding her sexy curvaceousness. Of course, not even the most tailored garments could disguise her feminine attributes, thank the powers of the universe. Lilith was one of those women who looked more tempting *au naturel* than clothed. And all her loveliness was on display for him and him alone.

Who could blame him for wanting to hang around?

Even as he feasted his eyes on her, Lilith drew away and started scrambling to gather her tossed clothes. Seeing her beautiful face now unsmiling, composed into a serious, professional expression, Rafe felt the room temperature, though not his own heat, drop several degrees.

She threw on her shirt and slacks, made adjustments to her makeup and ran her fingers through her wild tangle of hair. Then, before he could protest, she picked up a sheaf of papers and a pen. "The intake interview," she said, her voice so tiny and soft, even with his super sensitive senses, he almost couldn't hear. "I came here to conduct the intake interview."

He leered at her. "I don't believe that was on your mind

when you were coming right here." He patted the mattress next to where he lay and savored her blush in response.

She closed her eyes and appeared to be counting to ten, or maybe one hundred. Bloody hell, she was so stunning, especially now, when she was unaware of the effect she had on him. She appeared caught up in the work at hand, to conduct the ridiculous interview.

Her lashes fluttered as she looked down at the paper. "What are the three top qualities you value in a romantic companion?"

Was she serious? Did she really expect him to answer that question in such a cut and dried manner? Judging from the expression on her face, she did. He aimed to please. "Let's see. I want my romantic companion, interesting choice of words there by the way, to be totally like Lilith, completely like Lilith and exactly like Lilith." His lips curved up in a smile as he reached to touch her. She ducked out of his way.

"I don't think you're being at all serious about this matter." She laid down her pen without having written a single word.

He went over to her, cupped her chin and raised her face so they were eye to eye. "You don't? Hmmm. What do you base your opinion on?"

She rolled her eyes and wriggled free. "Rafe. Your pack has hired Fangly, My Dear to provide you with dates who are viable candidates to become your mate." Her face melted in a wistful expression that wrenched his heart.

He bent very close to her. "Right now, Ms. Lilith Graves, from where I'm sitting, you're the most viable candidate I'd want to spend quality time with. Part of that quality time includes not talking about or thinking about any other woman but you. Cripes, I thought women didn't like having their dates divide their attentions and focus on others."

Bloody hell, she looked so stricken, so sad, he wished he could take back his remarks. After he'd seen the naked pain in her eyes, she ducked her head and looked down. She'd better not cry. He could not stand it when women cried. He willed her not to cry.

Trying to resume the same light, bantering tone he'd used before, he continued, "But you're insisting I should speculate about women I haven't even met—and don't want to."

Head still down, she sighed. When she raised her head, he

saw she'd teared up. Oh, shit. She'd ignored his telepathic request. Not tears. He could deal with screaming, yelling, jumping up and down—even full-fledged diva tantrums. But tears? He could handle anything except tears. If the tears filled her beautiful eyes and spilled down her cheeks, he'd feel like a complete bastard. He'd want to lick each one away. Gritting his teeth, he gently wiped the unwelcome moisture away with his thumb and then with a kiss. She drew back and shook her head.

"Don't, Rafe. You're only making it worse."

"What? What am I making worse?" She was the one who seemed determined to short circuit the electricity between them and channel their energies elsewhere.

"I'm not even in the pool." She sobbed the last word.

"What pool? Who's talking about swimming? Hell, if that's what you want, we can head to the ocean, skinny dip."

She half-laughed, half-sobbed. "The pool of possible candidates to be your mate," she ground out. "You know it and I know it. Aah, this was such a mistake."

He didn't like what she said, not one little bit. How could Lilith call anything about their being here like this tonight a mistake? They'd been so perfect together, without any of the usual awkwardness or tentativeness people felt their first time. "No, it wasn't. Whatever else you believe, that's not true."

"Yes, it is." In a graceful movement, she drew away. He reached for her, but she darted out of his range. "It was stupid of me to think I could conduct your intake, especially here, with the two of us alone. I should have known better, should have told Dominique to take charge of this one. The smart, ethical, professional thing to do when one feels personal involvement is to withdraw. Contrary to all wisdom and even simple common sense, I ignored this truth. Now I've made a fool of myself and made Fangly, My Dear look unprofessional. Your pack will want their money back and we'll get a negative reputation in the area."

"Whew," Rafe said. "Hard on yourself, there, Lilith? As in, do you always take total responsibility for everything? If you do, I'd strongly suggest you stop. Even as my pack alpha, I realize I'm not responsible for everything that goes on."

She actually wrung her hands. He took them in his to stop her.

"Rafe, I'll admit I was attracted to you."

"Glad to hear it. Attraction's mutual."

She sniffled. "I'm glad to hear that. But, you see, I should have realized this attraction might interfere with the completion of my assignment, my sole reason for coming here."

"Baby, it takes two to tango. And to tangle the sheets."

Another blush. He wanted to lick the hot redness from her high-boned cheeks and then lose himself in kissing her, but in her current mood, he figured she'd probably rebuff him and say words they'd both find regrettable. He could sense her fragility and realized he had to proceed with caution to keep from messing up even more.

"Since you're the alpha of your pack, I am not a candidate to be your mate. We both know that." Her voice sounded strained, as if each word caused her pain. The longing in her eyes scraped at his soul. In that moment, he knew how much she longed to be a possible mate for him. His heart clenching, he could admit to himself that he longed for the same thing.

However, neither of them could ignore the truth. Lilith P. Graves was a ghoul. Even a demi-ghoul carried the full hereditary taint of that species. She was related on her father's side to creatures who fed on the flesh of the dead, graveyard grovelers. Also shifters who'd become hyenas and used their obnoxious laugh to trick the unwary before killing them and feeding on them. Lovely Lilith had hinted that she reined in her own ghoulish potential by being a strict vegetarian. If she ever slipped and just sampled the meat his pack favored, she could morph into a hideous monster like her father's relatives. So despite her spirit, her personality, her beauty and a hundred other desirable qualities, she was automatically excluded from consideration. Something about that reality was so fundamentally wrong, Rafe wanted to howl out his rejection of this injustice.

Though he could howl and protest until he was purple and blue in the face, the pack would never acknowledge Lilith as his mate. He had to have a mate to be an effective alpha for his pack—he'd come to accept that. And only he could guide his pack through the current turbulent times.

So, did the question come down to choosing between his pack and the chance to be with a woman who jolted him like a lightning strike to the heart? Why did he have to choose?

Lilith put the papers aside. "Tomorrow, I'll have to tell Dominique I failed, that I wasn't able to guide you through our intake interview. I'm sure she'll contact you to reschedule. And now, I should leave." She heaved a huge sigh and began to weep, more quietly than before.

Distressed and unwilling to let her walk away, Rafe took her in his arms. "None of that's important, baby. I don't want you to leave."

She held herself stiffly, resisting him for a moment, before she let herself melt against him. "Rafe, this is so wrong, but I can't tear myself away from you. It's like my legs have turned to rubber and refuse to support me."

He ran an eager hand along her thigh. "Your legs feel wonderful to me, except for one problem."

"A problem?" she echoed.

"Yes. You're wearing too many clothes. It's so much nicer when we can be skin to skin."

She sighed again. "It's the dumbest thing I've ever done, being here and then compounding it by staying. Rafe, I don't want to go. I don't want to go."

He traced her fine features with his fingertips. "So we're agreed on that. Stay with me, Lilith. I want you here. Nothing else matters."

"Oh, you're wrong there. Everything else matters. But Rafe, let's make it special for us. Let's agree. Tonight doesn't count. I'll stay here with you just for tonight. After that, we'll both forget whatever's happened between us." She locked eyes with him and, at that moment, he'd have promised her the world.

"Lilith, I can never forget you. I'd never want to forget you."

"You have to, Rafe. To be the alpha your pack requires, the alpha it's your destiny to be, you have to find your mate and be with her alone. I won't get in the way of that."

Every word she said dug into his heart like a knife. With her, he felt all the complications and conflicts of being his pack's alpha and of being a man. How much simpler if they could both assume wolf forms and freely live their animal natures. But Lilith, despite their soul affinity, wasn't any part wolf. She was part ghoul. She could never be his mate for all the parts of his journey.

Though he wanted to resist, he had to agree with the wisdom of her insight. They would have to snatch whatever chance they could to be together. She could never be his officially.

Lilith hadn't signed on for this. When she'd longed for an end to her current dry spell, she'd envisioned being caught up in a fling, maybe with some romantic fringe benefits, with a man she could share a no-strings good time with. Who needed the complication of this irresistible attraction to someone so wrong for her he might as well have come from another planet?

After tonight, Lilith knew she'd have to take a firm, irrevocable vow to avoid being alone with Rafe. After tonight. But she lacked the strength to leave him just yet, so she gave herself up to his caresses, to the hot passion of his touch. She wanted him and oh, goddess, he wanted her. If only that could be enough.

Rafe was right. Being naked with him felt right and as natural as breathing. How silly of her to try to form a barrier between them with her clothes. After all, it was a barrier neither of them wanted.

When she looked in his eyes, Lilith knew it would be easy to lose herself, just to drown in their dark depths. So easy.

His hands caressed the outlines of her face. Funny, it was new for her to regard herself as beautiful, as completely feminine, desirable and desired. She was living the romance Fangly, My Dear advertised to attract clients. She wanted this romance too, but she was the one client Fangly would never be able to service properly.

For right now, she could leave such sad thoughts behind. Her body celebrated being with Rafe. As if she were some latter day Sleeping Beauty, he awoke her with his sensuous touch. Only with him did she begin to understand that her whole body was an erogenous zone. This was true for her only with him— one of the many fantastic discoveries she made in his arms.

He tenderly kissed her closed eyelids, his touch light as a butterfly wing compared with the fierce strength of his embrace. As she lay, mesmerized, Lilith would have sworn he ran his tongue over every inch of her body, tasting, sampling, sniffing, marking her as his. Hyper-aware, she experienced every lick and nibble as if in slow motion. She visualized him scrawling his name all over her body in permanent ink, his claim bright for all to see.

His vibrant presence heated the bed and the air around them. Even if she'd wanted to try, she could not shield herself from the magnetism of his energy. Her response took root deep in her belly, in her pussy and in her heart. The warmth of her responding desire for him spread through her with the relentless determination of a conquering army.

"Lilith, you are so beautiful to me," he murmured. "I could drink in the wonder of you day and night and never want anything else."

She chuckled. "I think that wonder could wear thin when your appetite for solid food kicked in."

"Not when I have you to feast on." His fingers tweaked her nipple, followed quickly by his eager mouth.

Overwhelmed by the sheer beauty and simplicity of their being together this way, Lilith stroked his head. They had to try to compress so much life and love into their short time together, her mind skittered over all the experiences they'd never have time to share. For no good reason, she suddenly grew playful and wanted to lighten the intensity between them. She cleared her throat. "Will you have fries with that?"

He started to laugh, which broke their physical connection. Eyes wide with surprise, he asked, "What? You say that with such authority. Did you once work in a burger joint?"

There was so much about each other that they'd never have enough time to talk about. "The fate of the liberal arts major? No, I actually never had to hustle burgers."

"A pity, but only because you would look devastating in a grease-stained uniform. Of course, I'd immediately want to strip the uniform off you and—"

On that note, he slid down and buried his face in her hot, slick folds. She squealed with delight and her whole body reverberated with the erotic shock of the touch of his tongue on her sensitive, intimate places. Wanting to hold him to her forever, she ran her hands through his hair and pressed him to her there.

Chapter Four

He wanted to feast, to take his fill of her—but he could never have enough. Lilith's sweet feminine musk surrounded him as he moved between her legs to pleasure her. He loved her exquisite responsiveness, the way she reacted to his moves.

His cock was already full, achingly erect. Too bad he couldn't figure out a way to pleasure her with his tongue and his cock at the same time. Neither in man nor in wolf form could he perform such an act of magic which meant he had to devote himself to each sensuous delight in its turn. First the tongue, then soon, so soon after, he'd plunge his burgeoning dick deep inside her.

"Rafe." Lilith practically sang out his name. Despite the many other times he'd made love or had sex with or just plain fucked other beautiful women, this was the first time he ever understood the meaning of the word *intimacy*. Only now could he begin to appreciate the very special bonds that unite a man and a woman in their own particular world. Only between her legs and in her heart, could he find a refuge of comfort and respite—the fulfillment of physical and emotional hungers.

He and Lilith were completely intimate. If he had to answer her silly intake interview, he'd list the possibility of *intimacy* as the most desirable quality in any relationship with a potential mate. Hell, the word *intimate* contained the word *mate*. He'd never realized that before, but the connection pleased him. He would need an intimacy at least as complete as what he felt with Lilith with any woman he'd consider taking as his mate for life. Anything less would dishonor both them and the institution.

"Oh, Rafe," Lilith sighed, her breath like the flow of a sweet gentle breeze refreshing him. She maneuvered her lush, lovely hips so her clit slid between his lips and she gasped. "Mmm," she groaned in extravagant response.

What turned him on more, the musk of her taste or her rich scent? Fortunately, he didn't have to choose. With her, he could have it all—only not for much longer. He needed, wanted to come deep inside her. He tingled with the anticipation of his release, but his lady's pleasure must be first.

So, though he adored the richness of having his nose and lips pressed against her core, he needed to lead her to the climax she appeared to be very near. He swept his tongue across her clit and stroked her sweet, hot folds. With a hiss and a groan, she began to quiver and tightened her hold on him, quaking with the sheer raw power of the build-up to her orgasm. Then she whimpered his name, again and again— music to his ears as she expressed her need.

Stepping up the speed and intensity of his tongue thrusts, he almost missed the first tremors of her release. Vocal as she was at other times, Lilith now turned surprisingly subdued, as if she focused all her energy on the sheer physicality of coming. She announced herself with a series of sounds, soft and almost incoherent, a primitive language of desire sated. As her release grew in intensity, her heartbeat and blood flow increased, surrounding him with sensation.

She sighed and whispered, "Oh my God, thank you."

He raised himself and buried his face into the warm spot where her shoulder joined her chest. He could happily lose himself in her musky scent. "You're magnificent," he growled.

She fluttered her lashes. "You're pretty terrific yourself," she whispered. And then he heard her sharp intake of breath. "Oh, God, I'm being so selfish. I can't believe it. You must be on the verge of a case of blue balls."

Despite his crushing need to be in her, he threw back his head and laughed. "Blue balls? Where'd you dig that up?"

She tried to sit up, but he was so all over her that she couldn't. "I know it's selfish not to think about your partner's needs."

Geez, where was she coming from with this anxiety? He'd always heard ghouls were the most selfish, self-absorbed beings in the universe, but Lilith was incredibly selfless—even generous. He rubbed his dick against her leg, which radiated shock waves of pleasure through his groin. With super self-restraint, he stroked the side of her face with his thumb. "You're the most giving person I've ever met."

She smiled at that. "I want to touch you." She started to reach her hand down in the direction of his cock.

Too much. He'd reached the end of his self-restraint. With a groan that was half howl, he swung them both around so she was straddling him. Looking up at her beautiful face, Rafe felt his heart go into a funny hammering rhythm. "Baby, I want you to touch me and I want to touch you back. I want us to touch on every level known to man or beast. But we have to hold back on that right now so I can get inside you."

He bent his knees and she sat propped up, leaning back against his thighs. There was her gorgeous feminine core, teasingly nudging the head of his cock. It didn't take much nudging at all to convince him to plunge into her from below—especially when she raised her hips to provide him full access. "Oh, baby," he rasped as his cock wedged fully, deeply into her. She surrounded him with her sexy warm heat of welcome and they were transformed into male and female in the primordial forest. All they'd ever need was each other.

She looked beautiful as she perched, legs wide open to him in erotic invitation, straddling him from atop his groin. Her full breasts swung in provocation with each move, the nipples and the areolas winking at him any time he deigned to open his eyes. He longed to reach up and cup a breast and claim possession of her that way, too. First, though, he didn't want to disrupt the rhythm of her movements, so he settled for resting his hands on her hips.

"You fill me so completely," she whispered. "I was always so empty before you. Now I know what it means to be complete."

His heart wrenched at her words. A woman like this should never be so neglected, never left alone and empty. She moved in a tight circle around his cock, rotating her hips first one way and then the other. Pleasure shot up and down his penis, through his balls and seized control of his body. Hell, he felt like an enormous, throbbing cock with just one goal in life—to reach an explosive orgasm and a depth of satisfaction unlike any before.

A man could get used to this. But a pack alpha? How could it be—to find this degree of rightness in the arms of the wrong woman? A demi-ghoul vegetarian. This woman could never be anything to him but a lay, a one-night stand. He bristled at the prospect and couldn't bear to think of her in such terms. Though he couldn't choose her to be his mate, he refused to treat her with any less respect—even in his thoughts—than he would his mate. Maybe he'd choose a mate his pack would accept and have Lilith as his mistress.

No. That was not his way. Not the way of the alpha. Not what Lilith deserved. Besides, having a woman other than his mate, even a recognized and acknowledged mistress, did not fit with his understanding of having a mate for life. However, this was all he could offer this woman, who made his body vibrate with divine ecstasy.

"Rafe, I don't know what you're doing to me. Before you, I was amazed if I had one orgasm in a night. With you, I can't stop coming. I feel like I've turned into a fountain, gushing like some natural wonder all over you."

He winced at the nuance of apology he heard in her words. If he could do nothing else for her, maybe he'd leave her with the assurance of her beauty and how much she had to offer any man who was free to offer her the best. "More like a blushing fountain."

She turned even redder.

"Ah, Lilith, you have no idea who you are and what you bring to a man." He cupped her chin. "I wish I could give you that, wrapped up with a ribbon. Know who you are, Lilith Graves. Know that any man would be lucky to call you his mate."

He could feel her blood course more rapidly through her veins, deepening the crimson of her cheeks. "Rafe. Tonight with you is the best gift I've ever had. With you I have a taste of all that life could be."

"I wish it could be more. My inner beast wants to drag you into my cave and keep you there, away from all others. But I can't offer you—"

The possibility of any other male experiencing *his* Lilith the way he did would be intolerable. If he ever got wind of another male being intimate with her, Rafe would have to kill him. Lilith was his.

Except. Except he couldn't be hers in the same way he demanded she be his. *She's a demi-ghoul.* He had to remind himself of this inalterable fact again and again and again. He could stake his claim on Lilith, but she couldn't reciprocate. He couldn't give himself to her. Did he really intend to condemn her to a solitary, celibate life? Is this what he wanted for a woman he lov—dangerous turf.

These thoughts should have put him off, but instead, he became more turned on. It didn't take much imagination to realize he might never again be with this woman in this way— hell, in any way. If the pack leaders really got on his case, he'd have to give priority to finding a mate—and walk away from Lilith. Instead of cooling off, his desire for her ratcheted up. If he could be with her only this one night, it would have to be one neither of them would ever forget.

Lilith squeezed his balls, which amped up his erection. He wanted her to come again before he gave himself up to his release. He reacted without thinking, scooting his balls away from her talented fingers with a sharp intake of breath.

Confusion skittered across her face. "Shouldn't I have done that?"

He raised a brow. "Yeah, Lilith. You need to avoid providing such pleasurable touches which risk pushing me off the cliff."

She studied him. "It felt good?"

He chuckled. "Sugar, saying your touch feels good is like calling the Mona Lisa cute."

"Really?" She grinned before letting her fingers resume their previous play. At least this time he was prepared, so he didn't jump. And he didn't come. Yet.

"I don't want to come before you." Though he'd planned to deliver this sentence in a normal voice, his clenched teeth somewhat distorted his expression and his intent.

Her laughter pealed merrily. "You won't. I just came before... A short time before."

"Yeah, but that was by mouth. I want you to come again with me in you."

She licked her lips and the sight of her tongue ratcheted up his arousal. His cock throbbed within her, and he knew he wouldn't last much longer. "But," he gasped, "if you keep doing things like that, I may not get my wish."

She bucked her hips slightly forward, surrounding him with softness and warmth. "I'd hate to disappoint you," she murmured.

"God, Lilith, nothing about you could ever disappoint me." He put a hand at the top of her rear crease and began a gentle exploration of her there.

"You say and do all the right things." Moving with erotic grace, she swayed her ass from side to side so the pressure of his touch intensified. He enjoyed a woman who liked to get her ass stroked. Moving his fingers playfully, he explored her crease and darted his fingers down to her opening. She stiffened.

"Maybe you shouldn't touch me there."

"Why not?" He didn't remove his hand just yet. If she came up with a valid objection, he would move away. But he'd bet she'd never experienced this kind of stimulation before and was letting modesty inhibit her.

"It's not nice." Considering that she had relatives who were ghouls—talk about not nice—Rafe found her scruples a bit unexpected. Yet again, Lilith was turning out to be a surprise to him. He needed to find the balance between opening her up to newness and not offending her sensibilities. Right now, though, the way her body was responding to his touch, he figured her objections were more formalities than indications of actual distress.

"*Au contraire*, my little one. It's very nice and you're very nice. If I weren't otherwise occupied, I'd kiss you back there."

Her mouth twisted as if she was going to say, "Ewww." He lubed her with a wet finger and then played around her hole. Despite her scruples, her face reflected pleasure. In fact, this seemed to be the touch she'd needed to get her moving toward her orgasm.

A fast learner, Lilith tried the same maneuver on him, wedging her hand under his butt—a tight squeeze. When he felt her wet finger trace the outline of his cock, Rafe cried out with pleasure, which made her smile. He tightened his grip on her ass and began to speed up his in and out pistoning. At the same time, his finger rode the opening of her back crease.

"Oh, Rafe," she purred. "It feels so amazing being with you like this—" Her voice broke as the urgency of need impelled her forward.

She trembled in his arms with the force of her release and he heaved a sigh of relief. At last, he could allow himself to come—before he exploded.

She gripped his hips harder with her legs and panted out

her release. That was it. With the force of the big bang, he came and came and came. As the satisfaction of his release filled his body, Rafe yearned to hold on to the intimacy of his bond with Lilith. With a pang of regret, he clung to each sensation as the intensity began to recede.

Hook, line and sinker. Falling for Rafe Graywolf would be the easiest thing she'd ever done. Easiest and stupidest. Stupid, stupor. As Lilith lay on top of Rafe in a stupor that reduced her IQ to negative numbers, she willed herself to stop obeying her most primal instincts and start thinking. So what if she'd experienced the sexiest, most erotic interlude of her life? Aside from how fabulous she felt in Rafe's arms, there was nothing right about their being here together—and far too much wrong. Talk about potential for damage. Rafe could hurt her in ways that hadn't even been invented yet. She needed to gather up her clothes and her dignity and get the hell out. She definitely wasn't the right person to conduct Rafe's intake interview. How wrong she was bordered on the ridiculous. That was exactly what she would tell him, as soon as she could pull herself together enough to put some physical space between them. She now realized the futility of any other plan.

Summoning the remnants of her strength and will, she dragged herself off him. The separation hit her like a cold shock as air rushed to touch her all the places where she and Rafe had shared skin contact. It reminded her of when she'd tried to eat ice cream with a cavity in her tooth—only a hundred times worse.

"Where are you going?" Rafe reached out an arm to draw her back to where she'd been, on top of him.

She swallowed hard. "I have to get going." Her voice seemed soft and meek, despite her intention to sound determined. He'd intuit, for sure, how easy it would be to talk her out of leaving.

Eyes locked with hers, Rafe sat up. She adored the look of his body—along with the taste, smell and feel of it, and then there was the strong, silent stealth of his movements. His voice set off eruptions of goose bumps along her arms and legs. All her senses flourished in his presence, except common sense.

"Stay." He freighted that one simple word with a universe of meaning. He leapt out of bed and took her arm in his powerful grip. She snuck a peek at where his hand clamped onto her arm, his tan against her porcelain skin and she had to pretend

141

she didn't welcome his touch.

No way could she let herself continue with what they'd started. She wrenched away from him and closed her eyes in an effort to resist his charm. "Rafe, I can't." The words, each like a burning stone, came from her gut. "Look, this—"

He took her hand in his and her eyes flew open. She had to break the contact so she could say what she had to. When he held his hand out to her again, she shook her head and forced herself not to meet his glowering gaze. "I can't. What we just did was beautiful, but we both know it shouldn't have happened and can't be repeated. We each have lives filled with other demands."

"You say we know that, but *we don't. Those are your words."* There they both stood, still naked, the scent of their recent sex filling the air. She needed to continue looking away from him and shutting down her senses or she'd be lost. With great effort, she held herself aloof.

"I really mean it. I have to go." Her voice scarcely a whisper, she was begging.

"You were going to stay with me tonight." His voice was pitched so low, she had to strain to hear him.

She wished that could be. There was nothing in the universe she wanted more. If only there was a way she could stay with him until whatever spark there was between them played itself out. But she knew now that she couldn't. The longer she spent alone with him, the more impossible it would be to break away. "Rafe, I've gotta go. I'm sure you understand."

He exhaled hard and shrugged, and she could sense him begin to withdraw behind a wall. What a time for her empath self to wake up. Still, she needed those skills even if what they told her hurt.

"Sure. Use the wolf guy. Then when you've had your jollies, leave."

She shivered, his words shocking her like a punch. They had no possibility of being able to fulfill each other's needs in the real world and he knew it as well as she—maybe better. "You're joking, right? You have to be, Rafe." She could scarcely get the words out. "I'm not like that. You know that's not how things happened. You have to know that." Damn it, angry tears sprang to her eyes and her throat closed as if she were choking.

"Oh, yeah?" He cocked a brow and his voice sounded

flippant, sarcastic. "I know what I see. Damn it, Lilith, I thought we had something special. I know what my senses are telling me, but you're saying I can't rely on them. That for the first time in my life, I can't rely on scent, sight and touch, but should believe the words you can hardly bring yourself to say."

She sniffled back the coming tears the best she could. "You know why I came here." Her lip trembled, but she forced herself to continue on. "The words aren't any easier for me to say than for you to hear, but they're necessary." She failed in her attempt to smile, then bit her lip and turned her head. "I'm not the person to service your account in a professional way and for that I apologize. I'm going to tell Dominique to take over. I'm sure she'll call you first thing in the morning." Compared to the emotions and intensity of their lovemaking, their real-life roles and responsibilities seemed to fade in significance. She had to cut off that train of thought pronto.

"I don't want you to leave," he growled in his best big-bad-wolf mode.

"I know. I don't want to leave, but I have to." Lilith could sense that though he didn't say anything about not doing an intake interview, Rafe hadn't forgotten about it. Despite the emotional charge of this moment, Rafe wasn't losing sight of the duty that led him to Fangly, My Dear for an appropriate match.

Amazed and alarmed at the speed with which dejection took the place of elation, Lilith scooped up her clothes and rushed to the nearby bathroom.

He called through the door, "If you insist on going home, let me take you. It's late."

She sniffled again. Dignified, not. "It's okay, Rafe. I got myself here. I have no problem getting myself back home at any hour. Heck, I go out alone lots. I'm used to it."

Silence. She came out of the bathroom only slightly the worse for wear. Okay, a lot worse for wear. Rafe had thrown on jeans and a gray sweatshirt. His long feet were bare and even his toes looked sexy. Shit. She had to stop thinking like this or she'd be in major doo-doo.

All she needed to do was get out the door. She'd made it this far, so completing her exit shouldn't be an impossible challenge. She just had to get over her desire to linger, to hear one more word, to share one more kiss or touch.

He stood and watched, devouring her with his eyes. He

143

didn't say a word. He didn't have to.

It was the hardest thing she'd ever done, but Lilith got herself to Rafe's door and put her hand on the knob. Then, swallowing back tears, she opened the door and stepped out into the dark night.

He let her go.

After a sleepless night and oceans of coffee, Lilith dragged herself to her office the next morning. Though Dominique had never been other than sweet, generous and understanding, Lilith dreaded asking her friend to take over Rafe's intake interview. She imagined how the conversation would go. Her friend, who was rational, in contrast with Lilith's current insanity, would want to know why she didn't want to complete this particular assignment. Lilith couldn't begin to figure out how to explain. No matter how understanding Dominique was, she would probably have a difficult time dealing with Lilith's unprofessional—to put it mildly—conduct with Rafe.

To make an awful situation even worse, Lilith looked like hell this morning—an accurate reflection of how she felt. Sleep or tears—or the damning combination of both—brought all her ghoul genes to the forefront and made her resemble a cross between a frog and a troll. Red eyed and nosed, she had charming oversized bags competing for space with the black rings and shadows beneath her eyes.

Dominique took one look at her and could obviously see that something was wrong. "What is it?" She put a sympathetic hand on her friend's arm. "Are you sick? Maybe you should just go home and take care of yourself. I can handle anything that comes up."

Lilith shook her head. She should have known better than to think she could fake being okay with Dominique. The question remained, how much truth should she tell her friend? She hated putting Dominique in an untenable position *vis-à-vis* Rafe and the Wentworth pack. On the other hand, she knew Dominique had an unerring sense of how to zero in on what was going on. "I'm okay, fine to stay and work." The way her voice wobbled, she couldn't possibly sound convincing, which Dominique's skeptical look confirmed.

"You don't look or sound okay. Tell you what. Get yourself some coffee and come chat with me. If you feel okay, fine, stay. But don't hesitate if you need to go home. I looked over the schedule and there's nothing pressing here today."

Dominique's kindness and concern nearly pushed her over the line to tears again. "I'm really all right and I don't want any more coffee." She made another feeble attempt at a smile. "If it's okay with you, I just want to work. That would be my best medicine. Since I look worse than I feel, I'll hide in the back office if anyone comes in."

Dominique waved a hand in a dismissive gesture. "Fine, of course you can stay. Don't worry about how you look. You're being tougher on yourself than anyone else would be, as usual. Any time you want to talk, I'm here."

She nodded.

"How did you make out with Rafe Graywolf's intake interview last night?"

That was it. That question was all Lilith needed to lose her tenuous hold. Unbeckoned and unwelcome, more tears filled her eyes. She hadn't braced herself for the impact of hearing his name, though it was only logical for her friend to ask.

The flood arrived quick and hot. Even worse, Lilith found that she couldn't bring herself to say what was going on. Heck, she couldn't talk at all. Any time she tried, she started sobbing again. Eyes now full of worry, Dominique took her by the arm and steered her inside her office. She handed Lilith a much-needed tissue, which she demolished in nanoseconds. Dominique got the box ready. When Lilith had calmed down enough to catch her breath, Dominique said, "Please tell me what's wrong. Maybe I can help. Is it about Rafe? Did he do anything last night to hurt you?"

How was she supposed to answer? On the other hand, she'd better set the record straight right away. She didn't want Dominique to think Rafe had done something hurtful—Fangly, My Dear had a zero tolerance policy for disrespectful behavior. "No, nothing like that." She shook her head to indicate she wasn't going to say anything more right now.

"How about I make you a cup of tea? Nice, soothing herbal tea. Then, when you're ready, you can tell me as much or as little as feels right."

Lilith didn't want anything more to drink, but she also

didn't want to keep turning Dominique down. "Okay," she whimpered.

While her friend bustled and hummed, Lilith pulled herself together. She couldn't believe what a girly girl she'd been acting like with all the tears and sighs and shuddering. Enough. If she didn't stop soon, she'd undo all the good Rafe's fantastic lovemaking had accomplished for her.

Dominique brought back two cups of chamomile tea. One day real soon, Lilith would confess that she despised chamomile tea. But for now, she sipped the hot brew and let it calm her.

"Are all the tears about Rafe?" Dominique asked when they'd both taken few sips.

Lilith, who still didn't completely trust herself not to break down, winced and nodded.

"I hate to intrude where you don't want me, but I must know. After all, our clients trust us to screen out undesirables. If he's done anything to hurt you, if he's in any way a creep, tell me. I assume he didn't assault you. There are other, less egregious ways a person can inflict damage. I don't care if he's alpha of the Wentworths or the freakin' king of San Francisco, if he's bad news, he's out of here."

Warmth spread through her at her friend's generosity and concern. Too bad the situation between her and Rafe wasn't simple. "You're on the wrong track if you think my bizarre behavior this morning is because Rafe did anything wrong." If only he hadn't done so many things right. "He's quite wonderful and he'll be a dream match for the right person." At least she was able to get those words past the giant lump in her throat— something she could do right.

"The bad news is, I wasn't able to complete the interview. I apologize for that and promise I'll never again be so unprofessional. Please, you do the interview." She swallowed down more of the tea.

Dominique appeared surprised and confused. Lilith could understand her reaction, since conducting an intake interview was usually no big deal. "I can't believe you're so upset this morning because he didn't cooperate for the intake form. He seemed macho, but I didn't think he'd be that difficult. That's not it, though, is it?"

Lilith put down her cup and sighed. "No." More tears started to come and she swallowed them before she resumed.

"You see, I can't help Rafe complete the forms because..." She sniffled and scrubbed the tears away, then started again. "Because I've gotten personally involved with him."

Her voice had risen into a squeak, but at least she'd gotten the hateful words out.

Dominique sat still for a moment, obviously mulling over what she'd just heard. "You and *Rafe Graywolf?*"

Lilith nodded. "I know it was a totally wrong, stupid thing to do. But once we were together, it was like we got caught up in something bigger than both of us." She made a face. "Yuck, that sounds like such a cliché. I can't believe I said it."

Her friend shook her head. "I can't believe you did it."

Lilith snorted. "I know. My behavior was unprofessional and inappropriate, not at all the image for Fangly, My Dear. Ah, heck. If you want, I'll resign."

"Resign? Why in the world would I want that?"

"Because I, uh, got involved with a client?"

Dominique rolled her eyes. "You don't remember when Antoine signed up as a client so he could convince me to see him again?"

"That was different."

"Don't be ridiculous. My concern here isn't that you and a client got together. Goddess, I'd be thrilled if Fangly, My Dear did bring you and your soul mate together." She waved a hand as if to sweep away Lilith's objections.

"You would?"

"Oh, yeah. My concern is the particular client. Rafe Graywolf is about the most unavailable guy on our list. What with him being the alpha of the Wentworth pack. We know he's looking for a mate with very specific qualities. You, my darling friend, wonderful as you are, don't fit the required profile."

Like any of this was news to her. "Exactly."

Dominique hugged her. "Lilith, you'd be a fantastic life mate for any male. Heck, any one you'd pick would have to count himself one of the luckiest men in the world because you're wonderful. That said, Rafe has constraints on him... Those have been clear from the start."

"I know all that," Lilith sniffled. "We both do. Unfortunately, that particular slice of reality wasn't enough to keep us apart last night. He had me so knocked for a loop, for the first time ever, my empath skills failed me. I'll have to talk to Mom to see what's up about that." She swallowed hard. "Most of all, though I knew it was wrong, I managed to shut out the voice of reason. So did he, at least for a while. But we can't keep pushing away the real world forever." She shook her head. "I think I'm starting to fall in love with Rafe Graywolf. Oh, Dominique, what am I going to do?"

Chapter Five

"The Treglio pack is making noises about breaking our agreements and starting up a consortium with some other packs," the elder droned on.

The painkillers Rafe had had to resort to this morning hadn't yet managed to quell his monster headache. If he had to listen to one more speech he might go stark-raving mad and start leaping around the room, tearing the place apart. That would sure throw the elders for a loop. An insane out-of-control spree might almost be the perfect remedy for what ailed him—if he couldn't have what he really craved, Lilith. He'd wanted to spend the night with her, wake up with her. He so didn't want to be at this council meeting this morning when he should be at her side, convincing her to be with him.

After Lilith had left last night, after Rafe had failed to convince her to stay, his emotions had dropped him into an overwhelming cold emptiness. He'd transformed into wolf form to run off some of his frustrations, but the expected release from his emotions hadn't come. He'd run and howled, chased other wolves and been chased by them—everything that usually worked. Though he'd done everything he could to exhaust himself, he was still wired.

Just before dawn, he'd at last managed to fall into a fitful sleep. No surprise, though, he'd woken up far from rested. With her by his side, he'd have been able to sleep even without going into wolf-in-the-woods mode. Okay, so they would have spent half the night making passionate love, which brought its own kind of exhaustion. Good exhaustion. At least between bouts they might have gotten some decent rest. Then he wouldn't have felt like warmed-over shit from the pit of hell this morning.

It was all her fault. When would those damn painkillers start to work? His head throbbed on the edge of exploding. Hell, it wasn't her fault. It wasn't his fault. It wasn't anyone's fault. It was just the way things were. He needed to find and marry a life mate who could rule alongside him, the perfect alpha's wife. Lilith was a demi-ghoul. A vegetarian, which kept her inner ghoul at bay but complicated the situation for the leader of the pack. Those were the bald facts. Nothing could alter them. Nothing could be added to or subtracted from this equation to fix their situation. End of story.

The men around the table were looking at him in expectation, as if he had some magical formula to make the Treglio pack toe the line and live up to their agreements. Hell, he didn't blame them for looking to him for leadership—and he didn't even blame the Treglios, who were out to take advantage of perceived weakness. Business as usual. The miracles Rafe was supposed to perform as alpha weren't materializing—and there was no reason to expect anything to change. He'd heard the whispers. He couldn't even run his own life, couldn't settle with a mate. Maybe it was time for everyone to realize his becoming the pack alpha had been a huge mistake. If that happened, he and Lilith...

"What would happen if we just told the Treglios to go their own way, do whatever they think is best for them?" he asked. "What if we all agreed our previous accord is now null and void? That would just formalize the reality of the split that's happening."

The shocked gasps around him answered that question, but he kept pushing. "What exactly does having the Treglios allied with us accomplish? Why should we put any energy into keeping them in our orbit?"

One of the elders cleared his throat. "The Treglios may not do us any good per se, but letting people break away from our accord would hurt us."

Murmurs of agreement.

Rafe massaged his right temple. "Can you explain?"

"It's a fundamental principle of leadership. To remain in control of our position in the shifter community, we need to be able to count on the loyalty and support of other packs."

"Even when those packs are pretty much running on fumes?" Rafe figured with deadwood like the Treglios, the intelligent action would be to cut them loose and let them drift. Though holding on to their dubious allegiance cost the Wentworths far more than they were gaining, convincing the elders seemed on a par with planning a trip to Saturn.

He hated to see his pack waste so much energy on minor matters when a far greater danger—the imminent arrival of the Loups-Noirs from Vancouver—loomed. "Let's move down our agenda to more pressing concerns. We can come back to the Treglios later."

By the time he'd heard the latest, Rafe got into gear. The renegade pack had swept through Washington and were now in northern Oregon—headed directly to them.

Time to go into battle mode and kick some Loups-Noirs butt. For the first time since he'd become pack alpha, Rafe understood in his gut why he had to lead.

Dominique looked up from her computer screen and frowned. Even though Lilith swore she'd given up on her impossible dream of being with Rafe, she'd been moping around the office for hours. "Try to cheer up. Despite all the obstacles to your being together, my gut and my witch's instinct indicate you and Rafe are the real deal. We'll just have to find a way to make this work."

Lilith didn't want to hear any of it. Maybe obstacles didn't matter in a hundred cases, but she and Rafe were number one hundred one.

Dominique shook her head. "I don't know how to convince you, but trust me. When there's a soul-deep connection like there is with you two, obstacles tend to disappear. But first of all, you've got to believe."

Lilith got teary. "You don't know shifters like I do. I've studied their community dynamics. They treat ghouls with such contempt. It's like they consider us lower than the dirt they wipe off their paws."

"And you put up with that from any group?"

Lilith shrugged. "I suppose ghouls haven't had the best PR."

"You think witches have?"

Lilith couldn't help remembering that only a short time ago, Dominique had been anti-witch, denying her connection. "You've never been perceived in as bad a light as ghouls."

"Tell that to the witch hunters and all the witches burned or drowned."

"Sorry." Lilith grew hot with embarrassment. It wasn't like her to be insensitive.

Her friend shrugged. "Come on. I sure as heck hope you don't believe any of the nonsense the ignorant or the biased put out there. You know, the crap about the vampires being the nobility of the paranormal world. It's more like they have the largest, fattest advertising budget and know how to manipulate the media. I know you can see through the hype."

Lilith nodded. She also knew all the promotion in the world wouldn't rehabilitate the public image of ghouls fast enough to make a difference for her and Rafe. It would take several centuries or so to rehabilitate ghouls. Maybe she could help with some PR. That would be more productive than obsessing over Rafe or passively watching him hook up with his life mate—barf. "It's a moot point."

"Well, I'm going to give Rafe a good talking to when we meet for his intake interview. I'm almost tempted to tell him and the pack to get lost."

"You can't. It's not his fault his duty forces him…"

Dominique shook her head. "As long as we're alive, we have choices. Sometimes, even afterward… Actually, I haven't been able to reach Rafe this morning."

Lilith bent over her friend's computer screen. "I wonder what's going on. In the background material I read something about another pack posing a danger."

"Really? I didn't realize there were many other packs around here. From what I understood, the Wentworths are the head of a kind of consortium, which would make Rafe the alpha in charge of all of them. Pretty rare for a young, single guy. The common practice is that they're mated before they become alphas."

Lilith winced at the word *single*. "That's why he's got to take his duties so seriously," she said in a soft voice.

Of course, a leader with such responsibilities needed to have a refuge, a place to go to escape the pressures and let off steam. Rafe had hinted that taking his wolf form allowed him some of that space. Lilith knew lovemaking with the beloved of one's heart and soul provided another crucial outlet. The way the two of them had made love the night before. Her pussy creamed and her nipples hardened at the reminder. What wouldn't she give for even a few more moments of that intense intimacy? How she longed to touch him, to feel his touch bring her alive.

She had to stop her mind from wandering down such dangerous paths. Rafe Graywolf couldn't be hers. Now, with Dominique unable to contact him, she had to wonder if she'd lost him as a client for Fangly, My Dear. How unfair would that be to her friend? Heck, to both of them?

"Wait, look at this. The local packs have gone to a full-moon alert."

Lilith bent over Dominique's computer screen and stared at the updated message flashing on the Wentworths' home page. "What does that mean?"

"According to what they have written here, it's the pack equivalent of preparation for a major turf war."

Lilith gasped. "Do you have any idea what happens in pack wars?" As alpha, Rafe wouldn't be the kind of general who issued orders from the rear. He'd be right in the midst of the worst fighting. What if Rafe was seriously wounded in battle—or worse? What if she'd never saw him again? Her stomach clenched and fear grabbed hold of her nerves.

Her blood coursed through her with glacial iciness. She had to go to him. Now. She had to tell him...to tell him...what? She had no idea. She'd figure it out when she was with him.

She straightened up and ran to the office door.

"Where are you going?" Dominique asked.

"I have to see Rafe before...before he leaves."

Dominique nodded. "Of course you do. Maybe when you're together again, you'll be able to figure things out."

Lilith snorted. She was leading with her heart, not her head.

Once they began to mobilize for battle, Rafe was amazed and impressed with how fast the suits and the old codgers sprang into action. He'd thought the lack of activity and the years of passive paper shuffling had sapped the men's vitality. Now that they had to unite as they prepared to face the approaching enemy, Rafe sensed a new energy of purpose and animation in his pack—all for the good.

His own blood coursed through his veins at an accelerated speed. Leading his men into battle made all the crap that went with leadership worthwhile. The diplomacy and maneuvering, the politics, bored him. If he had a regret, it was that they had to move with no warning—which meant no time to contact Lilith before they left.

Maybe it was better that way. They'd be better off making a clean break, accepting that they had no future. Except that just the thought of her sped his heartbeat up even more than the coming battle, not to mention the relentless hard-on. When it came to Lilith, he turned into the randiest, rawest high school boy. The young and the horny. He was too old to act like either, but his body refused to behave.

The pack followed the guidelines Rafe's dad had laid down for preparation for warfare. He'd been an amazing alpha. Bloody hell, Rafe missed his father, especially right now. He'd give just about anything to consult with him, even for only a few minutes, about all the questions filling his head. How to lead so all his men came back safe and whole? How to balance toughness and compassion through the challenging times ahead? As to Lilith, what would his father tell him? Follow his heart, his head, neither?

Less than an hour before they were going to leave for Oregon, his cell rang.

"Someone here to see you," a voice announced.

He really didn't have time, but then he saw it was Lilith.

Rafe looked so harried, Lilith almost regretted coming. The last thing she wanted was to be one more unwelcome chore for him to deal with. No sense beating around the bush. "I understand you're leaving very soon."

He nodded. "A situation we'd been watching just went from potential to actual trouble. We can't wait any longer."

She closed her eyes and recited a little charm Dominique had taught her to keep him safe. "I'm sorry."

He put his hand on her arm, unleashing an electric storm to course through her. They both gazed at each other and said nothing, silently communicating more than a thousand words could have expressed. Even though she knew it was impossible, she wanted to go off with him, somewhere they could be alone. Who was she fooling? She wanted him to throw her down on the ground and cover her with his body, to make wild monkey love to her here, on this very spot where men were getting ready for battle.

Or, even better, he'd lie on the ground and invite her to take his erection. He'd grab hold of her hands and pull her to him so she could straddle his powerful hips, drawing his long, thick cock into her. She could see he was already hard for her. Despite the chaos surging around them, a wave of reassurance soothed her. He wanted her. Even though they couldn't do anything about satisfying their desires, knowing that he wanted her helped.

"I didn't want you to go without a chance to say good-bye." Though tears began to well in her eyes, Lilith forced herself to exercise control. She didn't want Rafe's last image of her to be tearful. She wanted him to remember her smiling, the two of them happy. She wanted to give him a reason to come back.

His eyes said so much. She melted, drowning in their depths.

"I'm glad you came. It means a lot." He put her hand over his heart. "I'll come back. To you. When the battle's over, when we've won, I'll come back and we can be together."

His heart was beating so hard. Just like hers. "I'm not asking for any promises," she whispered. "I just want you to know I'll be thinking of you all the time."

Neither of them wanted to be the first to break the contact, but Lilith realized they were attracting attention—none of it friendly. People were looking at her like she was some cheap whore trying to distract their alpha at the worst possible time. Goddess, she couldn't allow herself to get emotionally bent out of shape just because other pack members were glaring. At this moment, other people's opinions didn't matter.

When two old men came over looking as if they intended to drag Rafe away, Lilith admitted to herself that she had to let go. Grateful she'd had this chance to be with him, even though they hadn't been able to share even a decent good-bye kiss, she backed away.

They'd have walked into the ambush without the advance scouts' work. Rafe knew better than to waste time and energy on remorse about almost leading his men into such a lethal trap. *Almost* didn't count. The viciousness of the enemy, the readiness of the Loups-Noirs to resort to treachery—the upcoming conflict looked more and more like a major battle. He needed to focus on kicking their butt, booting them all the way back to freakin' Vancouver, but he couldn't shake the last image of Lilith's face.

He signaled for their convoy to stop right before they crossed the border into Oregon. Fortunately, one of the forested places that attracted few weekday visitors would do. The men who'd come with him parked their vehicles and circled around Rafe.

"We'll transform together and run as a pack." His blood heated and coursed along with the usual pre-battle adrenaline rush.

"But shouldn't one of us remain in male form to get more troops here?" Buck Gravatt, runner-up for alpha, asked. Rafe considered, then rejected Buck's suggestion. He needed all his men in wolf form to take on the greater numbers of Loups-Noirs. They'd have the element of surprise on their side—and the determination to defend their turf. The Loups-Noirs were not going to get past them and add the Wentworths to their empire.

No matter how many times he accomplished the transformation, there was a moment of shock, of newness. Additional adrenaline began pumping as his muscles contracted. His snout grew and his backbone altered to accommodate the needs of his wolf's body. In a matter of minutes, he was firmly cocooned in his fur, claws and teeth, ready for aggression.

As he and his men raced to meet the enemy, one last thought of Lilith flickered before him. How would she feel if she could see him now? How would she react to this side of him, the animal he would never let anyone tame?

That was his last thought before the Loups-Noirs sprang. The Wentworths were outnumbered, but not outclassed. When Rafe realized all the enemy had in their favor were superior numbers and primitive savagery, he knew his side would win. He made short work of the first attacker, a wolf whose huge bulk encumbered more than aided him. Though Rafe preferred to wound rather than kill, it was soon obvious that the Loups-Noirs were out for the ultimate defeat. Disgusted with the violence the enemy demanded, he tore out the throats of three wolves before checking to see how the others were doing.

After a short, quick battle, the outcome was clear—the Wentworths would defeat the Loups-Noirs. Then Rafe realized Buck was in trouble. A snarling beast had him pinned beneath his paws and was lowering his head for the kill. No matter how Buck moved, he couldn't outmaneuver the enemy. With a growl, Rafe launched himself at the attacker. Tearing at him with claws and teeth, Rafe managed to get the surprisingly strong wolf off Buck so he could go back on the attack. To his amazement, Rafe saw that the attack on Buck had been the Loups-Noirs' last gasp. Though carnage filled the forest floor, all the Wentworths would be returning home to celebrate their victory.

He heard the crack of thunder moments before the hot burning sting hit and everything went black.

Chapter Six

"Rafe Graywolf, leader of the Wentworth pack, has been shot. We'll keep you updated as more news comes in."

After she'd spent another fitful night of almost no sleep, Lilith bolted upright in her bed. When her clock radio woke her with this horrible news, at first she thought she was having a nightmare. Rafe shot? Not possible. She shook her head in an effort to clear the cobwebs and wake up fully. Then her phone rang. Hand trembling, even before she picked up, she knew she was about to hear the unbearable. *Shot* didn't mean *dead*, right? Maybe his injury was minor, exaggerated by the news...

She had to pick up the phone and face whatever.

"We just found out about Rafe's injury." Dominique's voice came over the wire. At least she'd said *injury*, not, goddess forbid, *death*. Lilith shuddered.

"I just heard too." To her amazement, her voice was steady, unlike her nerves.

"I'm so sorry. What can I do to help?"

Just like her friend, to come up with a practical response when the world was falling apart. "I need to know everything." Her voice wobbled with the realization of what *everything* might mean. Maybe she didn't really want to know after all—

"I already called the pack's information line and checked their website. They're not giving out much information."

That didn't bode well. "I need to find out where he is. Words aren't going to do it for me. I need to go to where he is, see for myself, touch him, feel him breathe."

"Yeah, I know." Dominique fell silent. "Funny, I just tried a new spell on my computer a day or so again. You describe a being, the computer tells you where he is. I've got it geared up right now—"

Lilith appreciated the prompt offer. "Thank you. That would be—" Now the tears came. She might as well get them over with before she saw Rafe. She didn't want to weep all over him. Salty tears might aggravate his wound...

"As soon as I find out where he is, I'll call you back. Meanwhile shower, eat some breakfast, drink coffee and get yourself beautiful. I'm sure seeing you will be just what Rafe needs."

Eat breakfast? Right now, that seemed almost as impossible as the directive to *get beautiful*. On the other hand, she owed it to Rafe to present her best self to him—even if all she'd get to do was say good-bye.

Rafe couldn't believe he'd been shot. From what the men had told him, the impact of the bullet forced him to go through his transformation in record time. As soon as the others realized what had happened, they'd taken out the gunman. One of the Loups-Noirs had retained his male form, adding human firepower to the arsenal of lupine fighting skills. This was a grievous violation of the shifter code. When the Council of Shifter Packs gathered for their annual meeting, the Wentworths would add their accusations to the growing list from other packs. The Loups-Noirs would face shifter justice. The prospect of that pack's future punishment didn't stop him from wanting to tear the bastard shooter's throat out.

Aargh. Right now he couldn't tear off a hangnail. He hated feeling this powerless, but he'd been lucky. The bullet lodged in his upper arm, not his head or heart or any vital organ.

Even more important, getting shot was like a swift, painful wake-up call. The bullet reminded him that life was finite—and he needed to figure out exactly what mattered most to him before he wasted any more time. Lilith. Being pack alpha. Though he hadn't wanted to be pack alpha, now that he'd led his people through a crisis, he knew this was the place for him. Lilith was his soul mate, but would the pack ever accept her? His head pounded worse from the need to choose than from his wound.

He'd led his men into battle and ultimate victory, even taken a bullet. They'd stopped the Loups-Noirs—it looked like permanently. With no immediate threat to his pack and some glory, he had breathing space. Now even the Treglios were mewling that they wanted to be back in the Wentworths' good graces. Smart move.

He didn't have to stay on as alpha. Buck had been primed to be alpha and would be ready in a heartbeat to take over if Rafe stepped aside. Though he hadn't been the man to lead during an emergency, Buck had lots of ability as an administrator and he'd shown himself to be a heroic fighter. With him in charge and their situation stabilized, the pack would be in excellent hands for the foreseeable future. Since he already had his life mate, Buck and the pack wouldn't have to face that hurdle.

Rafe hated like hell to give up, but he had to face reality. He couldn't have Lilith and be alpha. He toyed with the idea of asking her to wait for him. A year or two. Or ten. Right. That would be a great thing to do to the woman he loved. Loved. He loved her and that meant he wanted her to be happy—even if that meant she'd be with another man. He gritted his teeth at the prospect, but he could no more ask her to wait than he could stop being a wolf.

Just then, Lilith and Dominique burst into his hospital room.

Breathe, Lilith reminded herself. *Breathe.* He was alive, but so pale her heart lurched when she looked at him. Despite his loss of so much blood, he looked more gorgeous than ever. Lilith wanted to grab him and hug him breathless, but right now he was weak and she had to be careful not to hurt him. His unaccustomed vulnerability both scared her and made him more precious to her. "Are you all right?" she asked as she ran over to the bed. The huge bandage on his arm blocked her access.

"Lilith." He looked from her to Dominique. "So what, you're here to do the damned intake interview?"

Though she could appreciate that he felt good enough to joke, this particular one twisted her guts and heart like a knife thrust.

Dominique's eyes flashed with indignation. "When we heard the news, we panicked. I offered to bring Lilith up so she could see for herself you're all right."

"How'd you find out where I am? This location was blanketed by top secret security."

Lilith paced. She couldn't believe he was wasting time talking about routine security matters when he'd almost died. Didn't he feel it, too? Or had the taste of battle cemented his commitment to being the perfect alpha? "Some witchcraft she has up her sleeve," she muttered.

Dominique glared at her. Lilith, who usually tried to respect her friend's discretion about her witchcraft, was making a hash of things by flapping her big mouth, but she didn't care. The way things were going, Lilith would probably manage to alienate both her lover and her best friend before she left this room.

He raised a brow. "I'm impressed, Dominique. I'm also relieved to realize it took extraordinary means. We didn't figure on shielding our online presence against witchcraft, which shows me a weakness in our thinking. Thank you. Speaking of weakness, I'm tired of lying around in this bed. I'm getting up."

Lilith held her hands out to him. "I don't think that's a good idea, Rafe." She put one hand on his uninjured arm and the other on the forearm not too far from where he'd been shot. A wince crossed his face. Rafe's pain ratcheted through her and nearly brought her to her knees. Powerful empathy, a quality she got from her mother, surged through Lilith, making her one with Rafe. She remembered hearing that love multiplied the power of the empathy— She'd think about that later. Right now, she had a stubborn, vulnerable man to deal with. How could he think of getting out of bed when he felt this awful? Him and his macho stuff...

Rafe shook her hands off as he lurched to his feet. He wobbled for a moment before he stood, solid and strong. Lilith saw he'd replaced the traditional hospital gown with low-slung pajama bottoms that rode his hips where she wished her hands could be. "If you'll excuse me for just a minute, I'll get dressed. Then you two can help me blow this joint."

"Rafe," Lilith protested. "You shouldn't even be out of bed, let alone coercing us to get you out of here." She looked to Dominique for support, but her friend just shook her head.

Walking on less-than-steady legs, Rafe made his way to the small closet where he had his clothes. He reached for the hangers, gasped, stepped back and sat on the bed. "Would one of you ladies be kind enough to hand me my stuff?"

Lilith wanted to order him to get into the bed, but she realized she might as well save her breath. Without a word, she handed him his jeans, T-shirt and leather jacket.

He grinned and she knew she couldn't deny him anything— even the insanity of leaving the hospital in his condition.

When he was in the bathroom and they could hear water running—she hoped to the goddess he wasn't getting his bandages wet—Lilith apologized to Dominique for her slip of tongue.

Dominique waved away the apology. "It's all right. I know where your head is and where it isn't. Lilith, my dear friend, you don't sense it this time, do you?"

"Sense what?"

"The way Rafe feels about you. It's kind of ironic, how you know what everyone else is feeling, all the time. But now, when it really counts, your power fails you."

Lilith figured Dominique would say or do anything to make her feel better and discounted her hopeful words.

Far faster than she expected, he came out of the bathroom. "I couldn't get the T-shirt over the damn bandage," he grumped. He'd gotten the jeans on and had the leather jacket slung over his shoulders. She wanted to throw him down on the bed and straddle him. Judging from the bulge in his jeans and the look on his face, it wouldn't take much to persuade him.

"My shoes," he said. "On the floor of the closet." He looked deep in her eyes. His gaze turned from smoldering to wistful— and any appeal to sanity she could summon up crumbled. "Could you help me get them on?"

"Of course." She got the leather loafers out. No socks.

He perched at the edge of the bed. She hunkered down and took one of his feet in hand. The man had the sexiest feet and she'd love it if he'd use his toes to... She cleared her throat and forced herself to stop playing with his feet and her fantasies. He was in a rush to move on, probably to take up more of his alpha duties. After all, the pack's alpha couldn't take more than one day off, even after being shot.

"I don't think it's a good idea for you to leave like this, without the doctor's okay." Dominique's voice sounded firm, authoritative.

"I take full responsibility," Rafe said. No surprises there.

Lilith figured *Full Responsibility* was his middle name. "I have a lot to do."

"You were joking about that intake interview, right?" Dominique asked.

"No. I can answer your questions as you drive me back." Rafe had evidently regained power in his legs, for he strode out of the hospital room with both women following in his wake.

Despite Dominique's words, all Lilith sensed from Rafe was a determination to go forward with his life. She swallowed hard and willed herself not to cry. She knew getting shot had convinced him to make a life or death decision—what if he'd decided his future wouldn't include her?

If Dominique hadn't been in the room with them, he'd have made love with Lilith right there. Not that he'd ever objected to voyeuristic sex before, but everything changed when it was him and his mate. What he and Lilith had together was too rare and compelling to be treated with anything but the utmost respect and care. So, no witnesses to their erotic intimacy. Whatever happened between them would play out exactly that way—for the two of them only. He'd fight to the death any man who tried to interfere with them or intrude on their bond.

He clenched his fists and growled at the mere thought of someone attempting to disrupt the sacred connection between them. Despite all he'd heard of pack lore about how a man felt about his mate, he'd never completely believed this phenomenon existed. Until Lilith. She made a believer out of him as she opened up a whole new universe he was ecstatic to have discovered with her.

Now he began to think about the future in a whole new way. They'd complete the formal mating rituals of his pack— even include any from her tradition if she wanted—and then she'd be part of his family. Family. Children. Huh, he'd never thought about the children he would father.

Of course, their specialness would extend to their children. He didn't know whether to shudder or smile when he thought about any offspring they might have. Half-shifter, quarter-ghoul, quarter-empath. Their children would be unique. Now that he'd been with Lilith, he knew that no one else could be the mother of his children.

The pack wouldn't accept Lilith as the alpha's mate. He'd made his choice. If he couldn't be alpha and have Lilith, he wouldn't be alpha. After the bullet shot, he knew there was no contest. He'd choose Lilith, no matter what he had to give up or change.

Lilith and Dominique wouldn't let him drive. Any other time, he'd refuse to get in the car until one of the women gave him the keys. This time he growled because he thought he should, but he was just as glad to be able to take it easy. Leaving the hospital exhausted him. In the backseat, where he could sprawl in an attempt to get comfortable, he caught a glimpse of Lilith's profile. Since Dominique was going to conduct the interview, Lilith would drive.

Why wasn't Lilith protesting about him even going through the charade of the interview? He knew being a demi-ghoul had messed with her self-esteem. Still, as his mate, even when he was ex-alpha, she had a community status to maintain. She had to walk tall. Though he hated to hurt her, he couldn't help wondering how long the interview farce would have to proceed before she "got it", before she realized she was the one?

"'What is your top priority in choosing the being who will be your mate?'"

Rafe sucked in a breath as a wave of pain rippled through him. "Shared values," he replied. "She should also be beautiful."

He thought he heard Lilith sniffle. Damn. She had to realize how beautiful she was.

"How do you define 'beautiful'?" Dominique continued after she'd typed his answer on her keyboard.

"'Beautiful' refers to the woman inside and out. My top choice would be a blue-eyed blonde who cares so much for other people, sometimes she forgets to care about herself." Lilith snuck a look at him. She had one perfect brow raised and he could see she was starting to wonder about what he was saying... He'd love to know the exact moment when she realized...

"Describe your ideal date—as in, where would you go and what would you?"

He laughed for the first time since before the battle where he got shot. It felt so good, he decided to do it again. "My first response is X-rated, so I'd better skip ahead to the second. Let's see. I love excellent food, fine dining and romantic settings. So, I'd take Ms. Perfect out for dinner to a fine restaurant in a gorgeous place. Everything classy and subdued. We'd drink champagne and I'd sink my teeth into the biggest, rarest steak in the place."

Lilith kept her face turned resolutely to the road. He quickly added, "Of course, I'd never fail to respect my date's food choices and preferences—even if she was a bloody vegetarian."

Lilith let out a whoop and nearly drove them off the road. Cripes, he hadn't meant to have his answers kill them all. He just wanted to let out enough information so his mate would know...

"I see," Dominique went on as if nothing unusual had occurred. "And have you given any thought to which group your date or mate should come from?"

"Lots. My mate will be a vegetarian ghoul empath—and my mind is made up. No wiggle room."

Lilith drove to the shoulder of the freeway and turned off the ignition. "Dominique, I think you'd better drive."

She slid out of the front seat and got in to the back with him.

"You're sure?" his mate asked, her eyes wide with wonder and the smallest tear in the corner. He wanted to lick that tear away.

"Never surer in my life," he murmured. Despite his aching arm, his cock had sprung to full erection the moment she'd opened the door.

She wanted to kiss him hard. Oh, bloody hell, she wanted to do a lot more than kiss him, but she'd have to settle for that now, with Dominique in the front seat. Not to mention his injuries.

With great care not to jostle his arm, Lilith put her arms around his waist and brushed his lips with hers. He responded immediately, probing her mouth with his questing tongue.

When they came up for air, she withdrew. "I love the way

your lips glisten from my kiss. So much better than the glisten coming from tears." She trembled as his warm breath caressed her.

"What about your being the alpha?" Her voice quivered.

He stiffened slightly and she was afraid he hadn't thought things through until he told her his thoughts. "I've paid my dues. Now that we've gotten rid of the Loups-Noirs, I figure things will be stable for a while. Buck can do the job. He's always wanted to. So say yes."

Lilith grinned. "I don't know. Maybe you should persuade me some more." She licked her lips in invitation. From the look in his eyes, she understood that he knew exactly how to convince her. "It'll be three hours until we get back to the city. That's too long. I know the perfect place for us and it's a lot closer."

"Sounds like heaven," she sighed.

He nodded and whispered, "I'll take care of everything." More loudly he said, "Dominique, if you could exit the freeway at the next ramp. There's something Lilith and I need to discuss."

"I live to serve," Dominique muttered.

"Where are we going?" It didn't matter what he'd answer because if he wanted her there, she'd go.

"To my lair," he said in a menacing big-bad-wolf voice.

She had full body goose bumps at the prospect. They exited the freeway. "Which way next?" Dominique asked.

"At the bottom of the ramp turn left, then right, then pull over."

In moments, they were on the shoulder of a deserted road. "Thanks, Dominique." He reached for the door.

"Wait a minute, Rafe. Where are you taking Lilith? Do you want me to wait for you?"

"That's not necessary. Thanks for everything. You can head back to the office and close my file."

Lilith's heart fluttered. Though everything about being with Rafe glowed with romance, somehow she hadn't expected anything so romantic happening today.

"Lilith, are you cool with this?" Dominique asked. "Should I mark your file 'closed' too?"

"I didn't know I had one."

"You do. And I'm not going to leave you here with Rafe unless it's what you want also."

"More than anything else in the world."

"Romance is great, guys, but how are you going to get home?"

Rafe growled. "I'm in charge. I'll get Lilith home when we're both ready."

Heck, right now she didn't know or care when that would be.

Dominique waved as she drove off.

"So, Rafe, what and where is your lair?" They were in a wooded area. It always amazed her how woods and meadows could exist a short distance from the freeway.

He led her to a lone picnic table and sat her down. "I know it sounds like a joke, but this is my special place, somewhere I've never shared with anyone else."

Lilith recognized the great significance of what he was laying before her. Not only the terrain but everything about being with Rafe was new to her, a heady atmosphere she could get drunk on just from breathing the rich air. "Thank you for inviting me in."

Rafe put her hand over his heart. "I want you in every part of my life. Lilith Graves, I want you to be my mate. For life."

She wouldn't cry. "Are you sure?"

"One hundred percent. You're what's most important to me. I needed a bullet shot to make everything clear. It is now. With you in my life, everything else will fall into place. Without you, nothing would matter. So, I'll resign. Buck Gravatt will be a great alpha."

Though a little voice inside her questioned if he weren't making too great a sacrifice, her heart and her gut were screaming one word—"yes". Without any further hesitation or reservations, she accepted Rafe.

With Lilith by his side, he felt healthier and more whole with every step he took. The pain in his arm became a distant memory, along with emptiness, doubt and any hesitation about the rest of his life.

"Come on," he encouraged her. "We have to walk a bit, but it'll be worth it."

She came with him so willingly. He hoped she'd always look

at him with that same glow of trust. Please, forces that be, never let anything extinguish that light. He could sense her getting tired as they got closer to his lair, which involved climbing an easy hill. He'd have to help her get stronger.

Just after they'd stopped so he could rest, they came to his special waterfall. She stopped again, her face lighting up. The beauty of the sound and sight of the falling water had first seduced him to settle here. Impatient to show her the rest, he drew her onward to the small cabin he'd built himself. Just a kitchen, bedroom, small front room and bath. He knew and loved every inch. Over the years, he'd completely outfitted the place so he could spend days here with no need to leave. No telephone, no TV, no computer. He did have electric lights and a few basic appliances. It was an easy lope—just ten miles—down the road to the general store for perishables. Or not. There were enough canned and powdered foods for them to stay weeks.

"It's perfect," Lilith whispered, though there was no one near to eavesdrop.

He sensed that she understood everything about the attractions that drew him to this spot. "That was exactly what I hoped you'd say. Did I tell you about the bedroom?"

"No. But I can't wait to hear." She chuckled.

"I'm much more into showing." He ran with her to the bedroom, which a huge king-size bed dominated. Luckily, he'd done a reasonable cleanup last time.

"Life mate, let's seal our agreement in the best possible way." He drew her to him for their first embrace in his special place.

She hugged him back so hard she took his breath away. When they broke apart, he showed her the large picture window opposite the bed and the huge skylight over it. He loved having sunlight and moonlight pour into the room and to have all the wonders of nature surround him—them—here. He held her hand as they surveyed the magnificent panorama. Then he took her in his arms and branded her with a searing kiss.

"Oh, Rafe," she moaned.

His vegetarian empath demi-ghoul. He embraced all she was with gratitude and lust. His cock, half-erect since he'd first laid eyes on her, demanded precedence. With a thrill of dawning recognition, he realized there'd be many times for the two of them to make love here, in San Francisco or wherever the hell they wanted. There'd be many times to take it slow and wring every drop of pleasure from their union.

Right now, though, he needed fast and hard—and he sensed she did too. With his body and soul, he'd make her his. His teeth grazed over the soft skin of her face. Showing zero patience or finesse, he got them both naked. He needed to imprint her taste and scent on his inner man—and inner wolf.

He suckled first one breast, then the other, promising himself another time he would linger to savor her sweetness. At this moment, however, urgent needs had to be met.

"We have to be careful of your arm," she whispered.

"I'll be fine." He'd have promised her anything.

"This will be best." She pushed him off her and got to her hands and knees. "Take me from behind." She looked at him coyly, the round plump cheeks of her ass glowing with invitation.

He groaned.

"I'm so wet for you. I just want you to fuck me and fuck me until I'm seeing stars."

What was this? He'd expected their lovemaking to be a romantic interlude, but his mate was taking charge—and pushing them for a ride on the wild side. He loved that about her, too.

His cock close to bursting, he slid between her legs and right into her slick channel. Later, he'd taste her there and drink her up. But now, ah, the way her heat and tightness surrounded his dick had him ready to explode before he'd gone all the way in.

His stomach pressed tight to the crease between those gorgeous cheeks, Rafe willed himself to make this last, at least until he'd pleasured her. With his good hand, he reached between her legs so he could fondle her clit and massage her plump pink folds while he drove into her from behind. She anchored them both on the bed, which rocked with the increasingly rapid rhythm of their erotic dance.

Lilith pressed her clit against his fingers and rotated her hips. "That's it baby," he panted. "Do what feels good. When you move your ass like that, you give me so much pleasure. I want the same for you." He gasped the last words, lost in a haze of sensation.

"Like that," she panted. She lifted her head and leaned

back, changing the angle of the penetration and bringing him perilously close to the edge.

He did as she asked, so grateful that she told him and showed him where she wanted him and what she wanted him to do.

Far too soon, she was there. Her lovely pussy contracted around him and she called his name as she gave herself up to her release. He wanted to change position now, to experience her ass with his cock, but his arousal and her sensuous response were too great. Totally lost in her, he exploded and pumped his essence into her again and again and again.

Both of them shuddering with the power of their come, they fell together on the bed, which now bore their musky scent. This was where he needed to be to heal, not in some sterile, lonely hospital bed. Here, with this woman, his mate for life, Rafe knew he was complete.

Epilogue

Lilith was more nervous and excited than she'd ever been before—and why not. This was the most important day of her life.

"You look gorgeous," Dominique chided her. "But if you don't stop pacing, you'll wear a hole in the carpet."

Dominique, her attendant for today's ceremony, looked amazing—as always.

"I just can't wait until it's over."

Her friend rolled her eyes. "Before you know it, it will be over and you and Rafe are going to leave for your extended honeymoon. I can't believe you won't even tell me where you're going."

"If I tell you, they'll be able to force it out of you," Lilith said. "If you don't know, even torture shifter style won't be enough to break you down."

"I guess you're right, though it's hard for me to believe the council would resort to such underhanded tactics."

"Believe it." Lilith snorted. "As pack alpha, Rafe is on call twenty-four seven. Even though Buck Gravatt is covering for him while we're gone, we'd still get constant calls."

Dominique shrugged. "I guess by now you'd know the lay of the land."

"I do. Rafe and I thought the council would let him step down when we announced our plans—in fact, we were sure they'd make him step down. Fat chance. They actually changed the by-laws to let me be his life mate. Can you imagine that?" She'd made herself a sacred vow she wouldn't let tears ruin her mascara.

"Yes, I can," Dominique whispered. "Because you're worth

it."

Lilith swallowed back a sniffle as she hugged her friend. The music started and Dominique got into the procession behind the other attendants. Lilith knew Rafe was waiting for her at the end of the aisle so they could be joined together forever.

The procession began to move and she had to remind herself to breathe. Just a few more minutes.

"You're sure this mutt's the guy for you," her father growled as he came over to take Lilith's arms. As handsome as she'd ever seen him in the tux her mother had managed to convince him to wear, her dad squeezed her hand.

"I'm sure, Dad."

He muttered something in his ghoulish tongue.

"You promised, Dad. You're on your best behavior today, right? For me?"

He muttered something more then did something Lilith had never seen before—wiped away a tear. She kissed his scaly cheek.

"I'm real proud of you, hon," he rasped. "So is Mom. You want this guy, fine. But he'd better treat you right, or—"

Glancing down the aisle to where Rafe stood looking handsome and impatient, Lilith knew she'd found her perfect mate. "Thanks for saying it, Dad. It's time."

Her heart nearly bursting with joy and pride, with excitement at the future they were about to start, Lilith took her father's arm and glided down the aisle to Rafe.

Playing with Matches

Dedication

To all the Fangly, My Dear readers

Chapter One

"No!" A single gunshot slammed into the informant Gabe Morrow had come to San Quentin to interview. The air in the small office immediately grew thick with the smells of more gunfire and splattered blood.

Gabe threw himself to the floor. Where the hell was the guard they'd been assigned? Gabe thought he'd caught a glimpse of him, but then he disappeared. Moments later, Tom Lerner, his partner in the investigation that had brought them here, thudded down beside him. "What the hell—?" Gabe muttered between rounds.

Tom didn't respond. Staying as flat as he could, Gabe tried to drag Tom to shelter under a metal desk. He managed to move his friend only a few inches when he felt a sharp, burning pain in his gut, and everything went black.

Newly promoted San Francisco Police Inspector Tanith Kalinski glared at her ringing phone. She'd been about to head home after pulling a double shift, but when she saw the name on caller ID—her best friend, Sue Lerner—she picked up.

"There's been an incident involving gunshots at San Quentin!"

Tanith forced herself to focus. "Sue? What? When? Gunshots?"

"Breaking news, men down. Someone's smuggled guns to prisoners. Tommy's there tonight." Her friend's voice cracked.

Crap. Sue's husband was at the prison for his investigative series on police corruption. Though some cops denounced Tommy Lerner's work, Tanith supported his goal of weeding out bad cops. "Calm down, Sue. There are lots of people at San Quentin. Just because there's been an incident doesn't mean Tommy's involved."

"I just know he's been shot. I'll never see him again," Sue sobbed.

"Look, how about I come there? I'll stay with you until..." Until what? Her gut, what her Polish grandmother called her special sense, echoed Sue's fears. Tanith shivered.

Since her own car was in the shop, she'd hitched a ride to work this morning and had planned to do the same going home. Now she'd need to find a ride to Sue's house. Her new partner, Don Allen, lived in Sue's neighborhood. Tanith followed him into the break room to arrange the lift.

She started to open the door when she heard Don and two other guys laughing.

"So, Allen, you're the one who's stuck with the Ice Princess. You'd better stock up on de-icer." Smarmy laughter filled the room.

Ice Princess? Who was calling her that? She didn't recognize the voice. Beating back her impulse to leap into the room and confront the laugher, she waited to hear more. Her first choice would be her new partner coming to her defense.

He didn't. "Ice Princess? Maybe she just hasn't had the right guy heat her up yet."

Tanith clenched her fists.

"You're talking about the chick who mainlines Botox to her—" The first guy's voice grew too soft for her to make out, though the ensuing laughter crashed around her. "It would take some guy..."

She'd heard enough. If she didn't need to get to Sue's, she'd make these idiots eat their words. But she didn't have the time now. They could all go to hell. She might not show her feelings easily, but that was her choice. Besides, if this group of clowns were examples of who she should share feelings with, Botox injections sounded infinitely preferable.

Slamming the door to let them know she was there, Tanith relished the immediate silence. Keeping her voice steady, she told Don she needed a ride. Then she aimed her deadliest gaze at the other men in the room.

Once they were in Don's vintage Volvo, he asked, "Why are you headed out there at this hour of the night?"

At least he wasn't steering the conversation anywhere near what she'd overheard. She would deal with all that later. "My best friend's neighborhood. Would you believe, her husband's working at San Quentin tonight. She heard about the shooting, and she's scared." Tanith could barely get the words out without her voice cracking. Shit, she'd have to pull herself together or she'd be no help to Sue.

"Ever since the administration there started hiring vampires to be on the night staff, weird shit has started happening." Don chuckled, but the sound grated like a dog's hungry bark.

"Vampires at San Quentin?" Tanith echoed. How had she missed hearing about that? Her lifelong fascination with vampires—four parts sexy attraction, one part violent revulsion—she made a point of keeping up with any news about the creatures.

"Yeah. It hasn't gotten much publicity, but it's one of those outreach efforts to bring them into the larger community. I figure it's a stupid move, but hey, none of the high mucky-mucks asked me."

She didn't want to get into a discussion about vampires or anything else with him now. Fortunately, they were near Sue's house. Tanith gave him terse directions where to pull over and dashed out of the car.

When she got inside, she hugged Sue, who looked like red-eyed hell. How could she reassure her friend when she herself feared the worst? Once she got Sue settled into an armchair and searched for the remote, which was missing, as usual. Tanith navigated across the toy-strewn family room and turned off the TV. Overriding Sue's protests, Tanith insisted its constant yammer wouldn't do either of them any good.

"When was the last time you talked to Tommy?"

Sue shook her head and sniffled. "Would you believe we had a fight right before he left? I didn't even kiss him good-bye."

Tanith wanted to tell Sue she'd have another chance, many chances, to kiss her husband and even to have more fights with him. But she couldn't get the words out. "How about some coffee? You got any more of those chocolate chip cookies?"

Looking almost grateful for a distraction, Sue got up and

crossed to her kitchen, where she began to bustle. "Kids ate the chocolate chip. All I've got are honey nut bars nobody wanted."

Though Tanith hated honey, she accepted the cookies without complaint. Otherwise, Sue would set about baking other cookies and would fret and fuss if she didn't have the right ingredients. "Fine."

Tanith forced down one of the bars as she drank her four hundredth cup of coffee since she'd rolled out of bed twenty or so hours before.

"You don't have to keep me company," Sue said. "You look so tired."

"I finished writing a report on a tough one. I'm too wired to go home, so I figured I'd stop off and spend time with my best friend. We're both always so busy—"

Sue smiled weakly. "You need to get a life, girlfriend. Have a special guy to give you a massage, spoil you in other ways, as a reward for all your good work."

A special guy? Tanith didn't want to go there. Though even her best friend didn't suspect the truth, Tanith's most secret and long-held obsession was to be with a vampire lover—despite the revulsion that tinged her attraction. Even hearing the word "vampire" could trigger an unwelcome burst of desire, such as she'd experienced when Don talked about vampires at San Quentin. Tanith knew she had to free herself of this enthrallment or she'd never get a life. "Not now, Sue."

"Tommy's always telling me not to meddle." Sue appeared to shrink into herself, and Tanith regretted her sharp tone.

"Good advice for all of us to try to remember." Before Tanith could say another word, the doorbell rang. Sue jumped, looking terrified.

Tanith put her arm around her friend. "I'll go see who it is. Maybe just a neighbor who needs some help…"

"At three a.m.?" Sue's voice broke. "We'll both answer the door."

Tanith prayed that her instincts were wrong this time. But she and Sue opened the door to two grim-faced officers in uniform, and the bad news exploded all around them.

When Gabe regained consciousness, he had no idea where he was and, for a moment, could barely remember who he was. A tall, dark-haired man in what looked like a tux came over to the cot where he lay and sat at the edge. Gabe struggled to sit up.

"How are you doing, my friend?"

"What happened?"

"You were shot."

Gabe mulled this over for moment. "Shot? What the fuck? Where the hell am I?" Memory started to return. "Tom? Tom Lerner?"

The man's teeth glittered in the dark. "The two other men with you in the office were also shot."

"Shot? How the hell did somebody get a gun into the prison? We were all searched—Who are you?"

The other man held up his hands as if to hold off the barrage of questions. "I understand there's an open investigation in the events at San Quentin the night you and your companions were shot."

Gabe eyed the man warily. "Where are they? Are they all right?" He looked around. "I want to see them." He licked his lips. A thirst unlike any he'd experienced before seared his throat. "Can I get something to drink?"

"I need to explain a few things first."

Gabe couldn't understand what was so complicated about getting a simple drink of water. Maybe a doctor in a tux was too highfalutin for such mundane tasks. Why wasn't he answering the other questions? What had happened to Tom and the informant they were interviewing? "I need answers to my questions, too."

The doctor touched his shoulder. "Right. There's no easy way to say it. The two other men died at the scene."

Gabe's head was spinning. He couldn't make sense of the words coming at him. "Tom's gone? They're both dead? How can that be? What happened?"

He shook his head. "I don't know all the details yet. One of our guys was working a shift at the prison. He was able to save you but not the others. These things take some time."

Confusion muddled Gabe's thoughts as the recognition of Tom's death and his own survival took hold. Nothing made any sense, including that Tom was gone, leaving behind unfinished work and a grieving family. "Who are you?"

The other man—was he really a doctor?—held out a hand. It looked very white in the room's shadows. "Antoine Thierry. Don't call me Tony." His handshake almost crushed Gabe's fingers.

"Antoine, not Tony. So where the hell am I? What's going on?" He licked his lips again in a futile attempt to deal with his thirst.

"Listen up. What I say will be difficult to accept. But I'm telling you the truth." The guy's expression was piercing, almost hypnotic. Gabe felt a wave of discomfort and wanted to tear his eyes away, but he couldn't.

"You're in a halfway house for vampires in San Francisco— the section for the new guys. A place to learn the ropes."

Gabe sat bolt upright. "A halfway house for vampires?" He found that even harder to believe than Thierry's terrible words about Tom being dead.

The other man smiled wide enough for Gabe to see fangs, sharp and menacing, descend. Unless Thierry was a magician or in serious need of reconstructive dentistry, he appeared to be the real deal.

"Please tell me I've been wounded and am now hallucinating." Gabe crossed his arms in front of him. "I mean, I know vampires exist, but I've never wanted to be part of their world. Or vice versa."

Thierry, whose eyes shone with what looked like amusement, gripped Gabe's forearm. "No hallucination. Despite your previous intentions and desires, our worlds have come together. Welcome. You are now officially one of us."

Gabe blinked rapidly as he tried to grapple with Thierry's words. He held out his arms and looked at his hands, which seemed the same as always. He searched in vain for a mirror. Vampires didn't have reflections, right? With no handy mirror, he couldn't test this fragment of knowledge. He felt exactly like himself, except maybe for that strange thirst. "You don't look like the kind of guy to kid, not to mention the teeth. I'm a fucking vampire."

Thierry snorted. "Consider yourself lucky to be here in this halfway house, with mentors such as myself. In the bad old days when I started, we were on our own to figure out our

needs and how to fill them. I'll be right back with your drink."
With that, he rose and strode off.

Chapter Two

Once she'd left Sue in her mother's capable hands, Tanith dragged herself home. Her body screamed for respite. She wanted nothing more than to have someone big, strong and handsome soothe away her exhaustion. Unfortunately, what she craved wasn't just any random masculine someone. Her desires were more specific. She could just picture him—a tall, dark and handsome vampire with an amazing package, brains, a personality and the full range of vampiric powers. Too bad her obsession was steering her into dark waters that could drown her. Luckily, she had the will power and strength to overcome her weakness.

Several sleepless hours later, Tanith finger-brushed her hair off her forehead and sighed. She reread the last page of *The Vampire's Venice Adventure*, sighed again, and put the book aside. What was wrong with her, reading trash like these vampire romances—which she adored and gobbled up? Remembering Don Allen's comments earlier, she cringed. Her fellow cops really didn't get who she was, which suited her fine. If any of them knew how she spent her free time, they'd pillory her with contempt and disgust, the same emotions she felt for herself.

She turned off her lamp and pulled the light blue comforter over herself. Comforter. It would take more than a blanket to comfort her.

Lonely, horny and turned on by the love scenes in the book, she didn't have to be alone in her bed. Sex per se was never hard to come by. She turned down or ignored two or three offers a day, none of which tempted her in the least. Usually the would-be Romeos were married, old enough to be her grandfather or on their way to lock-up. Here she was, a healthy, red-blooded woman of thirty-one with normal needs and a sex drive—her pussy clenched hungrily just then, reminding her of how long it had been since she'd taken care of her desires.

Knowing there was no way she'd get any sleep if she didn't satisfy the hunger snaking up from her core, Tanith reached for Clyde, her friendly vibrator. In moments, the satisfying hum of his tiny motor assured her the batteries were working. Her pussy watered in anticipation. With a whimper of anticipation, she opened her legs and invited Clyde in.

Gratifyingly soon, her companion's steady vibrations shot sparks from Tanith's under-attended clit to her over-stimulated brain and back. She arched her hips and moved her thighs slowly to maximize the impact of Clyde's ridges. Biting her lip, Tanith closed her eyes but, once again, unwelcome pictures came to mind.

Of all the images that could possibly loom from within her psyche, why oh why was she stuck with fantasies of sex with a vampire—a wanton creature whose very existence was rooted in criminal murder and mayhem? She shivered, remembering the gruesome murder of a school friend, the victim of a rogue vampire attack. Her determination to fight such crime inspired her to become the best police officer she could.

Still, despite everything, she couldn't break the spell she was under when it came to vampires. Why couldn't she free herself from her fascination with the fanged creatures? No matter how hard she fought, she nightly succumbed to the dark phantom who dominated her dreams.

He would lower his full, sensuous lips to the tender area of her neck where her jugular pulsed. She arched her hips faster, harder, turning Clyde up to maximum speed. Her climax began somewhere deep, engulfing her as her mysterious lover took possession with his hard cock and his sharp teeth.

Shaken with the enormity of her release, Tanith turned Clyde off and put him aside. Her obsession blocked her from developing interest in any real man, someone she could build a normal life with. What ordinary man could possibly possess her as totally as her imaginary vampire lover?

Tanith sat up in her rumpled bed and hugged her knees. It wasn't like she didn't know the creatures for what they were. Police files were full of cases, complaints by women foolish enough to succumb to vampiric charm. Cruel, despotic destroyers. Masterful lovers who knew the art of seducing and satisfying a woman then tossing her aside.

She'd have to do something to move on with her life. Though Clyde could efficiently take the edge off, a battery-operated hunk of plastic had its limits. She needed a man who'd take charge, not carp at her success or expend energy asserting a phony mastery. One who'd captivate her the way her dream vampire did. To date, she'd never gone out with a single man who came anywhere close to meeting her needs—on any level. Hadn't even met one. She had to take charge of her life and, as she did in every other area, go after what she wanted.

Just then, something jabbed behind her knee. "What—?" She muttered as she reached down and retrieved the magazine insert she'd been using as a bookmark. Must have fallen out of her book. Tanith turned on her bedside lamp and squinted at the card.

"Want to date a shifter, a ghoul or a vampire? Who's the creature of your dreams?" The words practically jumped off the card. "At Fangly, My Dear, we can make any dream come true—satisfaction guaranteed." Tanith shook her head. Was this for real? She read the phone number and the extravagant promises. Dumb. Though lots of her friends went in for internet dating services, she'd always avoided them. She should do the same this time too, except...

Except that maybe dating a real vampire would help her get over her craziness and open herself to regular men.

She tried to push that idea out of her mind, but it kept popping to the surface. The thought of being alone with an actual vampire made her clit quiver—a delicious sensation, though mixed with a dollop of fear.

She'd call in the morning. That resolved, she at last fell asleep.

The next few weeks flew by. Busy with both work and helping Sue through the trauma of Tommy's funeral and its aftermath, Tanith put her own needs on a back burner. She also devoted a chunk of her limited free time to trying to solve Tommy's murder, even though it happened outside her jurisdiction in San Quentin. Finally, three weeks after she first saw the card for Fangly, My Dear, Tanith made contact.

Under the tutelage of Antoine Thierry and several other volunteers, Gabe learned the basics of vampire life. Once he'd become accustomed to his new diet and to spending his days in a coffin, a massive case of horniness and loneliness sprang to the top of his To-Do List.

"So," he asked Thierry one night, "how do I meet a girl?"

The other man grinned smugly. "This is not a problem. Women think we're hot."

"By women, what do you mean?"

He shrugged. "Females of all species. Do you require an anatomical description?" He raised an elegant brow.

Antoine Thierry had the damnedest ability to make Gabe feel like he had a single-digit I.Q. "No. I just mean, do we have to go out with vampire chicks only or what? I'm not into weirdo groupie types." Though it was more comfortable to act like he wanted only to get laid, Gabe was hoping he could meet someone who wanted to be with him for more.

Thierry laughed, a sound dry as brut champagne. "Who would dare impose such limits on us? My good man, you can go out with any female you deem worth the time and effort."

"Cut to the chase, man. Where do we meet chicks?"

"Many places."

"I'm looking for specifics here."

Thierry thought for a moment. "For a newcomer like you, I would recommend Fangly, My Dear. A dating service. Some say it's the best in the universe, or at least San Francisco."

Gabe raised a brow. "I have to say, Antoine, you don't look like a guy who'd use a dating service."

"I'm not." He actually cleared his throat. "Not in the sense you mean. Long story, for another time. Here's my advice. Talk to Dominique or Lilith, and they'll take care of the rest."

"Dominique or Lilith? They know about what vampires are looking for?"

He cleared his throat again. "In a word, yes. At this point, they know more on that subject than you do." His mouth tilted up in an almost smile. "To help you here, I'll call Dominique and set everything up."

With Antoine handling matters, Gabe got an appointment

for the next night. Despite the other man's involvement, Gabe still didn't know what to expect when he arrived at the offices of Fangly, My Dear for his interview with Lilith Graves, a demi-ghoul. Though Gabe had believed himself shockproof, the ghoul's role in a successful dating service caught him by surprise. Lilith, a beautiful young woman in a designer suit, was the picture of efficiency—nothing like the image the word "ghoul" conjured up. According to the laminated certificate on her office wall, she was a Harvard grad.

At first he stared. "I didn't know there could be beautiful ghouls, especially ones with degrees from Harvard," he stuttered when the silence had grown ominous.

She narrowed her eyes. "I think there's a compliment in there. Also, evidence of stereotyped thinking. I expect you'll get over that soon, or this might not be the right place for you."

He swallowed hard. "I apologize. To be truthful, all this is so new to me. I feel like I'm going through my adolescent awkward age again, and I'm thirty-five."

Her full red lips quirked. "Right. So, Gabe, tell me about yourself."

"What do you want to know?"

"You said you haven't been a vampire long. Tell me about your transformation."

What did this have to do with anything? "Condensing in the interest of time, I became a vampire as a result of being shot at work."

She sat back in her chair. "Let's not rush. I want to hear more."

His work for the newspaper seemed like it had taken place years before, or been part of someone else's life. "My partner and I were interviewing an informant at an office in San Quentin. Suddenly, we heard gunshots. Next thing I knew, I woke up as a vampire."

She typed notes on her laptop.

"I don't see how this impacts on my getting a date—"

The room lit up when she smiled. "I simply want to gather the facts so we can make a good match. To that end, please tell me more. Why did you choose Fangly, My Dear?"

Gabe explained about the vampire halfway house.

Her eyes sparkled. "Antoine is your mentor? I hadn't heard.

You must be a recent—"

"About three weeks."

"Brand new. And one of the first things you're looking for is a social life." She typed some more and looked at him. "Please be very specific as to what you're looking for from us."

"I want a date with a friendly, available woman. Blonde and gorgeous, though don't take that to mean I'm superficial."

She rolled her eyes and frowned at her monitor. "Would you prefer to date only vampires or are you open to females from other groups?"

"What's the difference?"

"Have you ever been out with a vampire?"

"My first encounter with any vampires was becoming one."

She nodded. "Going out with a vampire might be useful for you as a novice."

"What are the other options?"

"Shifter, hereditary witch, ghoul, demon, mortal... Some mixed-identity beings. You name it, we probably have it in our database."

"It doesn't make a difference." Maybe it did, but he considered himself a brand new learner when it came to the different kinds of beings.

She nodded again. "Good. That means you're open to a wide variety of experiences. Anything else we should consider?"

He thought for several moments. "How can I put it? I want a woman I can trust, someone with integrity."

"Ah. I'm sure we'll be able to find someone who meets all your criteria. At Fangly, My Dear we pride ourselves on making perfect matches."

"How long?"

"We should be able to contact you soon." She rose and held out her hand.

He stood and took her hand. "A perfect match or double my money back?"

"Absolutely. Count on it."

"Phone for you, Morrow," one of Gabe's neighbors shouted from downstairs the next night. This was the first call he'd gotten since arriving at the halfway house. He'd have to do something about replacing his cell he'd lost at the prison.

A woman with a Boston accent identified herself as Dominique LaPierre, calling from Fangly, My Dear. "Good news."

He perked up.

"Do you have a pencil handy?"

Gabe fumbled in the compartment under the phone and managed to retrieve a dull pencil and a note pad from a nearby hotel chain. "Shoot."

"Your date's name is Tanith Kalinski." Dominique slowly spelled the name. "Her phone number is 415-555-1205."

"How about her address?"

"You need to contact her. She'll provide that information if she chooses to."

"Okay. So, what else can you tell me about her?"

"Let's see, Tanith's a human who wants to date a vampire. She's a police officer here in San Francisco."

Gabe snapped the pencil in two. A cop? Some cops had threatened Tom and him with dire consequences if they continued with their investigation. What if Tanith had been one of the cops organized against him? What if she'd decided to come after him, to finish the job the ambush at San Quentin was supposed to accomplish?

What was going on with him? He'd have to ask Antoine Thierry if paranoia was a normal part of vampire thinking. After all, Dominique LaPierre, who evidently used both computer technology and witchcraft to make matches, sounded totally convinced that Tanith Kalinski would be a good date for him. Hesitant but curious, horny and lonely, Gabe dialed the lady's number.

Tanith liked the sound of Gabe Morrow's voice. Deep, husky. The woman she'd spoken to at Fangly, My Dear had warned Tanith that male vampires were in short supply, so she was lucky to be matched with one so quickly. It seemed women from all groups rated them the best lovers. Tanith's face grew warm as her imagination wandered.

She'd have one date with Gabe Morrow and majorly hot sex, after which she'd be able to get vampires out of her system.

Geez, what was with her tonight? Making wild assumptions had never been her style. What if Gabe of the gorgeous voice turned out to look like Nosferatu? Short, stoop-shouldered, beak-nosed, weird. Smelling bad. That would sure get her over vampires pronto. But if his looks matched his voice, she could well imagine herself ending up in the sack with him.

Not that she was the one-night-stand type, she reminded herself as she chose her outfit. But tonight was going to be an exception to her usual rules. Black leather skirt, black fuck-me heels, black sweater. Tanith put on full makeup, wiped half of it off, threw some more on.

On the chance they'd be coming back to her condo, she did a fast run through, straightening the worst of the mess. Realizing her Cinderella and the Prince linens would probably be a mood breaker, she rummaged for the black silk sheets she hadn't used since her last boyfriend took off. She smoothed them on and put a few candles on the night table and bureau.

With a yelp, she realized she'd be late if she didn't move her tail. They'd agreed to meet at a jazz club downtown. More nervous than she'd been since her first junior-high dance, she called a cab and rushed off into the night.

The moment Gabe saw Tanith walk into the club, lightning struck. He had no doubt the fox who'd just come in and was snagging all the masculine attention was his date. Blonde. Big green eyes, big breasts, long legs. A walk that highlighted all her womanly assets. His dick sprang out of hibernation and reminded Gabe how much was at stake. He winced at the image of a stake and pushed it away. Thank you, universe—and Fangly, My Dear.

The club was dark and crowded. The musicians kept up a stream of mellow jazz, nothing too challenging or lively. Conversations buzzed in counterpoint to the music, and the smell of booze nearly saturated the stale air. Gabe watched Tanith confer with the host. He crossed the room and held out his hand to her. "You must be Tanith."

Her eyes widened with a momentary flash of surprise before she composed her face to neutral. Like everything else about her, that coolness turned him on. "Gabe?"

He nodded. She took his hand with a stronger grip than he expected. "How did you know it was me?" Her voice aroused him as much as her looks.

"A beautiful face that matches your beautiful voice on the phone."

She rolled her eyes. "You actually get anywhere with lines like that?"

"It's the first time I've tried it." He steered her to his booth and they both sat. "You're saying it's not effective?"

Her laugh resonated through his body.

"So what are you drinking?" His fangs throbbed for the only drink he wanted.

"White wine."

He signaled a server and placed the order.

"Can I refresh that for you?" The server pointed at Gabe's untouched, flat and insipid-looking beer.

"Sure."

Gabe hadn't yet decided how much to tell her about his own background. He figured he'd wait to make that decision until he knew her better. After the server left, he asked Tanith first-date questions. "So, what's a nice girl like you doing in a joint like this?"

She chuckled. "I'm asking myself that same question. You come here often?"

So she was going to match him cliché for cliché. "My first time. But if I'd known great ladies like you hang out here, I'd have come years before."

The server's arrival saved them from exchanging astrological signs. They toasted each other. Though, since his transformation, beer tasted like used dishwater, he sipped some to be companionable.

"The folks at Fangly, My Dear said you're a cop here in San Francisco," he started.

Looking him straight in the eye, Tanith proudly announced, "Been on the force for eight years and just made detective."

A detective. Please, let her not be one of the corrupt ones he and Tom had been investigating. "Uh, you know I'm a vampire, right?"

Her gorgeous mouth twisted into a scowl. "Yes. I requested a date with a vampire." She took a long sip of her wine.

"You did? I guess that surprises me. I know some police officers don't look kindly on our mixing with humans." *Duh, smooth move.*

"That's an individual choice, not part of our credo. For my private life, I make my own choices."

"I see." He loved the way her eyes flashed when she put him in his place. How would those eyes look when they made love? His dick practically sat up and begged. He crossed his legs.

"Did you choose to date a human?" Her voice held a challenging note.

He shrugged, nonchalantly, he hoped. "Not specifically. I'm pretty open."

"Have you dated many vampires?" She finished her wine and he signaled the server to bring more.

"None."

One beautifully arched brow rose. "How come?"

"I haven't been a vampire all that long."

"Oh? Tell me about what you did before and what happened to you to...to make you a vampire."

Shit. Some day he'd learn to think before he spoke. "I'd prefer for tonight to be all about you." From her smile, he figured he'd just bought some time.

"Most guys only want to talk about themselves."

"I'm not most guys. I want to hear about you."

She motioned dismissively. "Not a whole lot to tell. As I said, I'm a cop. Native San Franciscan. Family's gone. No time for hobbies. I relax by going to the gym or curling up with a good book."

"Really? I'd think a job like yours would be so physical, you wouldn't need a gym."

"You'd think that, but you'd be wrong. Any exercise I get on the job is strictly unplanned. And I need regular workouts to keep me happy."

"Not to mention in incredible shape." When he looked deep in her eyes and did the vampire hypnotic thing Antoine Thierry claimed was foolproof, he could feel her warming to him. He took her hand in his and dropped a kiss on her long fingers. At the mere contact, his whole body shifted into an urgent plea for release.

Talk about being a sucker—funny word to pop into her mind with Gabe Morrow seated across from her. With his pitch-black hair worn on the longish side, chocolate brown eyes and even features, he reminded her of a cross between Johnny Depp and Orlando Bloom. As if his looks weren't enough, she melted into a puddle of feminine desire at the brush of his lips on her hand.

Heck, she'd always loved seeing men kiss women's hands. The men from Poland, her family's ancestral homeland, traditionally used this form of greeting. Experiencing it from a guy like Gabe Morrow, who could have been a movie star Dracula of the modern, hot kind—definitely not the Nosferatu kind—had her panties moist and her clit throbbing. He smiled, and her defenses crumbled. On the heat meter, he'd hit a perfect ten. She was so turned on she didn't know if she'd be able to stand up and walk.

He opened his mouth and she caught a sexy glimpse of fang. Did this mean she turned him on? So much to learn about the amazing creature staring at her from across a very small table. Was his penis hard too? Did the fangs and cock work together in real life the way they did in the novels she devoured? She was trying to shake free of the images these words conjured when he said, "How about we go somewhere more private?"

Chapter Three

When Tanith blushed and all that glorious blood rushed to her face, Gabe had to clamp down hard to keep from lunging across the table and grabbing her. He had to get them out of this club or he'd go crazy, make the kind of scene Antoine Thierry and the other mentors had warned against.

But where could they go to be alone? He hadn't thought things through. Obviously not the vampires' halfway house. Gabe thought regretfully of his former home, a rented cottage in Marin that would require major remodeling to suit his current needs. The reality was he had nowhere suitable to invite her. How uncouth would it be to invite himself to her place on a first date? Maybe the night air would stimulate his brain. "Let's go for a walk."

She looked at him from under half-lidded eyes. "Sure." She extended the one-syllable word like a drop of honey falling off a spoon.

To his fevered brain, moving slowly became impossible. Gabe sprang up, paid the check, took Tanith by the arm and steered her to the exit. Once they were outside, the evening breezes did little to inspire him. Hell, he could do it with her outside. And he would if they didn't get somewhere suitable soon. He couldn't remember ever before feeling so turned on. "I want to be alone with you."

"We're alone now."

Yeah, the two of them and everyone they shared the streets with.

He took her by the hand, rougher than he intended. Her wince told him he didn't yet know the full extent of his strength. He forced himself to relax his grip.

"You okay to walk?"

"Why shouldn't I be?"

He indicated her shoes. "Those don't look like they're made for much walking."

"Oh no? What do they look like they're made for?"

He turned to her to see if she expected a real answer to that question. Fuck-me shoes he'd heard them called. Tempted by the challenge in her eyes, he started to answer. Then he figured he'd show her. He put his arms around her and drew her close. In moments, he'd taken hold of her beautiful mouth with his lips. She responded immediately, inviting him to deepen the spontaneous moment.

Hunger for her gripped him. No way he could let go of her now, not until he'd satisfied the basic need pulsing through him.

His fangs, fully descended, scraped across her lower lip, and she moaned. He pressed her tight, hot body against his rampant bulge. Too friggin' much. Never breaking the liplock that joined them, he scooped her up and raced to the dark alley between two buildings.

Tanith kept her arms tight around his neck. Her murmured sounds of encouragement went straight to his bloodstream. Once inside the deserted alley, he set her on her feet between himself and the rough gray stone of the building. "I want you, now."

She whimpered in reply. Desperate to be everywhere on her and in her at once, he ran his hands from her shoulders to her lush breasts. More, he wanted more time to feel her, to watch her nipples harden in reaction to his touch, to watch her eyes register everything she felt.

But not now. Now it had to be fast and hard or he'd expire. He didn't want to take his hands off her, but he had to free his erection. Quickly, he unzipped his jeans and his cock sprang out. Tanith slithered her skirt up to her hips, and he nearly lost it. She was so amazingly beautiful, and every move tantalized. No panties, he was gratified to see. When she opened her legs, he stopped thinking.

Heat radiated from her innermost self, scorching her with the intensity of her desire. A momentary rush of air did nothing to cool her. She wanted his touch everywhere, his big, hard cock jammed deep inside her, touching all her most intimate places.

She didn't have to wait long. With a shudder of total submission, she gasped as he filled her so completely that she only now understood how empty she'd been.

At first, he moved with infinite slowness, searing her with the erotic magic of his movements. But she demanded more. Digging her nails into his muscular back, she rode him, wordlessly urging him on. Caught up in the whirlwind that was Gabe, she fell deeper and deeper into his embrace.

"More." Her plea sprang from her most intimate self.

He growled and thrust himself into her, taking her breath away. Hard and fast, hard and fast, harder and faster. Tanith held on for the flight of her life as Gabe's huge cock led her in a sensuous dance. The divine friction of his touch sent her spiraling into a new dimension. Ever closer, ever hungrier, she grasped his tight muscular back and held him tighter to her. With her legs wound 'round him, she surrendered to his pulsing dick, savoring the feel as he rubbed her clit and slid back and forth in her aroused folds.

Beyond any fantasy she'd ever imagined, he overwhelmed her senses with his presence, his scent, the strength of his arms holding her, the erotic link between them.

She bit her lip to hold back a scream of sheer pleasure that she was sure would alert people in a several block radius to what they were doing. If only a cocoon would envelop them both—hide them from prying eyes. As she glided from pleasure to pleasure, Tanith quivered, positive she'd arrived at an erotic peak never again to be scaled.

But then he lowered his mouth to her neck, and Tanith soon understood that before this moment, she'd only scratched the surface of sensuous delight. The initial prick of pain when his fangs penetrated her skin gave way to a heightened rush of sensation, a kaleidoscope of every color and scent she knew along with sensory amazements she had no name for. She felt her blood slowly pulse and stream, leading him to an intimate ecstasy only she could provide.

No way could she hold back from howling her joy—and she didn't give a damn who heard.

After all the women he'd ever had sex with before, how strange and unnerving for Gabe to feel like a virgin again. But this was his first time as a vampire. He thanked the universe for the overwhelming instinct that guided him.

Tanith Kalinski. The woman led him on a mystical magic carpet ride, introducing him to a whole new world in her arms. Trying to stay aware that he had her pressed against the hard surface of a building, Gabe cushioned her back with his arms and hands as he thrust in and out of her irresistible, hot, wet feminine core. The way Tanith grasped at his pulsing dick with her smooth fleshy muscles, Gabe knew the operative word this first time would be "fast".

Fast seemed to be exactly what she wanted too as she moved her hips hungrily, circling his cock alternately with large and small movements. Her breathing came fast too, shallow breaths that told him she wanted him. That and the hammering of her heart, the carnal caresses, the barely there sighs.

And then the need to feed thrummed in his head, a wave of red and dark he could no more ignore than the invitation of her warmth. With a predatory growl, he lowered his face to her neck, plunged in and began to drink.

The moment he tasted her essence flowing into him, his cock grew even harder—which he hadn't thought possible. Tanith, as if supercharged, began to move faster, more frantically. The double pleasure of their being joined in both intimacies spun his senses into a mad and dizzying swirl.

Can't drink too much or you'll hurt her, a small, insistent inner voice chided. Keeping Tanith's needs in mind, he forced himself to withdraw. Then he healed her wound with a flick of his tongue. Once again fully focused on his cock deep inside her, Gabe realized he could no longer hold back from coming.

The same sensation must have taken hold of Tanith, for she now began to tremble and shake, biting her lips and moaning his name, in her release. That was it. With a groan that came from the core of his soul, he let go and pumped himself into her deepest recesses.

"Oof." Tanith returned to earth when she began to fear the rough structure of the building would leave permanent imprints. Gabe set her on her feet and backed away, and the shock of cool air insinuating itself between them struck her hard. Never before had she done anything like fornicating on one of the city streets it was her job to police. Though the voice of reason kept trying to command her attention, all she could think was, "More." She wanted more of Gabe, she wanted to lose herself in the sensuousness of being with him. More, more, more. Again and again and again.

After they both adjusted their clothing, Gabe grinned at her ruefully, and her heart skipped a beat. If it weren't for his lopsided smile, she could almost resist him. But when she saw that grin, she was a goner.

He watched her minutely, as if he'd devour her. Tanith shivered, in part from how cool the night was turning, more from what she was feeling. "Let's take this inside," she whispered.

He hesitated for just a beat. "I'd like to say your place or mine, but mine won't work."

She had no patience for the usual dating games. "My place will. You want to grab a cab or walk? It's about a mile and a half. Or maybe you'd like to try some alternative transportation." Flying high above the city in his arms would fulfill another of her fantasies.

"I don't have the flying part down pat yet," he mumbled. Clearly he'd read her mind. "Let's walk. I'll carry you."

Before she could protest, he scooped her up and hugged her to him. "Where do you live?"

She gave him her address and snuggled against his chest. He practically ran. Though she was in great shape, she'd have been hard-pressed to keep up with his pace. Heck, she'd never been carried by a guy like this, and with a pang she realized she could get used to such pampering. Being sheltered in his powerful arms was seductive, romantic and very sensual. She leaned in harder.

Lost as she was in sensation and emotion, Tanith couldn't completely squelch the voice of reason. Mind-blowing as the sex had been, she was determined she and Gabe would be together for this one night only. Which meant she'd better get her fill of him tonight because there'd be no second chance. To satisfy all her vampire cravings, she had only the hours until dawn. She pushed away the suspicion that, having actually been with this vampire once, she'd be more obsessed than ever.

Was sex with vampires always this amazing? In his complete embrace she'd forgotten everything but his overwhelming masculinity. And that had been just their first time, when new lovers need to get to know their partners. Would subsequent sex be even more fantastic, hotter? Her clit vibrated at the prospect, though she couldn't quite believe any sex could be better than what she'd just experienced.

She burrowed deeper against Gabe's chest, amazed at how secure she felt in his arms.

They quickly arrived at her condo. Gabe set her down and she fumbled in her tiny purse for the key. With trembling hands, she unlocked the door and invited him in.

Stepping into Tanith's condo, Gabe was reminded of the normal existence he'd lost. A rush of regret swept over him, but, with her by his side, he couldn't remain sad. After all, they had hours yet before he'd have to return to his lonely coffin.

He liked Tanith already. The welcoming atmosphere of her condo made him like her even more. Best of all, they were both unencumbered, free to do anything they wanted, right?

"I guess there's no point in offering you a drink," she said softly.

"No. But please feel free to take one yourself."

She pointed to the loveseat and went to the kitchen. In moments, she returned with a glass of ruby red wine. She sat down next to him, took a sip and said, "Tell me more about yourself."

He still wasn't sure bringing up the work he'd been doing when he was shot was a good idea. "I'm really glad to be here. I always thought signing up for a dating service was stupid, but now I'm changing my mind."

She raised her glass to toast him in agreement and sipped some more. "I know what you mean. I looked at it as something losers do." She put her glass down on a cork coaster.

"Yeah, me too. But now that I've met you, I see why so many people swear by them." He took her hand again and kissed the palm.

"Mmm. I like that. Not many men realize how sexy it is to kiss a woman's hand. Where'd you learn that?"

Gabe relaxed, enjoying the compliment. "Just natural. Part of loving women's bodies."

"Sounds like you've been around a lot."

"I dated before—"

"Before?"

Damn, he was running at the mouth. He shrugged. "Before my transformation."

She nodded. "I really would like to hear all about that."

No way. "Never on the first date. Uh, how many rooms in this condo?"

For a moment, he thought she wouldn't let him get away with changing the subject, but then she said, "Just the kitchen, bath, this living room which is also supposed to be the dining room, and a bedroom."

He stood up and held his hand out to her. "So where's the bedroom?" Tanith put down her wine and took his hand.

Just the thought of taking him to her bedroom aroused Tanith. Despite her complete and utter satisfaction a short time before, her clit made its presence known again. Now she was really glad she'd changed the sheets. She didn't want housewifely concern to rear its ugly head at the wrong moment. "I'll show you."

Tanith had left one lamp on low in the bedroom. With the top sheet turned down, the bed invited them both. She lit one of the waiting candles and turned off the lamp. Gabe stopped her. "Wait. This time, I want to watch you."

She laughed nervously. "I thought with your vampiric vision you were able to see me back in the alley."

"As you might recall, we were both pretty busy then. And I had my eyes closed."

In truth, she wanted to see all of him too. She blushed again. She, Tanith Marie Kalinski, who'd served a rotation on vice and thought she'd seen it all. She'd been blushing a lot all night, and she wished she could stop.

So focused that she could swear he was committing each touch to memory, he traced the contours of her face with his fingers. "You're very beautiful. Extraordinary. But you know that, don't you?"

She needed to diffuse the warmth searing her at his touch, his words, his breath. If she didn't watch herself, his being with her would start to mean too much. She couldn't let that happen. She needed to be on guard or she'd be riding for a fall. "Yeah, yeah. Flattery will get you everywhere."

"I don't flatter and I don't lie." For a moment, his face took on such a harsh expression she was afraid she'd insulted him. "Everything I say to you is the truth, or I wouldn't say it."

Everything he said turned her on more and more. Was this just part of the vampiric magnetism she'd read about in the glossy magazines? *Ten Reasons Why You Need To Keep Your Guard Up When You Date A Vampire.* Or maybe it was just his way of hypnotizing her into believing whatever he said.

She wanted to do exactly that.

He touched her and she shivered. Never before had she been so aware of her body, every nerve ending, every beat and pulse. Never before had she realized—felt—her magnificence. His fingertips grazing here, pressing there, brought her to this new level of awareness. *Breathe*, she reminded herself. But even that most fundamental of acts took on an exquisiteness she recognized for the first time. Every moment felt magnified, expanded.

Tanith had never realized how slowly a person could move. Gabe drew off her shirt as if he were undressing a porcelain figure that would break at the slightest undue pressure. Goose bumps sprang up as he uncovered her skin, and she quivered.

Gabe flung her shirt aside. Braless, she inhaled with wonder as her nipples stiffened under his gaze. With teeth-grinding slowness, he brushed the palms of his hands over those nipples, seeming to hover a fraction of an inch from them. She moaned and strained toward him, attracted to his magnetism, wanting him to possess her breasts with his hands.

"Soon," he whispered.

Couldn't happen soon enough to suit her. Though she pressed her breasts harder against his palms and moaned her need, Gabe did nothing to increase his pace. She could have sworn he began to move even slower, which she hadn't thought possible.

Didn't he realize they would have only this one night ever?

Starting at her breasts, he slid his hands down her sides,

moving with such deliberation as to lay claim to every detail of her skin, her bones and flesh beneath his fingers. He unzipped her skirt and slid the cool leather down over her heated skin.

"Is this what they mean by vampiric control?" she asked hoarsely, startled by the sound of her voice breaking the silence.

"It's as new to me as it is to you," he whispered back. "All I know is I wouldn't chug fine wine. I'm not going to rush with you. No more slam-bam-thank-you-ma'am. Not with a woman like you."

She was getting to the point where a little slam-bam wouldn't be unwelcome. When he'd finished the first part of his exploration, down the outside of her thighs to her feet, he worked his fingers up the inside of her legs, finally pausing at the sensitive skin of her inner thighs.

Then, thank the universe, he touched her weeping labia, and her knees buckled. If she hadn't clutched his shoulders, she'd have fallen in a heap.

Her pussy was so wet, she could hear his fingers slide between her folds, around her clit—maddeningly around her clit—so close she wanted to scream. Finally, he brushed her sensitive nub with his fingertips just before she thought she'd expire. His exquisite holding back tortured her, and she whimpered her need. When she thrust herself against his fingers, he pulled back. Hunger built within her and she groaned her protest. She tightened her legs around his hand but couldn't keep him where she wanted him.

"I like these." He lightly touched her garter belt and stockings before unhooking the garters and smoothly rolling the stockings down her long legs, inch by agonizing inch, stroking her and kissing her flesh as he uncovered it. With a quick, deft movement, he undid the garter belt. Then he sat on the bed, drew her down on top of him and nuzzled the nape of her neck.

Immediately aware of Gabe's arousal, Tanith manipulated her bottom until his bulge wedged between her cheeks. His sharp intake of breath gratified her. Even though he remained fully dressed and she was naked, feeling his reaction helped her stay in touch with her power. She could give as well as she got, make him crazy too. She just had to focus and remind herself she wasn't totally out of control.

He lifted her off him, then massaged her arches, toes and

ankles. Part of her wished he'd continue playing with her feet for hours, but her pussy yearned for precedence.

"Gabe, I want you." Her demanding words startled her.

"I'm yours."

There she sat, buck naked, while he remained fully clothed. Something was definitely wrong with this picture. Despite her intention to maintain control, her hands trembled when she touched the waist of his pants and began to unbuckle his thick leather belt. He put his hands over hers to stop her.

The hell with that. She wanted him naked as she was. Now.

"I can do it faster than you can," he growled, standing them both up and moving back from her. For a moment, she felt bereft at the separation. As he flung his own clothes aside, she realized he was right. Another time she'd strip his clothes off as tantalizingly as he'd done to her. But her need and desire were too urgent now. And just for now she could promise herself there'd be another time, even if the reality would prove otherwise.

Though he'd been enjoying the slow and sensuous pace of their foreplay, Gabe had played that card to its limit. As much as he wanted the feel of her hands undressing him, he needed to be naked with her now.

With Tanith he finally became aware of the full extent of his vampiric senses. He felt like he'd entered into a full-color universe after a century in gray and sepia.

Tanith filled him, raising him up to ecstasy, sexually and in his feeding. Her scent, her taste, the feel of her skin brushing his. The way her feminine muscles contracted and relaxed, the pulse of her life beat. He took it all in like a parched traveler reaching a magical fountain.

When they were both standing naked, he drew her into his arms and held her tightly, the column of his erection pressed fully against her taut, flat belly. She enveloped him with her arms, and she burrowed her face into his chest.

With a groan and a sigh—was it his or hers?—they both fell onto the cool sheets of her bed. "I want it to be slower this time," he insisted.

In response, she kissed him hard, delving deep into him with a firm tongue.

He rolled onto his back, bent his knees and pulled her on top of him. She scrambled to sit with her labia touching the tip of his cock. He exerted the tiniest pressure to open her, and she threw her head back and hissed. With a slight rock of her hips, she swallowed him into her, taking his full length deep. "Hold my ass," she commanded.

Never one to turn down an invitation, Gabe took one of her taut smooth cheeks in each hand and drew her closer. The way she engulfed him with warmth made him want to stay exactly where he was forever—and made forever impossible. She contracted the slick hot surface of her sheath, scarcely moving her hips while the intimate massage drove him crazy. He had to move, but he didn't want to disrupt her rhythm.

"Incredibly good," she murmured. "You're so deep inside me, touching all of me."

"All *for* you," he whispered. His fangs began to throb, and he realized how integral a part of the intimate act feeding had become. He couldn't satisfy that part of his hunger, not in their current position. But he didn't want either of them to shift.

In a way, he was grateful his blood hunger was strong enough to distract him from the overwhelming satisfaction of their intimate contact. With that attention divided, he'd be able to hold off from coming until she'd been well and truly satisfied.

Then Tanith took hold of his balls—and all bets were off. He nearly flew to the ceiling and took her with him. Waves of pleasure rippled through him as she squeezed with one hand while she braced herself against his belly with the other. He thrashed hard and Tanith, looking cool and in control, grinned. "Like that, do you?" She gave his balls another squeeze before setting her fingers to a killer massage.

She loved sitting on top of Gabe, loved the power she felt as she straddled him so his amazing cock could wedge deep inside her. Just like everything else about him, Gabe's balls turned her on. Round, firm. She couldn't decide what was more fun—squeezing them or making him crazy with a perfect massage. So she did some of each and savored his reactions, his intense responsiveness. As he moved from side to side, she could sense him losing some of the iron control he'd had before. Good. When she replayed this night in her memory, she'd lick her lips over how she'd gotten to him.

Too bad this position had its limits. She wanted to taste his balls, to use her tongue and teeth and lips to play with them. But she was having too good a time to climb off him, and she was enjoying the ride far too much to bring it to an end. Yet.

She circled her hips around his pulsing dick, first in one direction then the other, stopping only when his groan set off the beginning of her climax. This was way too soon, so she'd slow things down.

If she'd had to identify what aroused her most—the way he looked, the way he sounded, the feel of him, his scent—she couldn't have said and she was too lost in sensation to think. All this and she hadn't even tasted him yet. She was climbing, climbing far too fast. The colors around her shattered into a million pieces like some celestial kaleidoscope. In a futile attempt to keep herself rooted on Earth, she grabbed on tighter to his balls.

Everything stopped. One moment she was flying to her climax. The next she was literally flying, her hips swinging back and forth in mid-air, her legs embracing nothing as his powerful arms held her suspended over him as if they were performing a weird gymnastics stunt. She froze in mid-thrash. "What the—?" In the midst of her confusion, an idea meandered into the tatters of her mind. "Did I hurt you?" Was it possible for a mortal to hurt a vampire? Of course, when it came to a man's family jewels...

Hell, he was making a strange, choking noise—like he was choking or crying. Did vampires cry? Maybe she'd put him out of commission for the whole night or longer, maybe for all of eternity. Though he didn't seem injured. Heck, he was so strong, he still held her up in midair.

Then understanding dawned. Far from crying, he was laughing so hard that he shook the bed. From guilt she advanced quickly to fury. How dare he? "Unhand me or you'll be sorry," she hissed.

The bastard actually bit his lip and appeared to struggle to stop laughing as he lowered her to the mattress. Great, she thought. Let me in on the joke. "What's so friggin' funny?"

He turned his head away for a moment, and she could tell he was trying to compose himself. "Did you hurt me?" He sputtered into more laughter.

Seeing his hugely erect cock wet with her juices bobbing up and down in time with his hilarity, Tanith fought back the urge to reach down and really hurt him. He seemed to catch a whiff of her plan and scooted his package out of range.

For two cents she'd get the hell out of the bed and pour a bucket of ice water over him—or worse. But before she could scurry away from him, he clamped his hand on her arm, which kept her effectively immobile.

"Let go of me," she threatened. Her pussy, deprived of the climax she'd been implacably building to, clenched.

He shook his head. "I suppose I should apologize. But the idea that you could hurt me by squeezing my balls...." With his other hand he cupped her chin and gazed deep into her eyes. "Lady, don't you know what dynamite you are? One more squeeze and I would have exploded. Only I didn't want to because you weren't there yet."

"I was on my way," she grudgingly admitted.

"Not good enough. I wanted you completely there before I came. And I couldn't think of any other way to stop what was happening than to remove you from me."

As if in confirmation, his cock bobbed. A drop of pre-cum glistened at the opening on top of the glans.

"How about we pick up exactly where we were?" he asked, his voice pitched so low it raised goose bumps on her arms.

Though part of her wanted to hold back, her clit voted down any stubborn resistance. "You want me on top again?"

"If you want. Only maybe cool it a little on the ball squeezing, at least until you come. Okay?" He got on his back again, and his dick stood invitingly up.

"I'll try to restrain myself." To Tanith's delighted surprise, they were able to pick up almost where they'd left off, only better. In moments, Gabe was even harder than she remembered him being before. Now her fingers itched to get 'round his balls again, but she didn't want to do anything to short-circuit the magical ride the two of them were sharing.

She'd never reached this level of intimacy and complete communication with any other man, not even during the best times in her two long-term relationships. Here she was achieving this closeness their first night together. Their *only* night together, she reminded herself.

Maybe knowing it would be only this one time added an

edge of urgency. Whatever. This time, when she began to feel her orgasm building, she'd scream bloody murder if anyone or anything interfered.

"Gabe," she gasped, plunging herself harder and harder onto him, "it's happening." He clutched her tighter and murmured words of encouragement as his cock filled her even more completely.

Then, just when she was about to let it all go in one loud, colorful burst, he began to massage her rear opening with his moist finger. Electrical impulses exploded all around her, sparking more and more lights and bursts of energy. Thrusting her hips ever harder, Tanith realized Gabe was snaking a finger into her back there.

Making incoherent noises and slamming herself against him, Tanith came and came and came.

Chapter Four

She was completely open to him, completely vulnerable, showing him who she was. Now that she'd so audibly and visually climaxed, Gabe let go into his own release. With her warmth and wetness beckoning him, his orgasm sprang from his deepest core. Everything he had and was went into her. Afterwards, as they both basked in the glow of awesome loving, he hugged her and enjoyed their shared collapse.

Tanith's warm breath fanned him as she lay sprawled in his arms. Given the totality of his release, still feeling any tension in his body astounded him. But his fangs ached, a sensation that resonated in his groin. Gabe realized on the gut level what other, older vamps had tried to tell him. Without a feed, no matter how minimal, the act of sex would never feel complete.

He raised her head slightly, just the small amount he needed to gain access to the warm pulse under her chin. With gentleness that surprised him, he slid his fangs into her and drank. Not much, an almost token feed, but what he needed to complete his climax. Two swift sweeps with his tongue sealed her wound. Content and more satisfied than he'd known was possible, Gabe allowed himself to fall into a peaceful doze.

"I almost forgive you," Tanith murmured some time later. Her voice startled Gabe out of his dreamless sleep.

"Forgive me? For what?"

"For the trick you played before." She kissed him playfully

on the lips.

He flung a leg over her hip so she could feel his renewed erection and asked, "Almost? What, my lady, do I have to do to earn your forgiveness?"

"I need to think about that." Right. Her ability to think was still lost somewhere in the sensory overload of being intimate with him. "I know. There's some chocolate chip ice cream in my freezer. You fed before. I want to feed on that now."

He inclined his head. "Your wish is my command. I'll find a spoon where?"

She explained. As he walked to the kitchen, she feasted her eyes on his ass, the way his muscles rippled when he moved. She almost didn't need the chocolate.

He returned in moments, carrying both carton and spoon. With two pillows propped between her and the headboard, Tanith sat up for her snack.

"With my lady's permission," he murmured, holding a spoonful of the icy confection to her lips.

Gazing at her intently, he watched as she opened her mouth and took her first taste. Hot as she was, the ice cream melted almost the moment it touched her lips. She'd never before realized how delicious it was.

"Is that hitting the right spots?" he asked.

With him feeding her, there could be no wrong spots. She was in a state of complete heightened awareness. The ice cream flowed through her newly awakened body with explosive sensuousness.

"That looks so delicious, I want a taste." He set aside the carton and began licking bits of chocolate off her lips.

She licked him back. Licks turned to nibbles and she quickly abandoned her desire for anything but him.

She encircled his waiting erection with two fingers and began to play. "I want this too."

"It's yours," he declared. "But there's something I want to do first."

With hot kisses and some major-league sucking, he worked his way down her torso to her labia. Just when she expected his kiss on sensitive folds, he coated his fingers and lips with ice cream and massaged her hot sex with the frozen dessert. Sizzling with desire, Tanith hissed and sputtered her surprise at his icy-hot embrace. With slow, sensuous tongue strokes, he licked the ice cream off her there, sending Tanith to an erotic paradise.

Speechless, Tanith ran her fingers through Gabe's thick dark hair as he continued to tongue her, tracing a route between her clit and the soft pink folds of her ravenous pussy. She opened her legs wider to him and pressed him closer, tighter. While he sucked and nibbled, his fingers massaged the sensitive skin between her inner thighs and her nether lips. Tanith, who'd never had more than one climax in a night, couldn't believe she'd turned into such an orgasm queen.

Too bad it would only be for this one night. Any lovemaking after tonight would be, well, anti-climactic. At least she'd always have this. She could always look back at the memory of how her vampire lover satisfied her. From now on she'd be able to tell everyone, from first-hand experience, that vampires were, indeed, incredible lovers.

To her amazement, Gabe managed to talk and suck at the same time. Or maybe he was communicating with her in some other way. With his words and gestures he encouraged her to tell him exactly what she wanted and how everything he was doing felt. Even if she'd wanted to, she could hold nothing back from him. She responded fully, with words and her body.

He raised his head for a moment, and she could see how her dripping juices moistened his mouth. He licked his lips, then kissed hers, letting her taste how he and she and the chocolate chip ice cream mingled to form a unique musk. When he broke away, she picked up the rhythm and pattern, licking his lips and chin, savoring the flavor of their loving.

Then he returned to her pussy, blowing hot air on the sensitive folds before he resumed his ministrations with tongue, teeth and lips. He alternated using his tongue and his thumb to play with her engorged clit. With a sob, she realized she was going to come again and no longer had the will to try to delay her climax. She tightened her hands and her legs, pressing up against him for that one final push before she gasped out her climax.

His turn. She fully intended to take him into her mouth, but her sexy vampire lover had other plans. He turned her around and pressed up to her back. She braced herself to take him in the ass, something she'd never done before. But Gabe stroked her pussy, then entered her there from behind.

This position was also a first for her. Though he wasn't stimulating her clit, Tanith enjoyed the feel of Gabe's powerful arms around her, the sensation of his hard dick moving in and out of her from this different angle.

No stimulation of her clit? Tanith should have known better. Within moments, Gabe was stroking her there with his fingers, teasing, arousing, playing. As she'd experienced all night, a panorama of sensations exploded in and around her as they made love. Each time, amazingly, she felt they were growing closer and closer, sharing a greater degree of intimacy.

Letting herself get caught up in emotions she shouldn't, couldn't allow into her world, put her in dangerous terrain. She shook her head to clear away such sentiments. All she could permit herself was the indulgence of erotic satisfaction. She wanted, she wanted, she wanted. Yet again, to her astonishment, she quivered into a climax—this time simultaneously with him.

Nearly breathless, she lay in complete surrender, nestled by him in a post-coital snuggle. She resented the way time was passing, flying. All too soon, she'd have to say good-bye to Gabe forever. She knew he had a strict curfew—he had to be at the halfway house by dawn or risk dying. Or whatever vampires did when they ceased to exist. Whenever he left would be their last moment together. She couldn't let anything trap her into breaking this solemn oath to herself. No matter how incredible being with him was, she couldn't let herself lose sight of the fundamental truth—Gabe Morrow was a vampire.

Despite the growing tolerance for these creatures in society, Tanith was not alone in regarding them as criminal by their very nature. No matter what attractive mask Gabe might don, no matter how much being with him surpassed all she'd expected, she couldn't let him become important to her. She had no room in her life for the kind of complications he'd bring.

But when she looked at him, dozing for the moment with a boyish, sexy grin on his face, her heart constricted. How could she possibly tell this man—this creature who'd been so good to her—she'd never see him again? If she tried, she'd probably get all weepy, and then he'd comfort her and try to talk her out of it. That would lead to yet more lovemaking, pulling her deeper into his thrall. Where was her tough exterior when she needed it?

Well, she was paying the dating service big bucks. Let Fangly, My Dear do the dirty work. Her conscience woke up and protested. Having the service tell Gabe there'd be no second date was the coward's way out, and she had nothing but contempt and loathing for cowards. Her on-the-job courage didn't count for much when the prospect of saying goodbye to Gabe turned her into a big, blubbering chicken, but she saw no other possibility.

Resolved not to think about the future or listen to the prodding of her conscience, she threw herself into enjoying what remained of the night.

For maybe the first time in his short vampiric life, Gabe began to appreciate the changes his transformation had brought. Had he met Tanith before, he doubted she'd have noticed him. He'd never have known the satisfaction in his arms that she now experienced over and over.

Hell, they still had hours before he had to head back to his lair. Lots more time to make love, tonight and after.

To think, he'd found this wonderful woman through a dating service.

Tomorrow night, he'd call the Fangly, My Dear ladies. He'd thank Dominique and Lilith, let them know that, as promised, the match met and surpassed all his expectations.

His heart hammering wildly, he turned back to Tanith and said yes.

Time was her inexorable enemy. Time and her body's need for sleep. Why should she waste even a moment of her night with Gabe by giving in to the ordinary? She could sleep every night for the rest of her life. Being with Gabe was a once in a lifetime experience.

But she couldn't bear to tell him that. So she couldn't protest too much when he dozed. She allowed herself to drink him in, to fill her senses with his looks, his scent, the whisper of his breath. Though she yearned to touch him, she didn't want to disturb him, didn't want to tell him why she so desperately longed to cling to each moment.

No matter how much she wished to hold time back, dawn approached. Sending him back to his shelter was the hardest thing she'd ever have to do.

Looking rumpled and satisfied, the scent of musk clinging to him, Gabe smiled drowsily at her as he dressed and prepared to leave. "You know I don't want to go," he whispered.

She knew with every fiber of her being because she also didn't want him to go. "We both have places to go, things to do." She managed to keep her voice level, neutral, almost emotion-free, when all she wanted was to get on her knees, clutch him around the legs and beg him to stay.

They kissed. Although her lips were swollen from the night's excesses, she still wanted more. But she'd never let him risk his safety. She practically pushed him out the door, then stood and watched until he disappeared.

Broken and bereft, she went back to bed and tried to get some sleep. She had a busy workday ahead of her. Later, she'd call Fangly, My Dear and tell the biggest lie of her life.

When he awoke the next night, Gabe couldn't believe he hadn't set up a date for tonight with Tanith—but he'd remedy that fast. He rushed through his first feed of the night, a bottle of B positive from the fridge, which was nowhere near as delicious and sustaining as her blood had been last night. At the thought of her, his wake-up erection and fangs tingled in harmony. As soon as he got out of the shower, he'd be on the horn with her. Horn, horny. Considering how they'd burned up the sheets, he was amazed to be so hot and ready again. He smiled to himself and whistled a little tune.

Someone hollered that he had a call on the house phone. Realizing it might be his lady, he rushed, his heart hammering, to pick up. Before he had a chance to say a word, he heard a woman ask, "Gabe, how are you tonight?"

Sounded like Dominique LaPierre.

A troubling thought began to take form in the back of his mind. He decided to ignore it. "Fine, but a little surprised. I didn't expect to hear from you." Maybe she was calling for a reason that would make him smile, but his gut told him otherwise. "Oh, you must be following up. I guess you didn't have a chance to read my email. The date last night with Tanith Kalinski was..."

She cut him off. "I read your message." She sighed. "This isn't any good. I have to be straight with you. Tanith has requested other matches. She's also instructed us to ask you not to contact her again. Ever."

"What?" He shook his head. Dominique couldn't be talking about the woman he'd been with. There must have been some sort of mix up.

She repeated the same awful words, and he began to get the message. How could he be that out of touch with reality? "I'm being blindsided here. I'm trying to get my head around what's happened between last night and now. Can you tell me what Tanith said?"

"You know, these things can be so one-sided."

"Her exact words. Please. It's important." He sat down on the edge of the chair and cradled the receiver in his hands.

He could hear Dominique shuffling some paper. "She didn't go into a lot of detail. Just said she'd been out with you, and it didn't work out. She doesn't want to see you again and wants us to give her the additional matches she's entitled to. Actually, she's requested no more dates with vampires." Dominique delivered these facts with no emotion in her voice. Then she added, "I'm sorry. It seems you had a different impression of the date."

He sprang to his feet. How could the woman who'd shared last night's intimacy with him turn around and say these things? There had to be an error somewhere. Hell, they had communicated clearly on every level—okay, much of the time without words, but still. If some problem had arisen, why didn't she talk directly to him, so they could work it out? "I just can't believe any of this."

"Tanith was very clear. We're really very careful, and we don't deliver messages to the wrong people."

"On a rational level, I know that. But we were so great together, so close..." He caught himself before he spilled his guts. "Maybe I should call her, straighten this out."

Dominique cleared her throat. "Really not a good idea. She explicitly asked us to tell you no more contact. That's about as clear as it can get. And, by the terms of our contract with you, something I must insist you honor."

Talk about having the rug pulled out from under him—the magic carpet. "What am I supposed to do now?"

"This kind of miscommunication doesn't happen often, but you're not the first. My advice is for you to move on. We're going to set you up with other matches, ones I'm sure will work out much better than the first."

The words sounded smooth and professional, but smacked him with the force of punches. He didn't want any other matches, and he didn't want to move on.

"Do you want to modify your intake form or should we go with the guidelines you gave us?"

All he wanted was to be with Tanith again.

"Not an option. We'll help you with anything except trying to contact her again."

Move on snorted a little internal voice. "Did Tanith say I did something wrong? Did I hurt her some way?" His mind replayed the night yet again.

For a moment, he wondered if the line had gone dead. Then Dominique admitted, "No, nothing like that. She didn't say anything specific about you. I'm sure it wasn't a question of your doing something wrong per se."

"Then what—" Not that Tanith was obligated to provide any sort of explanation, but why would a woman drop a bombshell and then just walk away? Didn't she owe him the courtesy of some clarity?

"Look, if it helps, I told you she requested no more vampires as dates. In our very brief conversation, she said she changed her mind about wanting to date vampires, who were her original first choice. It happens. Part of what we do at Fangly, My Dear is help people identify whom they want to date."

Damn. Talk about rejected. Down to his core. Tanith hadn't brought up any objections he could deal with, anything he could change. Had he fed too hard off her, taken too much? She'd seemed all right, seemed to encourage him.

"I need to talk to her once more anyway, even if she doesn't want to see me again. She's the first person I've dated since my transformation. There are things only she can tell me." He had to know about the feeding bit. If mortal ladies couldn't handle it, he'd have to cross them off his list the way she'd crossed vamps off hers.

"If you want, I'll pass along any messages you have to Tanith. But please don't contact her on your own. She made me promise I'd tell you not to."

Because he didn't want to make any trouble for Fangly, My Dear, he agreed.

"I'll tell you this. You shouldn't worry too much about what happened on your first date. We'll get to work setting up some new matches for you. We're sure we'll be able to find the woman who's exactly right for you."

You already did. Her name is Tanith Kalinski.

He glared at the phone after he'd managed to end the conversation according to the rules of polite exchanges. Suddenly the night, which a short time ago had seemed full of possibility, loomed before him like a wasteland.

Calling the Fangly, My Dear people to break off with Gabe started Tanith's day off on a discordant note. From there, it only went further downhill. Though she went through the motions of her work, nothing went right. The computer kept misplacing files, her partner Don Allen had the male version of PMS and the vending machines swallowed her money. She tried to connect with Sue Lerner for the evening, but she had commitments that couldn't include Tanith.

Determined not to spend the evening at home alone, Tanith went out for a solo dinner and movie. Alone at a table in a sea of couples, she tried to read a novel as she picked at a huge Cobb Salad—usually her favorite. Right then she could have sworn she was the only singleton in the city. After she had the server pack the salad in a doggie bag, she headed for the movies. At least there she'd be sitting in the dark and could ignore the couples around her. Despite the change of venue, she couldn't escape her loneliness. Maybe seeing the new vampire version of *Romeo and Juliet* wasn't the smartest choice. She should have gone for a kiddie feature, cartoons.

Getting home at eleven left way too many hours of the night to fill, especially in contrast to the night before. She poured herself a few fingers of vodka, just enough to guarantee she'd get some sleep. Drinking alone was a really bad idea, but calling Gabe would be far worse. After all, she'd put herself through the agony of having the service tell him not to call again. She didn't want to jerk him around, send him mixed messages. He deserved better.

She took a huge swallow and winced at the alcohol's burn as it went down, numbing her, but not enough. How could she have known she'd miss him so intensely after just one night? It was like he'd imprinted himself on every cell and nerve ending in her body. At least now she understood the appeal of vampires. She just had to convince herself it was all smoke and mirrors, illusion—that nothing about last night was true.

Looking at her empty glass, Tanith decided she hadn't taken enough vodka the first time. She poured herself more, then put the bottle back in her cabinet and walked away. Determined to make the drink last, she curled up on the blue loveseat, picked up a copy of a local daily, began to leaf through it and sipped slowly.

When her glass was again empty, she sternly ordered herself away from any more vodka. Feeling a slight buzz, she decided to go to bed. Maybe, just maybe she'd be able to sleep.

Both Dominique and Lilith at Fangly, My Dear had been so sympathetic on the phone. Sorry that her date hadn't worked out, available to hear anything she wanted to say. Finally, they'd understood that she didn't want to go into detail and hadn't pressed her. They even had Antoine Thierry, Dominique's significant other and a vampire mentor, call her early in the evening to make sure Gabe hadn't done anything that hurt or scared her. Antoine had assured her he wanted to know only so he could be helpful to Gabe, who was so new to vampire life. Tanith, feeling guilty, had thanked Antoine and assured him Gabe had not behaved improperly.

Dominique and Lilith had promised they'd give high priority to matching her up with three other great guys. Despite their enthusiasm and reassurances, Tanith realized she should tell them to put the other matches on hold. She didn't want to be with any guy other than Gabe, and she couldn't be with him again. Maybe, if she lived to be a hundred, she might be able to forget him. In her effort to get over her obsession, she'd managed only to make things worse.

Thank goodness she had her work.

She snorted. Tomorrow was scheduled to be a big day. She didn't want to look like a hag when she accepted her award for valor at the departmental ceremony. Rumor had it the TV news crews would be there.

She had to sleep. Most of all, she had to put Gabe Morrow out of her mind, her heart and everywhere else he'd crept into.

The next evening, Antoine Thierry stopped in to talk with Gabe. "You didn't do anything wrong on your date with Tanith Kalinski," the other man assured him as they walked in the neighborhood around the halfway house. "But maybe we jumped the gun a little with the dating business. Before you go out with anyone else, I want you to go talk to an old friend of mine, Mirella Proctor. She's been in San Francisco forever. She knows everybody, and she's the leading authority on social life—vampire or any other creature's style."

Not pleased at having to talk with a "social adviser", Gabe nonetheless agreed. Heck, he'd do anything to avoid messing up again the way he must have with Tanith. He gave Mirella a call and she invited him to come right over. As this was the only break in her schedule for the next three weeks, Gabe did as told.

Mirella lived in the posh Nob Hill section of the city. Gabe had to use a key card, supplied by the concierge, for the elevator to her penthouse. Mirella turned out to be a very glamorous woman with long black hair, impeccably manicured red nails and piercing violet eyes. She had the ageless beauty of a Sophia Loren. Despite being a vampire, she appeared as tanned as if she'd just spent a week on a Caribbean beach. She offered him an aperitif, domestic or imported blood of whatever type he preferred.

Sipping his B positive from a heavy crystal goblet, Gabe focused on his surroundings and on Mirella. He could see why Antoine Thierry was so impressed, and why this woman was a leader in vampire society.

"So I understand you've been one of us for only a short time," she said.

"How did you know?"

"Antoine has told me a lot about your background." She smiled, held out her hand and touched his arm. "I remember what it was like, those first few weeks. From what I can see, you're doing great."

Most of the vamps he'd met hadn't seemed too enthusiastic to talk about their personal histories. Mirella appeared willing.

"Tell me. When were you transformed? How did you get from the beginning to where you are now?"

She raised a beautifully shaped brow. "That's far too long a story for tonight, but I will tell you about the start. You see, I was a serving girl." Her lips curved into a graceful smile.

"Where?"

"Heavens, I guess it's not obvious anymore. My accent used to be so strong. In England, the city of Bath."

"How long ago?"

Now her eyes gleamed with mischief. "Surely you know better than to ask a lady such a question."

Given immortality, he hadn't imagined this question carried quite the same punch for female vampires as it did for humans. "I apologize. Tell me more about being a serving girl in Bath."

She nodded. The expensive lighting in her penthouse was probably designed to flatter, but Mirella appeared to have a special glow. "You don't know me well yet, but even after such a short acquaintance, you might be able to tell how ill-suited I am to serve in any capacity. Trust me, I was no better a candidate for that role as a young girl from an undistinguished family than I am now."

"I can see where that might be the case."

"To make a long story short, when a most particular visitor from Eastern Europe came to visit, he easily persuaded me to come away with him."

"You're not saying you were transformed by—"

She put a discreet finger to her lips. "Name dropping can be so tacky, don't you think?"

If he weren't so totally into Tanith Kalinski, Gabe could fall for Mirella Proctor. Hell, if he had any brains, that's exactly what he would do. Made him wonder if he was guilty of thinking only with the head between his legs instead of the one on his shoulders.

Yeah, maybe it was his prick acting up here. But it was

also his heart. Between those two organs, he felt like he had nothing to offer any woman other than Tanith. Still, he was beginning to enjoy the company of the fascinating Mirella. After all, he wasn't dead. Undead wasn't at all the same thing, as he was discovering.

"How did you end up in San Francisco?"

She shook her head now. "Another long story, and I'm tired of hearing my own voice. Tell me about you and how you became one of us."

Gabe toyed with his glass. "I was an investigative journalist. My partner and I were on a story about police corruption, and we were getting pretty high up in the ranks with what we uncovered. While we were interviewing an informant at San Quentin, someone shot the three of us. According to Antoine, a vampire working there transformed me. The others were beyond help." He swallowed hard.

A frown creased Mirella's perfect skin. She put a hand on Gabe's arm. "That's horrible. Have you found out who was behind the shooting?"

He thought about her question. "I haven't. It's funny how I lost the thread of that work, which was my life's passion before." The only passion he'd felt since his transformation was for Tanith.

Mirella watched him intensely. "That might be from the shock of the transformation. Vampires are known for being passionate. Once you settle more into your new identity, you might pick up that thread. Some of us reclaim our past identities and resume our work. I take it the people from your former life don't know about the change?"

"No. I haven't done anything to reconnect, didn't know it was possible."

"It is for some. Others resume their work with new identities. Maybe I can help you reclaim that passion, however you decide to pursue it. Tell me, Gabe, where do you live now?"

He told her about the halfway house.

"Yes, I remember Antoine telling me a bit about that place. Sounds dreadful, like a dormitory. I'll tell you what. You must move into the penthouse with me. Let me also be your mentor, teach you more of our ways and help you to reconnect with what's important to you." She held her hand out to him.

Tempting. He felt a pull to resume his work, and maybe

he'd move in that direction soon. As to Mirella's offer—who wouldn't want to live with an elegant creature in a gorgeous penthouse with panoramic views of San Francisco? Sure better than the bare-bones arrangement he currently shared with six other clueless vampires.

But what about having a place he could bring Tanith back to? How could he do that if home was a room in Mirella Proctor's penthouse? Idiot that he was, he couldn't let go of his desire to have future time with Tanith—or the belief that such would be possible.

"I appreciate the offer and, for about a hundred reasons, wish that I could say yes."

She nodded. "The offer remains open. Now tell me about this woman who's got your heart tied up in knots, the one Antoine told me about."

Gabe opened up to her. Hell, he hadn't talked so much about himself in years, maybe ever. As he put together the words that conveyed feelings from deep within, he came to realize how completely Tanith had taken hold of his senses. Next, he had to decide what to do about that.

"Tell me," he said when he began to wind down, "what do you think I did wrong on my date with Tanith? Am I so clueless to what women want that I hurt her? Did I feed too much off her, scare her?"

She took his hand. "I won't say it's impossible to feed too much, but I suspect that's not what happened. Usually the person indicates clearly when a feed has gone too far, which didn't happen with Tanith, did it?"

"How do they do this?"

"By sound or touch. It's an instinctual survival reflex people have. Tanith didn't give you any such indication?"

He thought hard. "No."

She nodded. "I think this is really a case of her decision being about her, not you. Just as the dating service people said. For whatever reason, Tanith appears to have withdrawn from what could have been a promising relationship. She may change her mind again. But you need to take care of yourself. In this case, it means, move on. Go on other dates. And don't hesitate to turn to me or Antoine or the other mentors with any questions that arise."

Though Gabe had hoped Mirella would come up with a way

for him to convince Tanith to see him again, what she said made good sense, even if he felt bereft.

In the guise of moving on, Gabe went out on dates with two other women. Jen Shafter had evidently been transformed into a vampire after a plastic surgery gone wrong. Though Gabe didn't judge books by their covers, in Jen Shafter's case the exterior paled in hideousness compared to the inner woman. She gave bloodsuckers a bad name.

The engineering student, Anna Leona, wanted to study the hemodynamics of his fangs. Not wanting to be anybody's case study, he declined and took her home early.

Gabe figured he might go down in history as the only male vamp to die of horniness.

Tanith had no difficulty resisting Dominique and Lilith's efforts to make other matches for her. Though she didn't admit the truth to them, she knew exactly who she wanted. Gabe. He haunted her thoughts and her dreams. Clearly, she hadn't managed to get vampires—well, him—out of her system with their one night together. Each night left her panting with loneliness, and she began to rethink her previous stance. Maybe she'd tried to accomplish too much too fast. Maybe one more night with him might do it.

With trembling fingers, she surrendered to her overwhelming impulse and picked up the phone to call him.

Chapter Five

Luckily, Gabe had already learned to fly, 'cause there was no other way he'd be able to get to Tanith's place fast enough once he heard her voice.

Don't blow it again, he repeated to himself as a mantra while he covered the short distance to her condo. Second chances were rare. He'd take his and run with it. In a matter of minutes, he was at her place and she was in his arms.

Not that he could figure what had gone wrong last time. His instincts had told him Tanith desired him as much as he desired her. Her phone call proved his instincts had been right.

The moment he saw her, Gabe felt like a pilgrim who'd caught a glimpse of the Promised Land. He started to speak, but she put a finger to his lips. He opened his mouth and sucked her finger in as she melted, shaking, into his embrace.

"What is it, Tanith? Why are you trembling?"

She looked so fierce and beautiful. "I don't want you in my life. I hate vampires." Her words came in a hot rush.

Though he didn't let go of her, he mentally recoiled. She remained molded to him in their embrace. "If you feel that way," he whispered, "why have you called me? Tanith, I'm a vampire. That won't ever change."

She laughed dryly, a sound close to tears. "Good question. Believe me, I've asked myself."

"And what did you answer?"

She leaned her face against his chest. "I didn't tell you much about my past."

He ran a thumb down the side of her face and pushed her hair back. "Tell me now."

"You want to know about me, even though this will be our last time together?"

"What do you mean? Are you leaving town?"

She shook her head. "Maybe I should, but no. Gabe, once dawn comes, we're history. Even if I have to have a chastity belt surgically attached."

Though he winced at the image, he refused to be discouraged. After all, she'd already said goodbye and changed her mind. It was a woman's prerogative, right? "I want to know everything about you, including why you're determined not to give us a chance. With the chemistry between us, I'm sure we can come to some understanding. Let's talk."

She snorted and he thought maybe he'd already said something to put her off, but then she led him to her couch and gestured for him to sit next to her. Thigh to thigh, feeling the warmth between them, he couldn't believe she'd stick to her threat. Though he'd spent years shying away from commitments, for this woman he felt ready to make pledges and promises. He knew, without a doubt, that being with her was completely right.

"It goes back to when I was ten. Ever since I snuck into my mother's stash of novels and read my first vampire romance, I've been fascinated with vampires. I didn't outgrow this fascination, the way I did others. I began to date in high school and transferred the fascination to regular guys until I saw an old DVD of Frank Langella in *Dracula*. Silly as it sounds, I became obsessed with vampire lovers. As an adult, I should be able to push those thoughts away. But I can't. No, I won't say *can't*. More like haven't been able to. Even though one of you brutally murdered a dear friend." She laughed. "That's why I became a cop, to make sure there are no more victims like Janelle. After her death, I began to despise your kind. Being a cop, I've seen lots more examples of vampire treachery first hand."

He frowned. "Can't you say the same about humans and other beings? From my experience, vampires don't have a monopoly on treachery."

"Yeah, but I can't cut myself off from the human race, not to mention humans are more evenly matched in their conflicts. What can an ordinary person do when her attacker has supernatural powers?"

He chose not to point out the holes in her logic, just continued to listen and try to plan his strategy to win her over.

"I figured I'd go out with a vampire once and get my stupid obsession out of my system."

He winced at her labeling their time together the result of a *stupid obsession.* "What happened with your plan?" He kept his voice low and level.

She shrugged and her mouth formed a grim line. "You happened. One night with you wasn't enough."

It amazed him that such a complex woman could be so blind to simple truth. "And you think a second night will be?" Of course, she took completely for granted that he'd be available for a second night and then walk away on command.

"It has to."

"I feel so used." He put a hand to his forehead in a damsel-in-distress gesture.

Tanith laughed. "Yeah, you big lug. Come here and let me use you some more."

He would go along with the bantering tone, at least for now. He scooped her up in his arms and, in true vampiric fashion, swept her off to her bedroom.

✧✧✧

Tanith clung to Gabe for dear life. Now that he was here and she'd confessed her obsession, she should have felt stupid and weak. To her surprise, she felt free and beautiful. Being with him had that effect on her. Vampiric hypnosis or—?

If he felt as horny as she did, and she suspected he did, she wouldn't have been surprised if they went right to slam-bam-thank-you-ma'am. After all, his massive erection was tenting up the fly of his black leather pants, making abundantly clear just how much he wanted her. She itched to get her hands all over his cock, to feel him surround her, to get him inside her. But Gabe hung back.

"First I want to touch you everywhere." He laid her down and her bed, then stretched out behind her and began to massage her back. Just the simple touch of his big, strong hands through the thin layer of her silk shirt nearly brought her to tears of relief.

"How about if we take your shirt off so I can massage deeper?"

"Okay."

She started to sit up to help remove the shirt, but he held her where she lay. "Let me," he whispered as he slid the cool silk off her, grinning appreciatively when he saw she hadn't bothered with a bra. At his light touch, her nipples pebbled and his erection throbbed. He was determined to impress her with his restraint and control, which grew more challenging by the minute. Maybe if she realized he was as able as she to walk away from what they had, she'd value their connection more and get over her objections to him. He moved his hands away from those tempting breasts.

Her neck, where she always held the most tension, had tightened into one massive hard knot. When he probed her there with his fingers, she gave up this small bit of her resistance.

He extended his massage over a wider area of her back and shoulders, as if he had some kind of radar, an unerring instinct for all the right places to touch. He alternated long smooth moves with deep, intense probes then he added butterfly kisses and nibbles.

Tanith moaned at the sheer sensuousness of the contact.

At last, Gabe moved his hands to Tanith's breasts, and she gasped. Wanting to show him how much his touch there pleased her, she slid closer to him, pressing the full length of her body against the erotic shelter of his taller frame. His erection, rock-hard under the leather of his pants, nudged invitingly against her ass. Her nipples budded even harder into the palms of his hands. "So beautiful and delicious," he whispered, his breath hot on the back of her neck. He kissed her.

"You feeling less tension?" he asked.

"Less and more," she murmured. He laughed.

"Here's to more of both kinds." With lightning vampire speed, he eased off her pants, reached between her legs and insinuated his hand into her mound, now warm and wet. Each move thrilled her heightened senses.

"How did you do that?" she panted.

"A woman of many facets, including curiosity. Ask me again later. I'm busy now." He proceeded to massage the oh-so-ready folds of her pussy. She released a pent-up breath and squeezed her thighs around his hand, at the same time moving her butt against his groin. How could he act as if he had all the time in the world before he got into her? Much as she enjoyed his touch, her capacity for foreplay was shortening like a lit dynamite fuse with mere inches to go.

"Why are you still wearing your pants?" Was that breathless whisper hers?

She heard the rasp of a zipper. After a moment's separation, scarcely more than a blink of the eye, he whispered, "I'm not." Must have been more of those lightning-fast vampire moves.

By now, hard as a slab of granite, Gabe gritted his teeth to refrain from plunging into Tanith until she begged. He figured once he got inside her, his brain would melt and he'd lose the overriding thread of what he was doing. Somehow, he had to convince her there was too much between them for one or two nights of fun and games. "I don't want tonight to be the last time between us," he rasped as control begin to slip.

"Oh, Gabe," she groaned. "Why are you bringing this up now?"

"I figure I have your full attention." He gritted his teeth.

"You do. You have that all the time."

She had to be honest with him—and herself—or they'd have no chance. "I want to know you can tell the difference between me and some abstract image of vampires."

"I can," she wheezed. "And, I admire your powers of persuasion."

He pressed himself against her ass, his hard dick wedged tightly into her crease. "Find me irresistible, do you?"

She was thrashing from side to side, and she seemed to lean with deliberation against his aching cock. "I want you. Now."

He was holding on to his resistance by his fingernails. "About seeing me again after tonight?" His voice choked.

"Get in me now." Her voice sounded icy and hot at the same time.

He quickly weighed the options. If he held back, she might agree to future meetings. She was so vulnerable to emotional blackmail at this moment. He groaned. Much as he wanted her, he couldn't take advantage of her that way. In addition to principles he couldn't ignore, his huge desire and her erotic response made short work of his resistance. With a shudder of relief, he slipped his cock between her thighs and thrust himself deep into her.

With a gasp, she wriggled herself back until there was no space between them. Though aroused beyond the point where thought remained possible, with his last scrap of will Gabe managed to force himself to be slow. He controlled the movement of his hips as he glided rather than bucked inside her hot silkiness.

Tanith moaned and ground the muscular, smooth cheeks of her ass against him. His fingers played with her clit and her slick softness, as his dick slid in and out of her. "Oh, Gabe," she groaned. She rotated her hips, and he gave himself over to the pleasure of her sensuous nature. When his fangs tingled with unfulfilled lust, he scraped them gently as he could along the back of her neck.

She sizzled, panted and whimpered his name. Gabe nibbled a path down her delicious back, running his tongue along the column of vertebrae. Her intimate muscles tightened around him, caressing him in an erotic massage. She pressed his hand tighter against herself, and her movements began to grow wider, deeper and more frenetic. He could feel everything in her tighten as her body prepared to climax. Determined not to come until she did, he continued leading her where he sensed she yearned to go. Teasing her clit with his thumb, he coordinated the pressure with the rhythm of her breath.

One moment later, Tanith tightened and shuddered. She came in a rush, with a whimper of surrender. Exercising great effort, he clamped his mouth shut over his fangs. He'd have her that way too, but not yet.

Still hard when she subsided, he withdrew. She shifted down from her side and reached back to stroke him, but he withdrew from her reach, moved her so she once again lay on her side and slid his lips down her butt crease to kiss her rosebud of a hole. She gasped at the first touch of his lips and he froze for a moment. Then she pressed back against him and, without words, told him she wanted him there. With great control, he scraped his fangs along the tender flesh of her cheeks and tongued her, lingering over the opening again. His cock pulsed hard, and he knew he couldn't hold out much longer.

When he wedged himself into Tanith's crease, his near-to-exploding erection got impossibly harder. Gently, he replaced his tongue with the head of his cock.

Rhythmically stroking her mound, Gabe slowly entered Tanith. Though she was so well lubricated from his kisses that he could have penetrated her much faster, he wanted to savor every moment, and he wanted it to be good for her. Moaning softly, she pushed back against him so the soft skin of her cheeks brushed his thighs and hips. He bit down on his lip as the tight feel of this woman, her silkiness and her scent of musk and vanilla overwhelmed his senses. The room began to pulse around him in a blur of colors and sounds and sights. He sank into the wonder of being inside her, his cock alive with the sensation of tight, hot contact. Tanith rode his fingers as he caressed her clit and folds, inviting him to touch her harder, deeper.

As his excitement built and surrounded him, Gabe never lost his acute awareness of her reactions. When he began to move faster, he made sure she was staying with him, stroke for stroke. They were together as he ascended the ladder of erotic sensation. With a groan and a shudder, he came at last. She was right there with him for the aftershocks and afterglow. When the wonder of their lovemaking began to subside, he slid his lips down her spine, back up to the nape for a magical kiss.

But his ecstasy remained incomplete because he needed to feed with an urgency he could no longer ignore. As she dozed, he turned her to him, just enough to get at the delicate base of her neck. All warm and cozy where they touched, Tanith continued to smile in her half-sleep as he plunged his fangs into her. Just a little. He'd drink a bit now so he could satisfy his hunger for her later. After he healed her wound, she stirred. Spoon fashion, he positioned himself behind her, his head buried against her back. For the first time since they'd last been together, he was at peace. She couldn't make this be their last time together. No way could she ever again deny the power of the chemistry between them.

Tanith awoke with the most intense craving for hot

chocolate. Okay, her craving for the sweet drink didn't begin to match the power of her craving for Gabe. She couldn't offer him any refreshments. Except herself. For some reason she couldn't have explained, the knowledge that he'd fed off her didn't creep her out. In fact, it made her feel proud. Weird. Must have been part of the so-called vampiric charm.

The moment she slipped out of the bed, he rose, completely alert. "Where are you going?"

She told him what she wanted.

"I'll keep you company."

She threw on her ratty old white terrycloth robe. He pulled on his black leather pants. Geez, he looked fantastic, sexy. She feasted on his amazing appearance, his chest and arms exposed in the dim light of her condo.

He stood over her, watching, as she nuked a mug of water, mixed in instant powder and topped the drink with miniature marshmallows. "Did you drink hot chocolate before—?"

He shook his head. "I was never big on chocolate or hot drinks."

Realizing how little she actually knew about him, she wanted to know—then and there—about his life before the transformation. What had he been like? If she'd met him then, would they have hit it off? What difference did it make? After all, he could never again be human.

She took a big, unthinking swallow, scalded her tongue and put the mug down hard.

"What's wrong?"

She stuck out her tongue. "Too hot."

"I can fix that." He gave her a searing tongue kiss that made the scald feel lukewarm. When he released her and she began to breathe again, her tongue felt fine.

"How'd you do that?"

"Secrets of the vampires." He cocked an eyebrow and looked cryptic.

"Yeah, right." More careful now, she sipped the rest of her hot chocolate.

"I've never shown you around my condo," she said. "Not that there's much here."

"I'd love a tour."

She indicated the space around them. "This, in case you

didn't realize it, is the kitchen. More accurately described in real estate circles as a 'kitchenette'."

"You mean because it's so small."

She nodded and smiled. "My friends who are into cooking roll their eyes in mock horror when they check out the facility. Personally, I'm into takeout." She opened a drawer crammed with menus.

"Me too." They both laughed at that.

She took his hand and walked him to the next spot on their tour. "Small but adequate bathroom."

He took a fast look around. "Perfect. I see you have a bidet."

"Pretty extravagant. It's what sold me on this place."

"I'd love to use it."

After a quick stop at the bidet, they opted for a long, long, hot shower—replete with fragrant soaps they used to great advantage.

Much later, the tour continued. "The living room. It's small, too, but I'm lucky to have an affordable place here in the city. A lot of my friends either have roommates or rent rooms in other people's houses."

"It's great. I see you have a lot of books. What are all those certificates on the wall?"

She blushed. She always thought displaying all her stuff made her look like a show-off. On the other hand, she was proud. "Just some different awards from work."

To her embarrassment, he read each and every one. Was it her imagination or did he start to distance himself right then? Of course, she should feel happy if he distanced himself. That was what she wanted—distance from him—right? So why did her heartbeat get all funny at the prospect?

According to the certificates he read, not only did Tanith take her policing seriously, she was very good at it. But after what he'd learned investigating police corruption, Gabe viewed all police cynically—even an officer as sexy and appealing as she. Of course, he knew many officers were completely honest, and his gut told him Tanith was one of that number. But he was far from objective when it came to her, and he couldn't afford to let his guard slip.

"Nice place," he said.

"Where do you live again?"

"Almost like a dorm. I'm with a group of vampires, some new guys and some old ones who are teaching us the ropes."

Her mouth curled with what he interpreted as disapproval, maybe disgust. It might not have been the Ritz, but he'd have been up shit creek without the halfway house the past few weeks.

"How long are you going to stay there?"

"Until I get my own place."

"When will that be?"

He shrugged. "Haven't made those plans yet. There's still so much I need to learn about—"

"Where did you live before? Why don't you go back there? Are you from San Francisco or did you only come here after you became a vampire?" She narrowed her eyes.

Damn, too many questions. He could see why she was a successful detective. But he hadn't decided how much he wanted to tell her. Luckily, he had a sure-fire way to redirect her attention. "Doesn't this tour include your bedroom?" He planted his hands on her butt.

"I thought you'd never ask," she purred. "Right this way."

In moments, he had the robe off her and he'd stepped out of his pants. In the lamp's soft glow, she could really look at him, feast her eyes. He stood half in light half in shadow, his muscles taut and his cock erect. She wished she were a sculptor and could capture his perfection in stone. But having him in the flesh trumped that, for as long as it lasted.

"Looking is fun, but touching is better." He closed the short distance between them. With his arms around her, he slid down until he knelt on the floor before her. "Tell me your fantasy, lovely lady."

Everything they were doing together was her fantasy.

No, her real fantasy would be for this night to go on and on. If only dawn wouldn't come to pull them apart. If only they could change the reality of who they were.

Instead of putting these wisps of thoughts into words, she held his face to the softness of her belly. He kissed her, long and hard, licking her skin, raising goose bumps even before he lowered his mouth to her waiting pussy.

"You are so amazingly beautiful," he whispered. "Is this part of your fantasy?" His lips closed over her in the most intimate of kisses.

Speechless, Tanith let her body speak for her. The way they both were moving—as if they'd fallen into a perfect rhythm, neither making a false move—exceeded her fantasies. Her feminine core pulsed like a heartbeat, completely in sync with his lips, tongue and teeth.

The scrape of his fangs there should have frightened her, but she trusted without any hesitation that he wouldn't hurt her. The light touch of his sharp teeth heightened her arousal. "I want to feel your fangs in me," she murmured.

He stopped suddenly and peered at her, wary. The sudden stop shocked her. "I don't know about that. I don't want to hurt you..."

Wanting to prove her point, she slithered down and got her lips around his huge erection, which she covered with love bites.

"You want me to bite you like that?" His voice cracked on the last word.

Her mouth full, she nodded.

But he was too close to coming. "I've got to get into you," he whispered, nuzzling her.

After laving his cock with a lick that nearly sent him to the ceiling, she gave him a provocative wink. Gabe lay her down on the bed and covered her with his body. He savored every point of contact, every place where their skin came together, where their essences mingled.

When his cock lay poised to open her, he felt her encircle his hips with her long, luscious legs and draw him close. In a blink, they were connected. Deep within her, his shaft throbbed. He had to move, had to touch every spot inside her, had to lay claim to her in this most intimate way. With each move, their sensuous universe shifted.

She had her fingers in his hair, holding his head to her. "Is this what you want?" he asked, but the words were unnecessary. He felt so completely bonded with her, he knew she would answer yes. Was he reading her mind or were they just incredibly in sync?

"Yes," she whispered, then contracted her erotic sheath in a caress that nearly sent him flying. "Yes, oh yes."

The familiarity of her touch did nothing to diminish the sexy surprise and pleasure of each contact.

They knew each other so thoroughly—and yet they didn't. It might have been a cliché for a man to seize on the "L" word when his cock was buried deep inside his lady, but he didn't care. For the first time ever, the word "love" expressed what he felt. He whispered the essential words. "I love you."

"Oh, Gabe," she moaned. "It's not supposed to happen like this."

What wasn't supposed to happen? He didn't ask because he didn't want anything to impinge on the unique beauty of the moment.

He poured all he had and all he was into their lovemaking, all he could ever hope for.

And she answered him back, stroke for stroke. She whispered the deepest, sweetest secrets of her body and soul with the glide of her intimate warmth around him, the divine friction of her touch.

"I want this to last forever," he confessed.

"Too much," she gasped, and he didn't know if she meant what he'd said or the new level of passion between them.

"I can't," she whimpered, "not now." Her movements became wilder, larger, faster, harder, drawing him into her frenzy.

In contrast to her softness, she sucked him in with such power that he could imagine they'd never be able to break the bond. "I can't," she repeated again and again with rising intonation, in a mantra of complete surrender—and desperation.

Soon, his control would be gone as Tanith's frenetic dance carried him with her. He rode her now, hard, holding nothing back, clenching his teeth to keep from shattering.

"Gabe!" She cried his name as the pulses of her climax rocked him, rocked them both.

With a howl that rose from his gut, Gabe let it all go. He exploded with sound and light, heat and ecstatic release. Then he lowered his mouth to her neck and fed, providing them both with the final jolt of a mutual orgasm.

Mind, body, spirit and soul-blowing—words couldn't express what she'd experienced. Tanith felt like she'd just taken part in an out-of-body ecstasy, except she was totally in her body. Great. What she'd wanted was to get Gabe out of her system. But how could she ever let go of him when he'd taken her to the mountaintop and given her wings to fly?

She had to listen to her inner voice, the tiny reminder of rationality. No doubt he was exercising some form of vampire voodoo to reduce her to a small quivering bundle of nerve endings. Like she was a walking, talking clit. But no analysis, not now. Now she just wanted to float on the glow of being with him, locked in an intimacy that nearly had her in tears. Tanith Marie Kalinski never cried.

She'd just let herself drift, savor the way his skin and hair felt to her fingertips, the warm touch of his legs between hers. Soon, all too soon, it would be dawn. Then she'd boot him out of her bed—and her life.

"I feel so close to you." His exhaled breath raised goose bumps on her skin.

"Me too," she admitted. Just for the space of the night, she'd let herself say and do anything she wanted to.

"Kind of ironic you being a cop with so many awards and all."

Despite the haze she was floating in, his words raised an alarm. Ever so slightly, she shifted away from him. "What do you mean?" Her being a cop was too sacred to fool around with.

Gabe's words seemed to come from somewhere deep inside. "You asked how I became a vampire. I didn't want to tell you because I didn't know how you'd take it."

Mentally, she prepared herself to hear something she didn't want to. "Go on." She was starting to have a sick feeling in the pit of her belly.

"I wasn't going to tell you yet. But tonight I feel so close with you, closer than I ever have with anyone else. And I don't want anything this important to remain a secret." He stroked her side, and she committed every touch of his fingers to memory.

"Whew! With a build-up like that, I'm starting to feel

nervous."

He frowned. "I might as well begin. You see, before I became a vampire, I was an investigative journalist. I was at San Quentin with my colleague, interviewing an informant about police corruption when—"

A shock ran through her. "Tommy Lerner. You were with Tommy Lerner at San Quentin when he was shot?"

He looked at her in disbelief. "You knew Tom Lerner?" His eyes narrowed. "Did he interview you for our investigation?"

Revolted that he could suspect her of being one of the subjects of the corruption investigation, she drew back. "Tommy was married to my best friend, Sue Lerner. I was with her when she learned of his death. How come he died at the scene and you didn't?"

Gabe's mouth twisted. "All I know is there was one vampire on duty in that part of San Quentin that night, and he found me in time to transform me. From what I've heard, the others were too far gone."

Tanith shook her head. Knowing Tommy might have been saved, but Gabe was the one to walk away... Of course "saved" was a questionable word to use in this context. Would Sue and the children have found it possible to accept Tommy if he'd been turned into a vampire? They'd never know—they'd never had the chance to try. If she'd been the vampire on the scene, whom would she have chosen to save? She shuddered at trying to imagine herself as a vampire. These were futile questions, ones it would be senseless to grapple with.

"Tom crossed all sorts of lines for our work, we both did, which netted us death threats. Crossing one of those lines brought the gunman to our interview that night, I'm positive."

"How did anyone smuggle a gun into San Quentin?" She couldn't get her mind around what had happened.

He peered hard at her. "Excellent question, one I can't answer. A friend has suggested that maybe the time has come to pick up the investigation where it so abruptly ended. Hell, what else can I lose?"

She shivered at how cold his voice had become. "That's a dangerous attitude."

"Your friendship with Tom's wife wouldn't have eliminated you from a potential suspects' list." Gabe's eyes glittered with an intense emotion that had nothing to do with their lovemaking. "Did he ever interview you?"

"I thought he interviewed only corrupt cops."

"No, he talked with lots of cops. What you said was a misperception."

"Tommy himself told me he'd had to narrow the scope to those whom suspected."

"I worked with him, so I know otherwise. But given what you say he told you, I repeat my earlier question," he muttered.

Pain stabbed deep in her gut. "You've seen the certificates on my wall. You know what being a cop means to me. How could you even ask such a question?"

"Let's just say my work turned me cynical. As in, you wouldn't believe how many corrupt cops have walls full of framed citations."

She sprang to her feet. "You just made it easy. Get out and never come back."

He grabbed his clothes, threw them on and, without a word, did exactly as she asked.

Fortunately, Tanith was able to swallow back her tears of anger and grief until after she'd slammed the door behind him.

Chapter Six

When Gabe awoke and realized seeing Tanith would not be on the agenda that night or any other, his first instinct was to crawl back into his coffin. He squelched that idea pronto. What had possessed him to accuse Tanith of being a corrupt cop? After all, even in the course of his research for the series, he had also met honest cops, lots of them. His gut told him she was completely honest. Why had he unleashed his cynicism and pain over Tom's death at her? Now, even if she allowed the sexual chemistry between them to seduce her, she'd keep her distance from him.

Though an annoying inner voice told him he could have avoided all his pain by keeping his mouth shut, he didn't regret his attempt at openness—just the way it ended. Maybe there were different rules for vampire relationships than for those between humans. Maybe he should ask a mentor.

No. It was up to him to find his way. He wanted to be in a relationship with Tanith, which meant being honest about who he was and what he did. As confused and confusing as she was, he knew she wasn't lying about her work. Maybe she was hiding from herself about her desire to be with him, but that was another story.

Their painful scene reminded him how important his investigative work had been to him for a long time. Now that he'd made adjustments to his new condition, it was time for him to resume the work he and Tom Lerner had started. The first step would be to discover who'd been behind the attack at San Quentin.

His first instinct was to go back to the cops, and he had a perfect reason to start with Tanith. On the other hand, maybe he should start by separating the personal and the professional. There'd be time for both later.

After an hour of spinning his wheels his gut kicked in with a name: Mirella Proctor. Antoine had told him the woman had tons of connections—including with the criminal element in vampire society. The last leads Tom and he had uncovered, the ones they were following up in San Quentin that night, hinted at a connection between several highly placed police officers and a vampire crime family. With Mirella's help, he could get his investigation restarted. Once he knew some answers, he'd kick start his career and be able to see justice done. Although the investigation of the murders in San Quentin was outside Tanith's scope, he thought she'd be interested in hearing the outcome.

Gabe dialed Mirella's number on the house phone. To his immense gratification, she agreed to meet with him later that week. In the meantime, he'd start getting organized to accomplish his goals—and take lots of cold showers.

Maybe her work would help keep her sane. Tanith, normally a workaholic, reported for her next shift determined to double her usual output.

But as she attacked a stack of paperwork, her mind wandered to Gabe. Remembering his insinuations, she stiffened and resolved to push him from her thoughts. She got a bit more work done and once again her mind wandered, so she gave in to temptation and Googled Gabe. In moments, his biographical information flashed before her. She quickly scanned the data about his age, residence, distinguishing marks, education and career. Columbia School of Journalism grad. After writing several prize-winning series on the East Coast, he'd moved to California for the series with Tommy Lerner just a year before. Both men had impressive records. If they'd been able to work together longer, she felt confident they could have been successful in their battle against corruption. No wonder they'd been targeted. Tanith trembled when she read that in the eyes of officialdom, Gabe Morrow was a dead man. Evidently, the vampire census was not up-to-date enough to include him.

He not only seemed more alive than any other man she'd

ever known, he made her feel more alive than she'd ever felt before. How weird was that? Just thinking of him made her panties go damp with remembered desire. Acute awareness that she was a responsible professional at work didn't stop the heat generated by memory.

Her mind had to be playing tricks on her. He couldn't possibly have been as fabulous as her memory insisted. But none of this self-talk sufficed to distract her from her erotic hunger.

She'd always remember the sensuousness he awoke in her, the ecstasy of their climaxes. The feel of his touch, skimming her, pressing her most sensitive places. The sensation of his cock deep in her, the movements of his hips. His lips claiming hers. The strange elegance of his teeth on her, in her, sucking from her.

Her clit actually throbbed. Tanith blushed and crossed her legs, hard and tight. Thank God she'd learned to keep a poker face.

It was a very good thing she'd be going to Sue's tonight. Tomorrow, she'd call Fangly, My Dear again. Maybe she should reconsider and go out with another vamp. This time, she'd keep her eye firmly on the goal of working those creatures out of her system. She wouldn't let herself fall in lo—. She had to get that idea out of her head real fast.

In the meantime, she would do whatever it took to keep from calling Gabe, starting with buying a jumbo package of batteries for Clyde, her reliable vibrator.

Over the next few days, working long hours and not getting to bed until she was nearly falling off her feet, Tanith had no problem going to sleep. If only she could control her dreams and banish Gabe from them as effectively as she had from her waking life. She couldn't. She awoke sweating, hot, turned on, bereft and shaking with the force of her need...

Tanith turned down the next two matches Fangly, My Dear offered her. Maybe, she told herself, she was no longer in the frame of mind to be matched up. Maybe she needed to take a break from any social life and give herself time to get over Gabe.

Mirella Proctor was not a woman to be rushed. After they toasted each other with AB negative and drank the rare treat, Gabe wanted to start his investigative work. But she wanted to talk more. "Tell me about this woman who's so clearly gotten to you."

Gabe had never been one to talk about one woman with another, but she waved his concerns aside. "Nothing I enjoy better than hearing a great love story. Even if it's not my own."

In a few words, he answered the question and told Mirella about Tanith—especially how she made him feel.

Mirella took it all in. "Sounds beautiful and rare. What can I do for the two of you, who appear to have so much together already?"

Then he told her about the conflict with Tanith, her contempt for him, the angry words they'd left between them when he'd expressed his cynicism.

"Hmm. So how can I help?"

"I plan to solve Tom's murder and restart my investigative series. Tanith will be impressed, but that's only part of my motivation. First of all, I want to see the people responsible for Tom's death punished."

"How can I help?"

"I understand you know people at every level of vampire society, even our San Francisco crime family. If you could help me navigate around them, maybe put me in touch with informants, I'm sure it would help me get to the bottom of what happened."

"You don't ask for much, do you?"

Had he pushed too hard too soon? No doubt Mirella wouldn't lose any time putting him in his place. He started to fill the silence, when she held up a hand.

"I can put you in contact with some of those people, though it can get complicated. You see, they're not always willing to talk to new people."

He nodded. "That's why I figured I'd need to ask for a guide. You're the woman."

She laughed. "I'll do what I can. Seeing how far you're willing to go, I realize this Tanith Kalinski must be a very special lady."

"Takes one to know one. But, aside from the impress-

Tanith angle, I want to restart my work. Picking up at the murder is the perfect opening."

Mirella arose. "When do you want to get started?"

"Yesterday."

"You know, it might really be easier for you to get your work done if you move in here."

Gabe was about to turn her down again when he realized there was no good reason for him not to move in. Truth was, he was growing tired of the halfway house. Though he'd prefer to get a place of his own, for now Mirella's penthouse was a far-from-shabby alternative.

"Okay. And, Mirella, thank you."

By dawn, he'd moved in.

The next night, Gabe got right to work. First, he figured he'd study the dossiers on the people he'd be dealing with when he connected with the vampire crime family.

"What are you planning to do?" Mirella asked when he'd ensconced himself in front of a monitor.

He told her.

"I hate to interfere with your work, but I have a small favor to ask."

Considering how much he owed her, he immediately said yes.

"I need to make an appearance at a function tonight. The California branch of the United Vampires Leadership is having a banquet. I'm up to receive an award, and, because of the presence of someone I'd prefer not to identify, I don't want to show up unescorted."

No-brainer. "My pleasure. The only thing is, I don't have any clothes that wouldn't embarrass you."

She waved her beautiful hands dismissively. "I have a friend who owns a high-end men's shop. Tell me your measurements. In an hour, he'll deliver an Armani tux tailored to your specifications."

Gabe told Mirella the relevant information. "What time do you want to leave?"

"The driver will come for us at one thirty," Mirella said. "If you'll excuse me, I need to get gorgeous."

"You already are."

Laughing, she left him to his work. It was ten o'clock now. That gave him three plus hours. Gabe thought with a pang about Tanith. He'd resolved that he wouldn't get in touch with her until he'd made impressive progress. His cock twitched in sympathy. He gritted his teeth.

Right on schedule, the doorbell rang. Mirella's friend was there to deliver the tux. Gabe got some work done, less than he'd wanted but a start, before he went to dress up. He was glad for this chance to thank Mirella. Heck, he might even enjoy tonight's shindig now that he'd taken the first steps to reconnect with his work—and with Tanith.

Tanith missed Gabe, and that was just too damn bad. She'd have to get used to it. In the meantime, she volunteered to work extra hours, glad for anything to occupy the endless hours until she could move on.

Several nights later, in her ongoing effort to resist Gabe, she stayed in her office extra late. At half past one, when dispatch called for a detective to investigate a suspected murder in a posh club, she was almost grateful for the distraction. It happened that her partner Don Allen was there, too.

Enroute, they encountered a traffic tie-up. "What's going on at this hour of the night?" she asked.

He scowled. "Would you believe there's a big vampire affair?"

Would she ever be able to hear the words "vampire" and "affair" without thinking of Gabe? "What kind of affair?"

He shrugged. "Some bigwigs from out of town. I can't believe the vampire scum actually had the nerve to request police protection."

"Did they get it?"

"Are you kidding? Even if our budget wasn't tight, the brass wouldn't assign cops to the likes of them. After the chief said no, I hear they hired some rent-a-cops. Fat lot of good they'd do if any trouble came."

She nodded. None of this had anything to do with her or Gabe.

They made their way slowly through the throng of limos the

vamps appeared to favor.

"Filthy fuckin' bloodsuckers," Allen mumbled.

She muttered something noncommittal.

When she turned her head, she spotted Gabe exiting a huge black stretch limo, wearing an elegant tux and looking breathtakingly gorgeous. Tanith's heart lurched and a jolt of desire rocked her. His smile dazzled her, though it wasn't directed at her. Why did he look so happy, so completely together? Damn, she wanted to stop the car and jump out. Claim him. *Mine.*

That would have gone over real big.

He wasn't alone. Far from it. On his arm, looking enamored and fascinated, was a beautifully groomed and polished older woman wearing a gown—Givenchy or some other French designer.

So even if Tanith hadn't been there for professional reasons, she wouldn't have been able to grab Gabe. He was obviously already taken.

It sure hadn't taken him long to find someone new.

When she and her partner finally got to the crime scene, Tanith tried to focus. She knew how vital the first few hours were for solving any crime, and she despised cold cases.

But no matter what she did, she couldn't shake the image of Gabe and that woman. Tanith had to ask everyone to repeat themselves. She nearly overlooked a crucial clue and acted like a bumbling amateur, the kind of detective she usually had nothing but contempt for. Grrr. It was all Gabe's fault.

Right. Of course, the only reason why he'd turned to another woman was because she'd booted him out. She'd driven him right to the arms of that filthy rich, older woman.

Geez. If Tanith didn't stop, she'd make herself crazy—and, along the way, blow this case. If all those award presenters could see her now, there'd be no certificates.

Using all the force of her will, Tanith focused on gathering every scrap of information from the scene—and getting it right. Only after every clue had been processed, the body removed and the scene taped off did she leave. Don had hitched a ride back to the station earlier and left the car for her.

As she passed the club hosting the vampire affair, she couldn't help noticing the full complement of vehicles was still there. Against her better judgment, she decided to wait in front until the vampires came out. She looked at her watch and realized they wouldn't be staying too much longer. In two or three hours, it would be dawn.

A tiny inner voice of reason protested that she should really go home and try to get some rest. But a competing instinct reminded her she had almost no chance of getting any sleep. The image of Gabe and that woman would haunt her if she closed her eyes.

Tanith—cramped, cold and in need of a potty—regretted the obsession that kept her rooted to the spot. She couldn't have explained why she lingered there. Was it just to glimpse Gabe and the woman once more? What earthly good would that do? Maybe he would come out alone, his "date" with an escort more appropriate for a woman of her advanced years. Or maybe he and the unsuitable woman would still be together. In which case, though Tanith wasn't proud to admit it, she would follow them to see where they went.

Tanith had almost convinced herself to leave when Gabe, with the same senior citizen draped on his arm, came out. The two of them got into the black stretch limo and headed off. After the limo stopped at a posh condo, he helped his date out and accompanied her into the building.

Now in physical and emotional agony, Tanith would have followed them in, but a fierce-looking doorman stopped her. Not even San Francisco's finest could enter such a building at this hour of the night without a damned good reason.

Exhausted and discouraged, she dragged her tail home. She might as well face it. Gabe Morrow was well and truly gone, and she had no one to blame but herself. Though her logical self said she should be happy he'd moved on and do the same herself, her heart disagreed.

Chapter Seven

After several nights of solid work, Gabe allowed himself to feel cautious optimism. He was beginning to understand the local crime families—vampire and other—and he saw a pattern of police collusion with those families that appeared to lead to the San Quentin incident. Though it might have been premature, he figured he had enough information to justify contacting Tanith for advice on how to proceed.

"My information might help us catch the perp responsible for the shooting that night at San Quentin," he announced when she answered his call. "I'd like to pick your brain on what to do next."

"Who the hell is this?" She sounded haggard.

All right, not the reaction he'd been hoping for. Could she really have forgotten his voice already? "Gabe."

Her laugh sounded harsh, almost tinny. "What makes you think I, potentially corrupt cop that you accused me of being, am going to help you?"

"I didn't exactly accuse you. I'm sorry for the misunderstanding. I know you're not corrupt." He gritted his teeth and continued. "I figured you'd want to know my progress and also help solve Tom Lerner's murder."

"Do you really have information, or is this just another bullshit attempt to get me to date you?"

He stared at the phone. His attempts to solve the crime were not a smokescreen for anything else. On the other hand, he wouldn't say no to a chance to be with her again. "I'd like to see you again to show you the evidence of collusion. Also to find out how you think I should proceed."

"Do you know who actually shot you and Tommy?"

"Not yet. But I'm closing in on it. Meanwhile, I have several leads that I need to develop."

"Any cop can tell you how to proceed. That is provided you trust any of us."

"I trust you already."

"It sure didn't sound like it when you told me how many rotten cops have citations decorating their walls."

He winced, hearing her pain. "I'm sorry. Please accept my apology. I was out of line. I never wanted my work to turn me cynical about good cops. There was no reason to splatter you with the dirt my investigation turned up."

"Right. Thanks for that. I really have to go."

This conversation was not what he'd envisioned. "Please see me and at least let me tell you about my evidence. Tell me if I'm on the right track to bring Tom Lerner's killer to justice." He'd just played his trump card. If she could resist solving that murder, all was lost.

She exhaled. "Fine. Fax me what you have, and I'll get back to you."

He stared at the phone. "There's no way to be sure who might get access to a fax before you do. This information is for your eyes only right now."

"A little paranoid there?"

"Look what happened in the middle of Tom's and my investigation."

"Okay. Against my better judgment, I'll meet you at the Starbucks around the corner from my place in half an hour. I can give you fifteen minutes."

Fifteen minutes? Generous of her. "I'll talk fast. See you there."

She'd already hung up. Luckily, Gabe had printed out the data. He organized it in a folder and raced off to meet Tanith. He'd better not blow this chance.

The tingle traveled up from Tanith's clit and took residence in her brain. She willed herself to be strong, firm, even harsh. So she was going to see Gabe in less than half an hour. So her panties grew moist at the thought. She was in charge of her life and, dammit, her libido. She was not about to let him get to her. Besides, he'd clearly moved on and had a new woman in his life.

What kind of evidence could he possibly have discovered? She'd spent a lot of her free time pursuing leads and had come up with nothing solid. She seriously doubted he'd done any better, but he'd appealed to her on a professional level. In the past, she'd met with less reliable informants than Gabe Morrow. This was business, not a date, so she refused to pay any special attention to her appearance. Jeans and a sweatshirt, no makeup, her hair in a scraggly ponytail. Just to ensure she wouldn't bring the sexy vampire home, on the outside chance he even wanted to be with her, she didn't straighten up her messy condo.

He was at a table reading by the time she arrived at Starbucks. She bought herself a grande mocha latte and sashayed over. With great deliberation, she ignored how incredible he looked, how he made her pulse jump and her pussy throb with need and desire. Casual, she reminded herself. This is a casual meeting.

Gabe looked up and smiled when she got close. Her insides clenched with such hunger she nearly gasped. She would not let him get to her. She repeated this mantra, which did little to help.

He stood and came around the table to pull out a chair. Didn't he know nobody did shit like that anymore? Then to compound his unfair assault on her senses, he took the drink from her, set it down and kissed her hand. Her icy internal armor began to melt. Perched on the chair opposite him, she gritted her teeth and amped up her resolve to stay cool and professional.

He locked eyes with her, and she hoped she'd managed to veil her emotions from his piercing gaze.

"Thank you so much for meeting with me," he said so softly she had to lean closer to catch his words.

She gestured to the drink. "I'll stay just long enough to finish this. Fifteen minutes."

"You must be a fast drinker."

She held up her wristwatch. "Fourteen left. After that, I don't care what excuse you give for calling me. I will not see you again. Is that understood? I want everything clear before we begin."

"You drive a hard bargain, but you're calling the shots." To her surprise and disappointment, he nodded. "I accept."

The image of him with his sugar mama, if that term existed, flashed before Tanith's eyes. Maybe he really wasn't interested in her except professionally. It's what she wanted, and she'd live with it. Somehow.

Incredibly, Tanith looked even more beautiful and enticing than he'd remembered. The moment she came into the Starbucks, when she headed straight for the counter and ignored him, he'd grown hard with desire and his fangs began to vibrate. He wanted her completely. But she appeared walled off from him. Somehow, in the short time she'd granted him, he'd have to change her mind.

Other more experienced vampires would know how to handle the situation better. In the future, he'd be able to hypnotize her into drinking the latte with infinite slowness. But he didn't know all those tricks yet. He'd decided to work on turning to mist before he got into heavy mind bending. As soon as he had the misting down pat, he'd perfect hypnotic spells. Right now, he wasn't sure he'd learn this skill in time to salvage any relationship possibility with Tanith.

On the other hand, maybe that was all for the best. He didn't want to rely on tricks—just the honesty of his feelings.

"What did you find that's different from what we knew before?" Tanith's professional manner contrasted sharply with her casual appearance.

He summarized what he'd learned about San Francisco's crime families.

Her brows shot up. "How did you get that kind of information?"

"Through a new friend."

"A friend? Who?"

"A wonderful woman named Mirella Proctor. She's got connections everywhere, and she's been willing to let me tap into them."

Tanith's brows furrowed together. "Mirella Proctor?" She

appeared to think for a moment. "Is that the older woman who was hanging all over you last night at Club X?" Her voice rose.

Damn. How had Tanith seen him and Mirella when they went to the awards banquet? "Older woman? I don't think of Mirella in terms of age. She's a good friend."

She snorted. "How good? Does she know you're here with me?"

"Yes, as a matter of fact she does. She agreed it's the perfect next step. You see, she's doing all she can to help me."

Tanith's eyelids fluttered several times, a nervous tic he hadn't seen before. "Why does she want to help you? And what does that help include?"

Her anger and jealousy hit him like a shock wave. "How did you happen to see us at Club X? We got there pretty late."

She squirmed. "Police business. There was a murder very close by."

"I see. Mirella asked me to escort her. In light of her generosity, I figured that was a small way to thank her."

"How else are you accommodating her?" Her question dripped icicles.

Her question caught him off guard. She must care if she could be so—jealous.

Before he could come up with an answer, she shook her head. "I'm sorry. What I said was totally out of line."

So, she was capable of backing down. But Gabe hated seeing the pain on her face. "Mirella really is a friend. She mentors lots of new guys."

Tanith held up her hands and waved his comment away. "At this point, the best way to follow up your leads is with the vampire squad of the police force. I can give you some names of contacts, but I've never worked with these guys. I imagine your Mirella Porter also knows people there." Her voice sounded flat.

"Proctor. Mirella Proctor. I'll ask her, but I'll also take the names of your contacts."

She wrote the information on a piece of paper in her small spiral notebook, tore it out and handed it to him. Then she drained her cup and glanced at her watch again. This time when she spoke, her voice sounded softer. "I really have to go."

Now or never. "I vowed I'd be completely honest with you tonight. I want to spend more time with you. Whatever there has been between us is still alive for me. I believe it is for you too."

A wary look came into her eyes. "We agreed this meeting was only about police matters."

Now he really regretted his lack of hypnotic gazes. "That was what we agreed. But as we're the ones who set this up, we can change our agreement. I realize how much I've missed you. How much I desire to be with you again." His voice grew hoarse on the last words. If his dick got any harder, it would explode. "Ah, hell, I've missed you so much. It's not something I just realized, and it's not something I'll get over."

She swallowed hard. "Won't Mirella Proctor get angry if she finds out her boy toy is with another woman?"

Her sarcasm set his teeth on edge. "We're very good friends, and that's all it is and all it ever will be. Friends don't dictate who their friends spend time with."

She studied him for several moments. He saw the exact moment when her anxiety gave way to relief. "You really mean it, don't you? There's nothing going on between you and this woman?"

"No. Hell, Tanith don't you know? There's no other woman for me but you."

She stood up abruptly. "If you really believe that, I'm sorry for you. I told you the ground rules for tonight. I'm sticking to them, and I expect you to. I don't know how I could have been clearer. There is no possibility of any relationship between us." She took a deep breath. "I'd love to hear what you find out when you pursue these leads. Seeing Tommy Lerner's murderer brought to justice would go a long way to helping Sue and her kids heal. God, I want to see the bastard fry. I'm only sorry the case is outside my jurisdiction. But aside from that, goodbye."

He rose. Before he could say a word, she'd turned on her heel and was hell-bent on getting to the exit.

Tanith's heartbeat sounded like a rapid drum solo. She half-expected people to turn around and stare as she raced to leave the Starbucks. If Gabe caught up with her and tried to get her to change her mind, she didn't know what she would do.

Hell, she wanted him so much she could scarcely move. It took every drop of fortitude and will she possessed to keep her walking away from him.

Once she got out the door and was sure he wasn't following, her knees buckled. She held on to the display window to keep from falling. Passersby were eying her strangely. Wouldn't it be a laugh if one of them called the police for help? For once, she hoped people would be too self-involved to reach out to someone in distress.

When she felt reasonably sure her legs would support her, she took off for home. If Gabe had come out of the Starbucks, she'd somehow missed seeing him. Why couldn't she stop thinking about him? Who cared whether or not he was still in the Starbucks?

As she walked, she reflected—always a dangerous game. She couldn't believe the emotional turmoil she'd been through since she'd met Gabe. Her mind skittered back to the night Tommy Lerner died, when Don Allen said her peers called her Detective Ice Princess and considered her devoid of emotions. If only. She didn't relish being on the roller coaster of feelings she'd been on since Tommy's death and her first date with Gabe. Funny how those two events seemed permanently linked in her mind. In a way, they were. If not for the crime that killed Tommy and left Gabe a vampire, she'd never have met him. Of course, if not for her stupid obsession with vampires, she'd also never have met him. She had to get off that roller coaster which meant really, permanently banishing him from her life. She'd taken the first positive step to doing that tonight. So why didn't it feel good?

All she needed was to exercise the strength everyone accused her of having. A little selective amnesia wouldn't hurt either.

Go after her, go after her. With every fiber of his being, every iota of his energy, Gabe hungered to stop Tanith from leaving him. Exerting a restraint that bordered on violent, he forced himself to let her go.

He wanted her, a yearning stronger than any he'd ever known. The need to be with her burned in him like a live ember that threatened to ignite and engulf him. He could overtake her, he could be with her. One more night. Hell, he could picture her stringing him along for an eternity of one more nights—after which she'd again reject him.

No. Though it killed him to stay away, the only way he'd ever be with her again was on his terms. She had to admit to him and to herself that she wanted him—for more than one night.

Chapter Eight

First thing the next morning, Tanith called Sue.

"Hello." Her friend sounded breathless, tired.

"Hey, babe, how's it going?" Tanith was never sure exactly what to say, what tone to take with Sue. She wished she had information about Tommy's killer to tell her, that Gabe's leads were strong enough to give them some hope. No sense getting her expectations up until they were closing in on the perp.

"I just miss him so much."

Tanith hated how powerless she felt to ease the other woman's pain. "I know you do," she murmured. "Anything I can do?"

Sue laughed mirthlessly. "Not unless you can raise the dead."

Tanith winced, wondering again if Sue would have wanted Tommy back as a vampire. Her mind flickered to the randomness of chance. How would Sue react to finding out about the truth about that night and meeting Gabe? "If I could, I would. How are the kids?"

"Doing about as well as can be expected. Better than me."

Inspiration struck. "How about if I come over tonight? We can order in pizza. If you want to get out for a bit, you could run some errands. I'll stay with the kids."

"That sounds good. The pizza part. And the kids would love to see you."

"You're on. I'll be there around six."

Good. She had a plan and a destination for tonight. Maybe she'd even stay over at Sue's. That would keep her from contacting Gabe, no matter how lonely or horny she became.

Despite her excellent intentions, Tanith got caught up in paperwork and ended up leaving the office far too late for dinner with Sue's kids. She phoned Sue to order take-out for them, her treat. She'd come over afterward for a late dinner with Sue.

Tanith got pizza and a bottle of Chianti on the way. The aroma of garlicky tomatoes, pepperoni and cheese filled her car. As she pulled up to Sue's house—she had to stop calling it "Sue and Tommy's"—she could have sworn she saw Gabe walking away. Hallucination. She shook her head to clear the image away.

But even thinking she'd glimpsed Gabe cranked up her heartbeat and respiration. She gripped the steering wheel and fought off the impulse to follow the hallucination. Maybe there actually *had* been someone who looked a lot like Gabe at Sue's. After all, he wasn't the only gorgeous dark-haired man in San Francisco. It would take just moments to catch up with him and learn the truth.

Sit, sit, sit, she commanded herself. She'd come to Sue's for a specific reason—to forget her own problems and help a friend whose situation was a million times worse.

She took a deep breath and resolved to act like a responsible adult. Loaded down with pizza and the Chianti, she rang the bell and braced herself. Last time she'd seen Sue, she'd looked haggard. But this time, to her amazement, Sue looked almost serene. Maybe she'd dipped into a cache of Valium or booze. She chided herself for her suspicious nature, an occupational hazard.

Sue stepped out onto the porch, hugged her and took the pizza and wine. "You must be starved."

"Yeah, I am." She followed Sue into her eat-in kitchen.

Sue had the table set. She sat down and cut them each a slice.

Tanith chewed her pizza and formulated her thoughts. "I have to ask. What's happened? For the first time since... Well, you look calm." She took a good swallow of wine.

Sue's eyes filled with tears, and she regretted her question. "I'm sorry."

Her friend waved away the apology. "It's okay. Cripes, I've been such a basket case for weeks now. But the most incredible thing happened earlier."

"Come on, give."

"A man who'd contacted me before came here and told me about being at San Quentin the day Tommy died." Sue choked.

"What man?"

"Gabe Morrow. He worked with Tommy on that last series."

Shit. "What did he want?"

"To offer sympathy and support." A faint spark of enthusiasm lit up her eyes.

"What do you mean by sympathy and support?" She tried to keep her misgivings from her voice. "And why?"

"Whew, why do you sound so hostile?"

"It's unusual for someone you don't know to show up out of the blue and offer you something without having an ulterior motive. What does he want?"

Sue shook her head. "You know, I wasn't exactly born yesterday."

Tanith raised a skeptical eyebrow.

Sue snorted. "Were you always so suspicious? Is that why you became a cop, or are you suspicious because you're a cop?"

"Chicken or the egg, huh? That's not the point, is it? So don't distract me. What does Gabe Morrow want?"

Sue nodded. "Okay, I'll try to tell you without tearing up." She put down her glass and took a deep quivery breath. "Though I'd never met him before, Gabe Morrow was Tommy's partner for the last series—"

"Maybe Tommy had a reason for not bringing him home." She couldn't refrain from interrupting.

"I think it was more a matter of keeping his work and his family life separate."

"Not a bad idea," she muttered through gritted teeth. "I don't understand why he came to you now." *So help me, if he's going to hurt Sue in any way, I'll personally put a stake through his heart.*

Sue took a bite of her pizza and chewed thoughtfully before responding. "Gabe wanted to tell me what the last hours were like. I appreciate knowing." She paused again, got teary, blew her nose. "What Gabe wanted to tell me was how brave Tommy was during all the investigations, how heroic right to the end." Sue began to weep. Tanith rose and put her arms around her friend.

"Don't torture yourself, honey."

"I'll be okay. I want to tell you the rest." She took a deep shuddery breath and patted Tanith's hand.

Her appetite gone, she returned to her chair. Though she wished they could change the subject, she encouraged Sue to continue.

"It's weird that Gabe survived. My understanding was everyone there died."

"That was my understanding too."

"But somehow Gabe managed to..." Sue shook her head.

"Too bad it wasn't Tommy." Tanith instantly regretted the thoughtless remark.

Sue turned aside, sniffled, wiped her tears away.

"I'm sorry. I shouldn't have said that."

"I don't want people to walk on eggshells around me. You can't be afraid some remark is going to hurt me."

"Thank you."

"If Tommy couldn't be the one to survive, I'm glad Gabe did. He's a real gentleman, you know? After he told me how brave Tommy was, he asked if our finances are okay and offered to help fix things around the house, whatever he can do."

"That's something all right." Even though she didn't want to admit it, Gabe's offer moved her. "How did you leave things with him?"

"He gave me his number, said I should call whenever."

"Do you intend to call him?"

"I don't know. I'm just so happy he took the trouble to come. Best of all, he plans to continue the series—including Tommy's byline in whatever he writes—and to bring Tommy's killer to justice."

Tanith considered bringing her friend fully up to date, but she hadn't yet found out all she wanted to about Gabe's interaction with Sue. "He didn't tell you, by any chance, how he managed to survive, did he?"

Sue looked so uncomfortable, Tanith once again regretted her impulse.

"No. What are you driving at? Is there something going on I'm just not getting?"

Leave it to her to disrupt Sue's calm mood. She couldn't see what Gabe could gain by helping Sue, and he certainly didn't appear to be planning to hurt her. Tanith needed to learn to keep her suspicions to herself. "Now who's being paranoid?"

Sue actually laughed. Not long or hard, but probably the first time since Tommy's death. "Well, enough about me. What's going on in your life?"

As if she'd be able to tell Sue any of details.

Why hadn't he thought of connecting with Sue Lerner before? Touching base with her made so much sense, Gabe regretted how much time he'd wasted. He was resolved to help Tom's widow however he could. Bringing the killer to justice would be a big step forward for all of them.

Well aware that Sue was Tanith's best friend, Gabe was determined not to use his contact with Sue to try to change Tanith's mind. He would win her on his own terms, unlikely as that appeared now.

At least the search for the perp was going well—better than he could have hoped. After conversations Mirella had set up—off-the-record chats with people who knew people—evidence pointed to the guard assigned to protect him and Tom Lerner, a man named Stan Corona. Gabe's mind skittered back to that night, and he remembered that Corona seemed to have disappeared. Strange, Gabe had felt his hackles rise the moment he met that man. Too bad he hadn't followed his instincts. Now his gut told him Corona either was their man or knew the identity of the perp. Next, Gabe would have to locate him and get the truth out of him.

He'd promised to share any new information with Tanith. Even though she was a highly skilled cop, Gabe's protective reflexes kicked in. He couldn't shake the feeling that Corona posed a danger to her. Maybe he should hold back telling her. On the other hand, if she found out he'd withheld information, she'd probably add it to her long list of grievances against him.

His cell phone rang. Not too many people knew the number yet. Maybe it was Tanith.

The moment she arrived home, she dialed Gabe's number. "Why did you contact my friend Sue?"

"I'm glad I finally had a chance to meet her. She's a great lady."

"If you hurt her..."

"What's with you, Tanith? Why would you even think that?"

"I'm just warning you."

"It's not necessary. I won't hurt her. In fact, I've got a credible lead on the perp."

She felt she was hearing him on a delayed broadcast. She was about to continue bawling him out when his words registered. "You know who—"

"Right. I assume you want to know."

"Tell me."

"In person for news this big."

She closed her eyes. She wanted him here with her as much as she wanted to know the name of the scum behind the crime. Well, bringing the perp to justice would be a form of closure. She'd see Gabe one more time, get the name, close the case and close the door on their being together.

"Come to my condo. Bring everything you've got about the perp."

"You're welcome," he muttered.

"Right. Good job. See you soon." She put down the phone and prepared herself for the last time she'd ever see Gabe Morrow.

When Tanith opened the door, she saw Gabe was carrying a small package. Though he looked more gorgeous than ever, there was something different about him, a new edginess. "What's in the package?"

Without a word, he took out a pair of handcuffs.

She took them from him and put them down on a table. "I use these at work, not after hours."

"Closed mind." He shook his head, walked past her and sat down on the couch.

He looked so damn good she wanted him to stay. She had to find a face-saving way to tell him that. "Actually, I'm glad you're here."

"Me and my handcuffs?"

She'd ignore that. "Tell me what you found out about the killing."

Some tension in him appeared to unknot. He sat back on the couch and crossed his legs. "Just like that? No drum roll?"

"I hate to burst your bubble, but your lead may not pan out. Tell me what you've got, and I'll make sure the right people follow through."

His mouth formed a straight, hard line. "I'm glad there's something you'll remember me for."

"What do you mean, remember you for? Are you going somewhere?"

He nodded. "Isn't that what you want—for me to be gone? Never to darken your door again? Plus I'm handing you the name of the perp."

Her heart pounded so loud, he had to be able to hear. "We're still not sure if you have the right guy, but I believe you if you consider your lead credible. As to the rest, of course. That's what I've told you all along." That was exactly what she wanted. Hearing him say it threw her.

"I figured I'd just beat you to the punch tonight. Maybe we get to have sex once more, as long as I'm here, right? Isn't that the game? One come each before you boot me out."

Tanith had never heard him sound so blunt. He rose from the couch, took her in his arms and put his face very close to hers. "You hate vampires but you want this one in your bed. I wanted more from you, but hey, I'm not that slow a learner. I finally get it. So let's go out with a bang. I figured I'd handcuff you so I can have you exactly where I want you for once. Then we can both move on." He seized her lips with his and took her breath away with a crushing kiss.

His eyes glittering dangerously, he backed away. "Take your clothes off. Now."

"No."

His laugh scalded her. "Want some foreplay? Want me to say sweet things to you? Well, I haven't got all night."

A strange mixture of excitement and dread filled her. Now that he mirrored back the way she'd been behaving with him, Tanith felt mortified. "Maybe you should just leave now. Right after you tell me the name of the perp."

"Stan Corona. The guard assigned to protect Tom and me at San Quentin. Isn't that rich?"

Her eyes fixed on him, she speed-dialed the cop in charge of the investigation into Tommy's death and relayed the information. Gabe nodded and walked to the door.

"Thank you. If he's really the one, Corona will pay for what he did. Thank you for bringing me his name and everything." She couldn't bring herself to say what she really felt, all that she wanted to tell him. Praying that he wouldn't leave, she opened the door.

He stood so close, his breath warmed her face as his eyes bored into her. "Without even one last fuck for old time's sake? I want you, Tanith. But I'll walk out the door if you say the word. And trust me, it will be the last time."

Her body practically screamed for the release she knew only with him. She held her head up high. "Wait." She hated her need for him, the weakness that came over her in his presence, but she couldn't fight it. She didn't want to fight it. "The last time." She licked her lips and shut the door.

He picked up the handcuffs like a trophy. "And we use these."

Nothing was going the way she wanted. "Fine. If you want, I'll cuff you."

His laugh sounded almost sinister. "Not on your life. Besides which, these don't work on vampires. We're too strong. Tonight, we're together on my terms. I cuff you."

His words made her quiver. "We can start with them, if that's what you want." Her voice went soft and seductive. She'd do a sexy strip, distract him from his weird mood.

Moving as if to the beat of some raunchy bump 'n' grind, Tanith slowly pulled off her T-shirt. The moment she uncovered one breast, her nipple beaded under his intense scrutiny. He ran his tongue over his lips, and Tanith knew soon it would soon be playing with that nipple—which grew painfully hard at the prospect. She fingered her breast, swayed her hips and slid her tongue over her dry lips.

Picking up her beat, he began to move his hips provocatively, teasing her with the hard bulge of his still-zippered cock.

Tanith's pussy creamed in response, and her clit began to

vibrate. With every cell of her being, she knew she'd climax in his arms soon.

He grabbed her ass and ground his erection against her in a sensuous rhythm. Sparks of pleasure shot from her core, and she wanted more.

Gabe captured her nipple in his lips and suckled hard. Tanith threw her head back and howled. His fangs lightly touched the tender skin of her breasts, unleashing shivers up and down her spine.

He scooped her up in his arms and ran with her to the bed. Before she'd blinked he had them both naked. His eyes gleaming, he reached for the cuffs. "On the bed, now," he ordered.

Too lost in desire to protest, Tanith got on the bed and took a spread-eagle position. She knew he could see the moisture glistening on her intimate folds. No matter how strangely he was acting, she wanted him. For some reason she couldn't have explained, she trusted him. He was the only man in the world she'd allow to cuff her.

Tanith's beautiful face reflected the many changes in her mood, the emotions animating her. Surprise, desire, anger, need. Each took a turn in her eyes, on her mouth. He wanted her in all the moods. He loved her so totally, but he'd have to stick to his guns. After they'd made love, before she could throw him out, he'd leave. He wouldn't come back until summoned—for more than a one-night stand.

"Very nice," he whispered. "Raise your hands over your head."

She started to say something, then evidently changed her mind. He had her wrists cuffed to the headboard. Now her breasts rose in invitation for him to feast, but he needed to make this time last as long as possible.

"I want to lick you everywhere. I want your taste imprinted on my senses," he whispered. The little pink nipples beaded at the touch of his fingers, his tongue. Gently, he traced the contours of each breast with his fangs. He needed to feed, and he needed to get his cock in her, but he'd postpone that gratification until he couldn't stand another moment of delay.

From the way Tanith was moving, Gabe could see how difficult it was for her to be restrained. Without her hands, she became more creative about moving her feet and legs. Another time, if there was one, he'd vary their play by binding her legs. For now, he enjoyed the pressure of her feet on his ass.

Hard as she tried to hold him, he freed himself from her leggy embrace. He tongued and fanged his way down her torso to her waiting pussy. "The nectar of the gods," he whispered, licking and sucking as he continued to massage her breasts.

She moaned his name, louder and faster as she shuddered her climax and cried out.

Good, because he couldn't have waited any longer. He lifted his hips to get his cock exactly where he—where they both—wanted it. He had a momentary regret that she couldn't use her hands to squeeze his balls and to trace the contours of his shaft. On the other hand, having her exactly where she was added an extra nuanced dimension of pleasure.

"Oh," she gasped when he was fully, gloriously deep inside her. He slowly began to arch his hips, gliding in and out of her in an intimate rhythm that soon had them both panting. With her legs around his back, she pulled him tight. He stroked the swollen nub of her clit, feeling her shiver with the pleasure of the intense stimulation.

"Love me," Tanith demanded, her voice soft and low.

"Oh, baby." He lowered his head and inhaled the mixture of her natural scent and the musk of sex. She surrounded him, exciting him as she engulfed his cock with her silky slickness.

"I want to hold you," she whimpered.

"Next time," he said, knowing there was no guarantee of a next time. Fine. He'd be in the moment, show her his love, his passion for her, with his body.

She whimpered, seizing up into a second climax that gripped him into his own orgasm. With her shuddering beneath him, Gabe exploded deep inside her.

And then he fed, the taste of her like a sacred promise in his mouth.

At last satisfied, they shuddered together in a final burst of mutual ecstasy.

Tanith wanted to stay exactly as they were, but her arms were beginning to ache. Funny that she'd never before known how cuffs felt. Though they'd added a different nuance to their lovemaking, she didn't know if she'd ever want to use them again.

If there ever would be an again.

"I need you to take off the cuffs," she murmured.

Gabe lazily looked at her and stroked her side, raising goose bumps. "I kind of like them."

"My arms are going numb."

"Okay." He reached to the night table next to the bed for the key, then stretched over her to unlock the cuffs.

"Whew." She shook her hands and arms to get the circulation going. He rubbed her arms to help.

"So what did you think? Did you like the cuffs?"

She started to answer when her phone rang.

"Ignore it."

"I can't." When she picked up, her partner spoke rapidly.

"What do you mean he's holding them hostage?"

Gabe frowned at Tanith.

"My God." She jumped out of the bed. "I'll be right there."

She threw on clothes, pausing only to get her gun. "My partner's going to pick me up in two minutes. Stan Corona is holding Sue and her kids hostage. He wants two million dollars and plane tickets to Brazil. He'll release the kids, but he wants Sue to go with him. Christ, she must be hysterical."

He leapt out of bed. "Corona? But how could that be? You just phoned in the information."

"I don't know. There must be a leak. If anything happens to Sue—"

"Shit. How could this have happened?"

"Doesn't matter right now. Don said Corona believes Tommy has evidence against him hidden at his house. He broke in to get it. Sue and the kids came home from a party and caught him ransacking the place. I can't friggin' believe it. If only we'd had his name yesterday. But we're going to get that bastard and make sure he doesn't hurt another innocent."

"I'll go with you," he said, his face and voice steely hard.

She shook her head. "You're a civilian. Nothing you can do but get in the way."

He scowled. "I'm a vampire, remember? I can't get hurt. You can."

She shook her head. "We're wasting time. I can't be worried about you when I've got them on my mind."

"Don't push me away again," he said and put his hand on her arm.

She had to summon up all her strength. "We said this would be the last time. Let's stay with that."

The honking of a horn cut off whatever else Gabe was going to say. She ran down to the street and jumped into the car.

Tires squealing, the car Tanith had leapt into flew down the street. Gabe gritted his teeth. This wasn't the way tonight was supposed to end. Trust the asshole who'd killed him to surface again. But no way was he going to sit this one out. Especially not with Tanith in harm's way.

Taking a deep breath, he focused on assuming the mist form to follow Tanith's car. Still not completely comfortable with this skill, he took so long he nearly missed his chance, but was able to catch up. The driver sped through the city at a dizzying speed. Gabe could hear the buzz of radio communications from within. In fifteen minutes they'd arrived at Sue's small house. Many vehicles, both marked and unmarked police cars, filled the street. Tanith and her partner jumped out of their car and ran over to the knot of officers conferring curbside. One officer with a bullhorn announced, "Come out with your hands up, Corona."

Still in his mist form, Gabe hovered above the police to observe.

"It's over, Corona. Send them out, come out with your hands up and we'll work things out." Suddenly a shot rang out from inside and everyone rushed to cover.

"Why should I?" Corona shouted back. "I've got this nice family. Pretty wifey, three cute kids. Should be worth it to you to give me what I want in return for letting them live. But there's a time limit. I start shooting in thirty minutes."

"Shit," an officer said.

"He's going to kill them." Gabe recognized the fear in Tanith's voice. "Tell him to let them out. I'll go in. He can use me as a shield to escape."

"Kalinski, we can't risk it."

"I know Sue. She can't take much more. Do you want to be responsible for her breakdown or worse? I'm a professional. Tell him I'd be a better hostage. Too hard for him to ride herd on four people."

Tanith finally managed to convince the officer in charge to go with her plan. *Crap.* Well, no way would Gabe let her get hurt. Corona, that pig, at first refused to let any of the hostages go. When one of the children vomited and Sue got hysterical, Corona agreed to the plan. He let the children out and Tanith got ready. Hands in the air showing she had no gun, Tanith approached the house to serve as Corona's shield. He let the children out, but reneged about freeing Sue.

"Get in here, or I'll shoot her," Corona shouted.

"I'm here at the door. I'll cross the threshold when Sue does." Tanith's voice sounded cold and steady. Gabe's instincts were screaming. Corona would kill Tanith. He couldn't let that happen. He could swoop down and take Tanith up with him, but then Corona might act out of desperation and harm Sue. He owed it to the family not to let that happen. When Corona let Sue out and Tanith went in, Gabe would act.

Corona shoved the very distraught Sue out. "I'm so sorry!" she cried out to Tanith as they crossed each other. Gabe's heart sank. Would he be able to act fast enough?

Tanith wanted to reassure Sue in the quick moment when they passed, but Corona's pointed guns argued against even that small gesture.

Later, she and Sue would talk over what happened. But right now, she had to focus on disarming Corona and getting out safe so she and Sue would have a chance for "later".

She walked into the familiar living room with her arms raised high. Corona stood next to the curtained picture window, the gun in his right hand aimed at her and the other poised to shoot out. Two more guns lay at his feet. "Stop right there," he ordered. Tanith could practically smell the fear and anger rising off him.

Was he right handed? She tried to calculate her chances of disarming him if she rushed him. Would she be able to get hold of one of the guns on the floor?

"I've trained myself to shoot with both hands."

She shivered, uncomfortable with his answer to a question she'd only thought. Of course, he'd know how any officer trained for this situation might approach it.

"I'm unarmed. Let's talk this through, Corona. If you surrender now, I'll work with you to get a fair trial."

"Right. And you also have a bridge to sell me." He cocked his gun.

The desperation she saw in his eyes might work in her favor if she used it right, or it might push him over the edge. If she miscalculated, she might not walk away. She'd never again see Gabe. She'd never have the chance to tell him she loved him or make up for how badly she'd treated him.

If she lived, she'd cut out the idiocy and her hypocrisy about being with him. He was her soul mate. What a time to realize that truth.

She had to live.

To get in to the house, Gabe, still in mist form, slid through the back window into the kitchen. Corona and Tanith were at the front of the house, in the living room. He assumed his form as a man and silently made his way there. When he saw Corona holding two guns—one aimed out the window, the other at Tanith's heart—his blood ran cold.

Tanith saw him first. She almost imperceptibly shook her head, motioning for him to back off.

He had to protect Tanith from that murdering garbage. He leapt to grab hold of Corona. In the confusion, Tanith grabbed a gun and shot Corona in the head.

Corona's last act was to fire the gun he held to Tanith's heart.

Pain below and white light above. Tanith felt herself being drawn to a place where sunlight and music flowed, and huge sweet-smelling flowers waved in a benevolent breeze.

She wanted to embrace the white light and the music, to smell the flowers. The nearer she got to them, the better and more whole she felt. But something powerful and insistent pulled her back, something she couldn't leave behind—even though there was pain when she went back. Everything was so hard to understand. A voice spoke a language she no longer understood. Tears, great sadness. She didn't want the sadness, not when there was so much joy all around her. Most of all, she wanted to bring light and love to the sad being holding her.

Such a struggle. She was too tired and in too much pain to continue. Most of all, she longed to tell the sad being it was all right. Using her last slim reserves of energy, she said the one word she understood he longed to hear: "Yes."

Lord, who'd have believed saying one word could tire a person out so? She sank into an exhausted oblivion and let herself float down a dark and peaceful stream.

"No!" Gabe cried out to the heavens and the earth. Then, pushed by instinct, he grabbed the dying Tanith to him, kissed her lips and fed from her. When she was a heartbeat away from death, he slashed his wrist with his teeth and held the pulsing veins to her mouth. At first, she didn't respond. His heart pumped faster, harder, as if he could animate her with his own energy. He pressed his wrist closer to her lips, feverishly begging her to take just one drop, then another.

After what seemed like an eternity, he felt a weak flutter of a response. He bent his head to whisper words of love to her, words of encouragement. She shuddered, then began to suck from his wrist with a bit more strength, and then a bit more. When she'd taken all he could give her, he still didn't know for sure if he'd succeeded.

Gabe clasped the unconscious Tanith to him and flew her up and away from the horrendous scene, far from the police storming the house. Maybe he should have let her die, should have let the natural processes flow, but he couldn't. Couldn't stand the thought of the world without Tanith, even if she hated him forever.

In his lowest moment, all he could think to do was to transform her. He'd asked her, and, scarcely breathing, she'd agreed. Had she known what she agreed to? Had he performed the procedure correctly? Did she sleep the sleep of death or merely that of exhaustion?

Desperate to know that he'd saved her and not hastened her death or condemned her to an eternal hell, he flew with her in his arms to a safe haven—Mirella Proctor's condo.

Fortunately for his sanity, Mirella was home. As soon as he arrived, he laid Tanith down on Mirella's couch.

"What happened?"

Biting back tears, Gabe told her everything. "But I don't know if I transformed her correctly." Pale and lifeless, Tanith still hadn't moved. "If I haven't done it correctly, if it's not too late, maybe you can complete the process?"

"What did you do?"

He snorted. "I tried to dredge up what happened at San Quentin. Antoine Thierry also once described the transformation process to me. But he also said I shouldn't attempt it for at least the first year."

"Tradition." She shrugged. "It's our custom for new vampires not to transform others immediately, but there's no real rule. Try not to worry."

Gabe laughed hollowly. "It's too late for that. But if I messed up... Hell, I keep thinking about everything that happened tonight, wondering how it could have had a different outcome."

She touched his arm. "We have to deal with what is, going forward." Mirella, face serious, checked Tanith. When she was finished, she looked up and smiled. "You can relax, Gabe. She will be fine. She just needs time to recover. You did right by her."

He sagged with relief. Tanith would continue to be in his world. Of course, she might despise him and refuse to ever see him again. After all, if he hadn't gone into Sue Lerner's house, maybe Tanith would still be alive. Or maybe Corona would have killed her and she'd have gone on to a mortal death.

They would never know.

When Tanith regained consciousness, she felt very weird. Snippets of strange memories kept swirling around in her mind. And she felt hugely thirsty.

In addition to how peculiar she felt, she had no idea where she was. Why was she lolling on an unfamiliar couch? A woman brought her a glass of tomato juice.

"Where am I? Who are you?" Tanith croaked. She took the glass and drank deeply before realizing it wasn't tomato juice.

Now Tanith recognized the woman—the one she'd seen that night with Gabe at Club X.

Gabe. She'd been with him when she'd gotten a phone call from her partner. Told Gabe it was the last time. Again. Corona had his gun drawn on her... "Sue and the little ones?"

The other woman nodded. "They are fine."

"Why is everything so weird?"

"I'm Mirella Proctor, a friend of Gabe's. What I have to say will probably be difficult for you to believe at first."

Sue and her children were really okay. So far, so good. But then, in growing horror and disbelief, Tanith listened to Mirella tell her what happened. She, Tanith, was dead. Undead.

Too big for her to fathom.

And then she realized how much her story resembled Gabe's. Suddenly, more than anything else, she wanted to see him, talk to him, tell him she understood.

"Where's Gabe?" Tanith asked.

"Are you really ready to see him? Because, I have to tell you, he's worried sick about you. And I won't have him hurt, not anymore."

Tanith knew she had a lot to think about, but right now, she was going strictly on instinct. "I'm ready to see him."

Mirella, still not appearing completely convinced, went and got Gabe. He looked so gorgeous when he came in, but so sad. He must have been the sad being in her strange vision, the one who kept holding on to her. She wanted to take that sadness from him.

"Why did you do it?" Tanith asked him after Mirella left

269

them alone. They were both sitting on the couch, not touching.

Gabe braced himself. "I couldn't let you go. Not even if you hate me for eternity."

She looked at him sternly for one moment and then moved closer to him. "I don't hate you," she whispered. "I love you."

"Oh, Tanith. You don't have to say that just because…"

She put a finger to his lips to hush him and smiled, complete with the strange new feeling she guessed were her fangs. Tentatively, she reached up and touched one. Here was her new reality. She couldn't wait to learn it all. "I never really meant it when I said it was the last time. You knew that all along."

"Yeah, but getting you to admit it was tough."

"I love you, Gabe Morrow."

"I love you so much, Tanith Kalinski."

"Now how about you kiss me."

She didn't have to ask twice.

About the Author

To learn more about Mardi Ballou, please visit www.MardiBallou.com. Send an email to Mardi at Mardi@MardiBallou.com or join her Yahoo! group to join in the fun with other readers as well as Mardi Ballou! http://groups.yahoo.com/group/RedHotRomance

GREAT cheap FUN

Discover eBooks!
THE FASTEST WAY TO GET THE HOTTEST NAMES

Get your favorite authors on your favorite reader, long before they're out in print! Ebooks from Samhain go wherever you go, and work with whatever you carry—Palm, PDF, Mobi, and more.